The Stability of Everyday Objects

Pearl Watkins

For C.E.W.

"And so there was this willingness to try again with me,
and to see what it would bring in."

Rosemary Tonks: *The Halt During The Chase*

The way Bryn and I got back together again was via a letter.

It was the summer of 1977. I was newly alone, separated from my husband Ian after five years of marriage, with a possible divorce looming. Unemployed, my contact with friends having waned, I had a kind of freedom....not the best kind, where each day is a sunny, wide open meadow just waiting to be entered and enjoyed....still, free of the need to please one man, to "honour and obey" — free of that. I had made my escape from the kingdom of marriage — for it is a kingdom, whoever heard of a queendom? And yet....I still needed someone. ...Didn't I?

I was living, if you could call it that, in a room in Gloucester, a cheap boarding-house room to which I had retreated to lick my wounds after leaving Ian. Initially I regarded the situation as the "failure" of my marriage, as if the union itself were a kind of imperfect being who had let me down. But it didn't take long for me to start thinking of myself as the failure. I had failed at marriage. The only people who knew precisely where I was were my parents, and the only letter I received in the three miserable months I was there was forwarded by them. It was from Bryn.

Dear Lowri,

I'm not sure of your current address so I'm sending this to your Mum's. Talking of Mums, that's where I am at the moment — at home. I always seem to miss you when I get back here to the jolly old Welsh valleys.

I get really restless sometimes so I find I come home quite often, never really wanting to, as I'm sure you will understand (!), but it's the only place where I can sit back and see things as they really are. You know, the Dylan Thomas "womb with a view" thing. The only other situation in which I can think is when I'm out alone in the car. Probably the reason is that in both cases there's a sort of pseudo-security about it. I've often thought that it would be a great idea for a play, where a fellow lives out his whole life in a sort of limbo, aimlessly driving round the country in his car. Well, perhaps not!

Anyway, after all this catharsis (I've just learned that word), what I really wanted to do was to ask you if I could see you some time — you know, just <u>see</u> you. I've no idea of your present situation, where you're living or what you're up to these days, but if you'd like to get together, write and tell me when. I'm living in London now and I have to work some weekends but that shouldn't present too much of a problem. I really hope that you're happy.

Much love, Bryn

And I had immediately written back: *Yes, you can see me, yes, let's get together, I'll come up to London. Yes.*

Bryn and I first met when we were thirteen and all through our teenage years we had an on-again/off-again relationship that never involved sex. We became very close and, with increasing frequency, Bryn made it clear that he yearned to make love to me but I refused to be persuaded. After my older sister's shotgun wedding at the age of eighteen my parents had wordlessly hammered into me a terror of getting pregnant that was more effective than any conventional birth control....and Bryn began to look elsewhere for what he needed.

But we remained friends and, as time went on, when faced with the challenge of being an adolescent with parents who had unassailably Victorian values, it was to Bryn I turned, so that he began to occupy the space in my life where my parents belonged, supporting me and encouraging me as I struggled into adulthood. In that way he saved my life. If I had to give that space a name, it would be — a haven. Bryn was my haven.

Then, returning to Wales after the completion of higher education, we took off to Southampton and started living together. We were twenty and I was still a virgin but slowly, in jerks and starts, I began to submit to Bryn's advances. The only thing missing — a crucial shortcoming — was physical desire, meaning my physical desire for him. Although his kisses excited me and the sensation of his hand on my neck sent shivers down my back, he could not unlock my inhibitions sufficiently for me to enjoy sex.

Meanwhile, my mother, who openly disapproved of my choice and was the invisible, ever-present force behind my inhibition, never tired of reminding me there were plenty of other men around, a whole world of potential partners, just waiting to be found. *Plenty more fish in the sea…*

Eventually Bryn and I parted, simply, without fuss and without acrimony, almost without emotion. It hadn't worked, that was all. Happens all the time. *Fini.* He had supported me emotionally and I had indulged him sexually but it had not been enough. Now it was really over.

I let Bryn make love to me just once after we parted: he was so desperately inflamed, he climaxed the instant he was inside me. And I felt only an overwhelming sense of pity, that Nature could allow such inequity of passion between two people who had so much else in common.

The arrival of Bryn's letter changed everything. I immediately felt less alone. And the prospect of rediscovering the emotional solace of a warm and familiar male shoulder was instantly restorative. I could return to my haven and everything else would simply fall into place after that.

Ignoring the splinter of doubt I still felt, I replied to Bryn's letter with a "yes".

And the sheer vigour of Bryn's greeting when we met up again after so long was enough to sweep away any misgivings I might have had about moving backwards, about attempting to reposition myself in an equation which had proved insoluble.

Bryn rang as soon as he received my reply. The boarding-house landlady, Mrs. Glashan, came and tapped on my door to tell me I was wanted on the telephone, "by a man." Up to that point the only person who had rung me had been my mother.

After Bryn and I had talked on the phone and arranged to meet — when I told him I was standing in Mrs. Glashan's hallway, he took the hint that she was probably eavesdropping, so our conversation was rather formal and impersonal — I stood there, staring into space, a feeling of optimism creeping into me. Then, on an impulse, I dragged the phone directory from its shelf under the phone and made an appointment with a prestigious hairdressing salon in nearby Cheltenham for a cut, colour and body wave. I now had someone to impress.

When Roland had finished with me, I scarcely recognised the person with the bouncy copper-coloured hairdo who looked back at me from the salon mirror. As I handed over the three ten-pound notes to the receptionist I kept glancing up into another mirror behind her as I struggled to absorb this new image....then as soon as I stepped out into the street, I was reminded of the astonishing power of looking glamorous, of its ability to boost one's self-esteem, and I felt the corners of my mouth turn up.

So there I was at the end of September 1977, stepping off the long-distance luxury coach that had carried me from Gloucester to London and waiting to meet me was the most appreciative audience imaginable.

"Your hair! It's great!!" Bryn exclaimed when he saw me.

That was another of Bryn's talents — enthusiasm.

He took me to The Pomegranate in Pimlico where I ordered the French dishes I liked, pronouncing the French words unself-consciously — Coquilles St. Jacques, Truite Amandine — while Bryn listened, beaming with delight. We talked and laughed and drank wine and smiled across the table at each other. And dis-covered that, at that particular moment in our lives, ten years after going our separate ways, there was nothing to prevent our getting back together.

In the course of that dinner, Bryn showed me a photograph of himself, taken when he was decorating the living-room of his house in south-east London. I studied the photograph closely: there was Bryn, tall, medium build, dark hair, dark eyes, wear-ing a thick brown sweater and white dungarees splattered with paint, standing on a stepladder, paintbrush in hand, grinning. He had brought the photo along in order to show me the out-landish purple he'd chosen for the walls. But all I saw was him, as if for the first time.

What is it about a photograph that helps us see something that we cannot see otherwise? Because for me the image was so appealing I felt a surge of warmth which was irresistible. Perhaps it was the spontaneity of the shot, or the joy demonstrated by Bryn that he had the freedom to paint his living-room any colour he pleased. Or perhaps my vulnerability and longing were at a dangerously weak point.

Whatever it was, in that moment I was sure I loved him, with that powerful sinking feeling of gladness and relief, so intense that I thought my skin must have changed colour. A drug, that feeling.

So there we were, in a Pimlico restaurant, both thirty years old, both single, or almost — Ian had told me he was preparing to file for divorce — bound by a mutual past and an uncertain future.

Over dinner we talked about our individual histories, confiding in each other the details of our personal lives, details we might not have mentioned to anyone else for fear of boring them. I complained about Ian's drinking and Bryn bemoaned his inability to find the right woman. We did not try to make sense of what we were sharing. It was tacitly agreed all that was now — history, and we had "returned" to each other. After years of dissatisfaction, we suddenly saw an avenue open up and, almost without discussing it, we were a couple again. We were thirty years old and couldn't quite believe our luck.

...Ten years earlier we got as far as the registry office in Southampton. We intended to get married; for all I knew the forms we filled in were still there in the files, forgotten, still awaiting verification of our ages, because we were both under twenty-one at the time. I was not in love with him then, I was in love with the idea of a haven and he had said he would take care of me....but we did not go back with the proof of our ages. I had sensed that a haven was something but it was not enough.

After dinner we went back to Bryn's house, where our love-making was an exquisite combination of the familiar and the unfamiliar: the many unsatisfying times it had taken place before were lost as in a distant dream and all that remained of that dream was the fact that we were not strangers, we had touched before; all other sensations arose as if for the first time.

And after ten years Bryn had become a skilful lover — he had all the time in the world — and I had never been more receptive to male tenderness, allowing his gentle caresses to soothe away the invisible scars left by my failed attempt at marriage.

Next morning I lay in Bryn's bed and watched the thin, pale mauve curtains shiver and twist in the light currents of summer-warm air circulating through the open window. My clothes were piled untidily on a plain wooden chair next to the bed with my skimpy floral undies on top like a dash of colourful froth. Bryn was downstairs on the phone.

"Lowri's here," I heard him say. "Yeah, she's staying for a few days," and I could hear the smile in his voice. "Tonight? Yeah, sure, where are they playing?"

Ten years ago we came very close to getting married and here I now was, older, but perhaps not much wiser, trying him out again.

That evening Bryn took me to the Tufnell Park Hotel because there was jazz on, the Stan Tracy Quartet. The room where they were playing was off the hotel lounge bar. It was already packed when we arrived — you could see the wavy layers of smoke drifting up towards the ceiling — so we had to squeeze in beside an elderly, nattily dressed gentleman who sported a beribboned boater and a broad smile. We were making a space for one into a space for two but the old gent didn't seem to mind, he edged over a few critical inches, nodding and smiling, as if the important thing was not one's personal physical comfort but the privilege of being present to hear the music.

Stan Tracy, his eyes screwed up and a lit cigarette between his lips, jabbed at the piano keys as if any moment one of them might burst out of the instrument, escape and take on a life of its own. He was a keen young sheep-dog, nipping at the heels of any sheep who looked as if it might be so much as thinking of straying.

Bryn turned and pulled me closer:

"Stan's the only person I know who actually plays the piano like a percussion instrument," he shouted into my ear, "which it is!"

I nodded vigorously. I had never seen anyone play the piano like this.

The alto player, Art Themen, stepped to the edge of the low stage for a solo. Diminutive and curly-haired, in a tight black T-shirt with "GOOD AS IT GETZ" emblazoned in scarlet on the chest, he played the sax as though in the grip of some musical devil, a shouting, kicking devil who could not decide if he loved music or hated it. Either way the struggle was exhilarating.

The musicians stopped for a breather and the room thinned out. I glanced around, absorbing the excitement of my surroundings while trying to look as if I went to this kind of event practically every evening, when Bryn said, "Here's Len and Alan."

I looked up to see two forty-something men making their way towards us.

Bryn introduced us. The three of them played in the Goldsmith big band, an ensemble for amateurs led by Don Rendell who apparently had once played with "all the greats".

Len shook my hand and smiled, and Alan, the more formally dressed of the two, took my hand and kissed it, saying, "Enchanté. Are you well?"

"Yes, thanks," I said automatically.

"And I, too, am well," said Alan. "So we're both well. Well, well."

"These guys have been in the big band much longer than I have," Bryn explained. "Len plays tenor sax and Alan plays the trombone. Watch out for him, he's a charmer."

"As are all trombone players," added Alan, warmly, his eyes twinkling, "as you well know." Bryn also played trombone in the band.

"You must come and hear us some time," said Len. "We're *almost* as good as these guys." He grinned and gave a despairing look at the musicians who were now standing at the bar with pint glasses in their hands. Then he looked back at the three of us and said, "What's everyone drinking?"

The boatered gent beside us excused himself, saying, "You can have this seat now, I've got to get home to the wife. It's our night for kinky sex."

"That's the spirit!" exclaimed Alan, "never say die!" and we all laughed.

Len went off to the bar, Alan sat down next to me and said, "You're here, I, too, am here. So now we're both here. Hear,

hear! You look like an interesting sort of person. Tell me some fascinating things about yourself."

"Oh, do you think so?" I said, charmed into flirting. And I thought, I'm being accepted, I'm becoming part of things...*je suis arrivée*....I've arrived.

After about ten minutes Stan and his men came back and started the second set, this time playing a slow number, during which I let my imagination race off into the future.

...The great metrollops....that's what Bryn had called it when I spoke to him on the phone after he received my "yes" letter. "I'm living in the great metrollops, I don't think I could live anywhere else now."

London....but what am I going to do for work? What am I going to do for money? Because this time I knew I could not just hand myself over, as I had the first time; that would mean hand-ing over all my choices as well and I had only recently realised that I had choices. This dress, this drink.

This city....this man...

The following day Bryn took me on a tour of London. Not the usual tourist circuit of world famous sights but one preferred by someone who has chosen to live in London, has got to know it a little and has connected emotionally or spiritually with certain areas, places whose charm is not so immediately obvious. So — no Buckingham Palace, Houses of Parliament, Trafalgar Square, Piccadilly Circus, St. Paul's or Tower Bridge for Bryn, no. These were places to be avoided simply because they were over-run by tourists and their atmospheres annoyingly punctuated by the strobe-like flashing of snapshot photography.

Instead he began by driving north past Regent's Park, turned off into a residential area and proceeded along streets lined with sedate Georgian houses, to the base of Primrose Hill, a high, rounded, grassy knoll dotted with clumps of ancient oaks and crisscrossed with much-trodden footpaths that fanned out from a central point like compass bearings. Here and there a wooden bench had been thoughtfully positioned so that one could sit and appreciate the view.

We walked steadily up to the highest point. To the south, practically the whole of central London was spread out in front of us, its bustle and noise muted by distance so that the far-off wash of sound only added to the feeling of calm. It was there, on that day, at that moment, that I was amazed and moved by the way the first impression of some parts of London was one of serenity. To find oneself in the peaceful middle of one of London's mild green spaces was reminiscent of being in the womb, untouched for a while by all the endless activity of the world outside but comforted by its muffled hum, and I wondered if this was also Bryn's reason for liking that spot. The city was like a great engine, never still, never quiet; one could take it or leave it, but it would never stop, never be still. For a fleeting moment, standing there with the vast expanse of London at my feet, I imagined myself a gentle god filled with compassion for the incessant busy-ness of human lives.

From the high point Bryn pointed out some of the distinguished landmarks — the Post Office tower, the spire of Brompton Oratory, the dome of St. Paul's — stretching out his right arm and indicating them not with the index finger of his hand but with the long middle finger — a quirk I had forgotten — while from the grounds of London zoo, situated in Regent's Park below, the occasional squawks of exotic birds could be heard issuing from the airy confines of the enormous Snowdon aviary.

"We are in the middle of all this," said Bryn, sweeping his arm around in a semi-circle, "and yet it's so bloody peaceful." And I realised I had guessed correctly: Bryn liked the place for the same reasons I did and I was so happy I could not speak.

Afterwards we plunged back onto the city streets, briefly joining the mass of other vehicles in fume-filled, traffic-clogged Oxford Street in order to reach a quieter street behind Claridge's Hotel where we had a lunch of beer and toasted bacon sandwiches served up by a friendly barmaid in a cramped, dimly-lit pub that had been there for over eight hundred years.

After two pints of beer in quick succession, Bryn became effusive and started talking passionately about his restlessness and confusion. We had got on to the subject of self-expression and when I told Bryn I would be lost without my attempts at poetry, he nodded his head slowly, and gazed out across the pub: "You're lucky."

"I am?"

"Yes. At least you have something to show — for — for being alive." His mood seemed to change and he gave a long sigh. "I'm just so confused all the time because I can never work things out."

"Work what out?" I asked.

He ignored my question and turned to face me. "You know, you probably don't remember this, but you once said to me that I had a restless spirit."

"Actually I do remember saying it," I said.

"Yeah? Well, it's not really restlessness. It's a kind of — frustration, I think and just recently I finally came up with exactly what it is that's really screwing me up. About a month ago, I was up in Birmingham, at this new Exhibition Centre they've just built up there. It's all very modern, you know, very 'cool' architecture with lakes and fountains, all really nicely laid out. I was up there for a conference, so I was in my suit and tie, and I went out first thing in the morning for a walk around the lake. It was really bright and sunny and really *quiet*. So there I was, leaning over this bridge, having a ciggy and looking out across the lake at the fountains, when this jet came really slowly over the whole picture" — he described a high arc with his left arm — "making that incredible sound that jets make when they are flying low and the whole scene was just — utterly surreal."

He paused, reliving the scene in his mind's eye. "Anyway," he went on, "at that moment I was really moved and inspired by the whole thing — the landscape, the sound, and just the mood of it all — and I really wanted to — you know — capture it or something. But then I realised that I couldn't express it. I had no way to express what I was feeling, not then, at that moment in time, but not ever. Do you know what I mean?"

I nodded. "I think so."

"I'm not a painter or a writer, I'm not even a very serious musician, and I think the restlessness is just a constant struggle to find a way of expressing what goes on inside me."

"So that someone else will understand it?" I suggested.

"Maybe that's what it really is, a need to communicate. I'd just like to be able to share it, somehow. It's so bloody difficult to find someone to share things with."

"Well, it *is* a struggle," I said, prepared to expound on the emotional drain of turning out a handful of poems a couple of times a year.

Bryn was not to be deflected. "That's why I'm so glad you're back in my life again. I don't have to explain things to you so much. Wait a minute, I'll prove it to you. Look at this." He pulled his wallet out from his back pocket and flicked through its contents until he found a piece of folded paper which he handed to me. I unfolded it, it was a picture of a young punk with outrageously spiked green hair holding, of all things, a small, very fat piglet. I gave a squeal of delighted laughter and Bryn laughed with me for a few seconds.

"See!" he protested, folding the picture carefully back into his wallet. "No-one else I've shown that to thinks it's funny."

His expression changed suddenly and I thought he was going to cry, and my heart went out to him. But no, instead he gave a rueful smile, exhaled loudly and said, "I feel quite worn out after explaining all that! I think I'll have a brandy to pick me up. Want anything else?"

I shook my head and the conversation was over, for the time being.

As we left the pub, Bryn stopped dead, turned and stared intently at me: "Let's go and find out what's on at the Festival Hall tonight. That way you can see the view from Waterloo Bridge."

Between Westminster Bridge and Blackfriars Bridge, the Thames makes one of its great serpentine curves, turning through almost ninety degrees and — instead of continuing north — flows east, until it makes its next dramatic change of direction at Rotherhithe, where it nonchalantly meanders in a huge semi-circle before flowing east once more and out towards the sea.

From Waterloo bridge, which spans the river in the middle of that monumental curve, one can see as far as the Houses of Parliament to the west and Southwark Bridge to the east, a vast urban vista of central London on the banks of an equally impressive body of water, a sight that makes one glad to be alive. It became for me one of the joys of living in London. It was one of those places where you felt London opening its heart to you — or at least that's how it seemed to me that day when Bryn and I walked across Waterloo Bridge together.

He parked just above the Strand, whisking the car with a triumphant "Aha!" into a tight space that another car was vacating, and we strode across the bridge, dodging the streams of people headed in the opposite direction. Bryn pointed to the collection of monolithic grey concrete buildings on the opposite side of the river which made up the South Bank complex, the most beautiful of which — perhaps because of its expanse of sparkling windows facing the river — was the Royal Festival Hall.

He seized my hand and started walking a little faster: "Good god, I feel wonderful today," he exclaimed. "Let's hope there's something decent on tonight."

We managed to get tickets for a performance of Chopin's First Piano Concerto with Marthe Argerich and the London Symphony Orchestra so that, only a few hours later, we were slowly surging into the auditorium of the Royal Festival Hall along with hundreds of others. We had cheap seats off to the side and I could not see the pianist's hands while she played, but the changing expressions on her face, with her long black hair flowing around it, spoke volumes and reinforced my deepest convictions: life is beautiful, life is hell, but music helps. Art, music, books....these are things that can help soothe you.

Also views from the top of high hills....and having someone to talk to about your innermost yearnings.

Next day I was due to leave but not until the evening.

Bryn and I rose very late, went to a greasy spoon caff in Lordship Lane for breakfast then drove up to Hampstead for a long walk across the Heath where we watched people fly kites and sail their model boats on the Round Pond.

Back at Bryn's house just before four, he unlocked the front door, saying, "Before you leave, I'm going to make you a really good cup of tea. I've learned how to do it — you make the tea really strong then put lots of milk in." He stood at the kitchen sink filling the kettle, plugged it in and disappeared into the downstairs loo. The phone rang and Bryn shouted from the other side of the door, "D'you mind answering that?"

When I picked up the phone, a female voice said, "Is Bryn there?" When I said he was not available just then, the voice said, sharply: "Who is this?" and when I said my name and that I was a friend of Bryn's, it said, "Oh. Well, this is Julia. Would you tell Bryn I rang and I'll be at the usual place this evening."

I replaced the phone, faintly ruffled, and turned my attention to Bryn's books: Amis, Waugh, Wodehouse, Chandler, Le Carré, a large dictionary, an A to Z. An unfamiliar title caught my eye and I was removing it carefully from the shelf when Bryn reappeared.

"That's a really good book," he said. "You can borrow it if you like. It more or less sums up my ideas about relationships. Who was that who rang?"

"Julia?" I said, looking up from the low bookshelf with an expression I hoped did not demand a complete explanation.

Bryn smiled, came over and kissed me lightly on the top of my head: "Julia plays trumpet in the big band," he said. "Don't look so worried. She doesn't have a car so I usually give her a lift to rehearsals."

The book was called *Open Marriage.*

On the coach back to Gloucester I looked down at the vehicles we passed on the M4 motorway and at the segments of the drivers visible inside them. I saw male hands on steering wheels, trousered thighs, the sleeve of a shirt or sweater, sometimes a slice of white at the wrist of a sombre tailored suit....and the occasional woman driver, usually seated in a more upright position closer to the steering wheel, one of the things that men liked to make fun of, the way they also did when a woman threw something.

My brother taught me how to drive and how to throw stones — "properly", as he put it, "not like a girl" — but it still filled me with an almost uncontrollable fury to hear a man ridicule women in these particular areas, while conveniently ignoring his own shortcomings in others. Added to which, any criticism of a male on the part of a woman had her labelled an unfeeling bitch. Too incensed, when such a situation occurred, to be able to offer a coherent reasoned statement of how unfair this was, I would give an inward snarl of annoyance and simply seethe silently.

As far as all this went, Bryn was an unusual mixture: he was what might be described as a man's man and did not hesitate to use crude labels when talking about women in general —

breasts, for example, were "knockers", a word which shocked and appalled me. And as with other men his age, his ambivalent feelings about women — the desire for them and the desire not to be controlled by them — were often thinly disguised by humour. Yet I had never once heard him make fun of an individual woman for so-called "typical" female behaviour or ineptitude. He liked women too much for that. In other words, he objectified womanhood but had enormous respect for the individual woman. And his criticisms were genderless; rather he disapproved of stupidity or a lack of sophistication or banal taste in music, failings that could afflict anyone.

Nevertheless, Bryn's one concerning trait was that, while professing doubt about his capacity for true love — "I don't know what it's like to fall in love!" — he was continually stupefied by attractive women, and I knew the one consideration I was refusing to contemplate as I tentatively planned my immediate future was the fact that Bryn, without any shadow of a doubt, had a roving eye. I knew I occupied a very special place in his heart because of our long shared history; I was also aware that his appreciation of the opposite sex was not limited to me. And never would be.

The coach pulled into a motorway service station near Swindon for a ten-minute stop to pick up passengers and on an impulse I jumped out and purchased a *Sunday Times* newspaper. As we thundered steadily onwards towards Gloucester, I perused the classified columns under *Accommodations*....and there it was, in among the ads for cottages in the Lake District, holiday chalets in Devon, luxury mews apartments in Kensington and other more modest offerings: a two-line ad for a flatmate in south-east London at a rent I could afford — once I found a job.

Bryn had tactfully not suggested I move in with him. He recognised instinctively that I needed to re-establish a certain degree of autonomy before making another commitment to intimate cohabitation. Besides, I wanted to be able to tell Ian — truthfully — that I had found a place of my own. I tore out the ad for the flat, tucked it into my purse and sat staring out at the growing darkness as the coach neared Gloucester, imagining myself nervously picking up the phone in the morning to answer the ad and everything going along swimmingly after that.

When I got back to the boarding-house, I climbed the two flights of stairs to my room and unlocked the door, still thinking about Bryn and the events of the weekend and the ad and having something to look forward to doing first thing in the morning.

I switched on the light and saw a small white envelope on the worn carpet of my room just inside the door, obviously slipped under while I was away — probably another invitation to have a quiet cuppa with Annie, the occupant of the room next to mine, a delightful old lady with ancient clothes, impeccable olde worlde manners and an affectionate overweight cat which the landlady grudgingly tolerated. But instead of the uncertainly formed capital letters which Annie used to write my first name, I found myself staring at my full name neatly typed in the centre of the envelope.

Mystified, I dropped my overnight bag on the floor, sat on the edge of the bed and studied the envelope with narrowed eyes, as if that alone would force it to reveal its origin. Then I turned it over and saw the discreet embossed crest on the flap: *BK*.

Knowing that I would not settle in Gloucester once I was no longer attached to Ian, when I broke away from my marriage, I also broke away from my job. Not that *that* was saying much. One of the things that had helped our relationship on its down-hill course had been the dearth of work opportunities available to me in sleepy Gloucester.

When we moved there, the Ministry of Defence had a job waiting for Ian. I ended up, the squarest of pegs in the roundest of holes, in the typing pool of an enormous ice-cream factory on the outskirts of town, one of a dozen women, all of them mid-dle-aged, whose conversations revolved around cooking, cloth-ing sizes, oafish husbands, disobedient kids, diets and the mean-dering storylines of various television serials.

This was the job where a major portion of my daily energy was expended in quelling the urge to scream as I listened to the banalities that flew around the room to the staccato accompa-niment of a non-stop barrage of key-strokes on a dozen electric typewriters.

The only person to whom I was drawn was the pool super-visor, a short, portly woman in her late thirties who ruled her flock with unwavering strictness but who occasionally revealed glimpses of a kind heart and an educated mind. She seemed to appreciate the fact that, while I was incapable of joining in so-cially with the other typists, I was capable of fast accurate work. When a typing job came in that required swift and immediate at-tention, she usually gave it to me, a gesture which did nothing to enhance my popularity, but she understood that it was the work and not the society of my fellow employees that kept me sane. A mutual unspoken bond of affection had developed between us.

After three months of supervising me at work and drawing her own conclusions, she had invited me — *"and spouse"* — to afternoon tea at her thatched cottage in the nearby village of Hardwicke. Ian was not interested in having tea with a middle-management factory employee so I went alone. Over tea, served in exquisite porcelain, she told me that her husband was a long-distance lorry driver, was often gone for days and nights at a time, that they had no children and she was often starved of interesting company. After that I saw her in a more sympathetic light.

A few weeks later I invited her and her husband to dinner. This time Ian did not protest. Unlike afternoon tea, dinner meant he could drink.

When we had finished eating, the two men lingered at the dining-table over brandy and cigars while we women took our liqueurs into the living-room. In the course of conversation I hinted at the difficulties I was having remaining married to Ian.

When, two months later, I told her I was leaving my job and gave the absolute minimum notice and no explanation, I think she understood that outside events had precipitated it and wished me well, giving me a slim box of three snow-white lace handkerchiefs as a parting gift. Her stout, inflexible body had earned her the unkind nickname of "the Barrel" but her real name was Barnell King. This was what she wrote:

Dear Lowri,

I felt I just had to write to you, I couldn't just let you disappear without saying something. We saw Ian recently and he confirmed what I had suspected. I had an inkling what might be on the cards — you had appeared so very unhappy for the last couple of months at work — but I felt it was none of my business, so couldn't say anything.

As I said, I guessed what was going on but when I was told for real I was very upset, and I've spent many hours thinking about you. I really do hope you will find real happiness and get to do all the things you want. With your skills, I'm sure you can find a job that is more interesting than typing replies to complaints about ice cream!

I hope you won't take offence by my writing to you and if you should be coming out anywhere near this quaint little hamlet of ours, please pop in for a chat. Meanwhile, I would like to make you a gift of the enclosed. As you know, I have no children on whom to lavish my spare cash so it gives me great pleasure to lavish some of it on you. Money isn't everything but it can be very helpful sometimes.

All my best wishes, Lowri, chin up

Barnell (King)

She must have delivered the note by hand, though how she had found me I had no idea....perhaps Ian had given her my parents' address.

I unfolded the cheque; it was for fifty pounds.

I fell back flat on the bed, my mind racing. Then, holding the cheque out at arms' length, I said aloud to the room, "I shall be moving to London very soon, to live near Bryn, I shall be sharing a flat in south-east London and this is the deposit."

His hair looked as if someone had snatched up a fistful of loose hay with short stalks sticking out at all angles, dumped it down on the crown of his head and left it there, but his eyes were friendly, I liked his Australian accent and it seemed the most natural thing in the world to be considering sharing a flat with him. There was a strange object in front of the television, a thick black solid rubber disc, about twice the size of an LP, fixed on the central stem of a tripod base. A small stool stood beside it.

"What's that?" I asked.

"That's me practice pad," he said. "I'm a drummer."

"Oh," I said, suddenly having to readjust my ideas about him. Another musician…

"I used to be a professional but I got tired of carting me drum kit all over London. Now I just do the odd gig. But I still have to practise, see, and with that little set-up" — he grinned — "I can watch Panorama and practise at the same time."

His name was Phil Miller and the flat was on the ground floor of one of those once very imposing but now rather dilapidated three-storey Victorian houses that lined the streets of south London. Once the homes of large families, whose servants lived below stairs, most had since been converted into flats and bed-sits.

"Have many people come to look at the place?" I asked, thinking I should keep the conversation going.

"A few. That's why I put the ad in *The Times* — to keep the riff-raff out. First time I was looking for a flatmate I put up a card in the local newsagents and in the colleges, you know, and the phone never stopped ringing. And I swear half of them came round just to see if I had anything worth nicking. So I thought I'd be more choosy this time. This is the kitchen." He led the way around a corner into another cavernous room.

"I get milk delivered but I forget to use it up." He opened the fridge to reveal four unopened pint bottles in the bottom shelf of the door, their contents varying shades of greenish-white and suspiciously solid-looking. "Science projects," he said, with an amused snort. "Bathroom's nice and big, plenty of hot water. Oh — and I've got a steady girlfriend — in case you're wondering."

He was neat and clean and energetic, about the same age I was, the corners of his eyes crinkled up when he smiled and I liked the way he didn't waste words. The flat was spacious, sparsely furnished; the white-washed walls, white plaster frieze of vine leaves along the edges of the ceilings and enormous high windows gave the place the air of an artist's studio. But the place could have been a pig-sty for all I cared. Its most persuasive feature was that I could afford it….and it was about a half a mile from Bryn's house.

We went back into the living-room.

"D'you have much stuff?" he asked.

"Not much," I said. "I'm leaving nearly everything behind — with my soon-to-be ex-husband." I managed a wry smile.

"I see," he said, slowly, looking at me and nodding. "Didn't work out." A statement, not a question.

Extraordinary how the slightest hint of sympathy had the power to release all the pain I had pushed down inside myself. But what do you do with memories that you don't want to keep? You hope they will be crowded out, elbowed back, that they will eventually fade, but no, they continue to stand there, hovering silently in the wings, going over the script, and sometimes they push their way with full force, unannounced and uninvited, into the spotlight, and the same, horribly familiar lines of dialogue emerge from their mouths: *How could you? I trusted you. Why, why, why?* I started to cry.

"There now," said Phil, "it's a bit of a dump but it's not that bad, is it? I'd make you a cup of tea but... " He jerked his head towards the fridge.

I gave a little gust of a laugh and wiped the tears away with the heel of my right hand. "Sorry. No, I really like the flat. Especially the science projects."

He smiled. "A woman with a sense of humour. Look, it's yours if you want it. I didn't much like the other two who looked at it anyway and you sound as if you could do with a spot of good luck. You can move in as soon as you like, I just need the deposit and a month's rent and you can have the key today."

"Okay," I said, feeling my optimism returning. "All right if I write you a cheque?"

"Absa-bloomin'-lutely — with a bank card." Friendly, but also business-like.

As he saw me out of the flat, Phil grinned and said, "No worries, eh?" and I smiled back at him with my lips tight together because the wraith-like echoes of my broken marriage were still milling around, spouting unwanted words and mocking his kindness.

....*No worries? That'll be the day...*

I walked slowly, fingering the key to the flat in my pocket, to the end of the street where Bryn was waiting for me in the Fox and Hounds. I thought, I have somewhere to live, I have somewhere to live....now I just need to find a job....and all my face-pulling, scenery-chewing memories were relegated once more to the wings.

Bryn said, "How did you get on?" but he could see from my face that things had gone well.

"Now, all I have to do is look for some work," I said.

"You could try the Temp agencies," he said, "while you're looking for something permanent."

Pleasant, young lady, nicely dressed, a little reserved…

That was as much as I had time to read before Mrs. Barraclough, the intake interviewer, returned to the room after being called away in the middle of the interview. I quickly drew my head back and looked out through the window to my right, as if I had taken advantage of her absence to admire the view, which had the campanile of Westminster Cathedral in the middle of it. So much beauty in this city…

"I do apologise," she said, smiling, smoothing her skirt against her generous bottom as she sat down again. She resumed her perusal of my CV and, still looking down, asked, "What kind of work have you done most?"

Fabricate my work history, I wanted to say, but I overcame this impulse and answered, "Secretarial work, personal assistant, that sort of thing."

She looked up and fixed on me her light brown eyes which were kind but also shrewd: "And what sort of position are you looking for at the moment?" I thought it must be some kind of tactic, the eye contact, the removal of it.

"About the same," I said, unable to manufacture even a semblance of ambition.

As always I had little or no faith — not with regard to my skills but in my ability to tolerate office life: the hours that were carved in stone, the necessity to dress neatly and conservatively which, once established in the job, one took immense delight in ignoring, the stealthy desk snacks, and the vulgar, incredibly biased and bigoted jokes and anecdotes that passed for humour, told and retold by male co-workers in the presence of female secretaries who sat at their desks with fixed smiles on their faces and glazed expressions in their eyes. But what was the alternative? Start at the bottom of some colossal professional tree and work for a pittance, shackled to a career with which one might easily become disenchanted overnight?

Temps Unlimited, Alfred Marks, Brook Street Bureau, Manpower — all the big employment agencies had unmissable ads on the walls of the Underground stations, especially the stations in central London. It was impossible to wait for a tube on the Circle Line and not be confronted with their names in letters a foot high on the posters plastered to the grimy concave walls of the tube tunnels. I had registered with three of them.

"Don't bother with Manpower," advised Phil. "Unless you want to work for peanuts and get shunted from one side of the city to the other every week *and* deal with all their bloody paperwork into the bargain. I was with them for three months last year — bloody well near killed me."

So here I was at Alfred Marks, one of the more reputable agencies, and the interview, like all such interviews, was going along like the strange species of ritual tango that it was.

What do you have to offer? asks the one with money.

Everything you want, replies the one who wants money.

This is what we want, says the first.

And how much will you pay me to do that? asks the second.

They dip and sway...

We will pay handsomely for the right person, observes One.

I am that person, says Two. *I can be yours.*

And Number One throws out the challenge: *But you have so much competition. What makes you think you're the best person for the job?*

...The Temping Tango...

"I see you speak French," observed Mrs. Barraclough.

A wave of anxiety swept over me and a jabber of French slang flashed through my brain — *ça m'énerve,* that gets on my nerves; *petite salope,* little slut; *je m'en fous,* I don't give a damn (polite translation)....should I tell her I had once been an au pair in the south of France? ...*Fais gaffe à lui, il a la main baladeuse,* Watch out for him, he has wandering hands. That one might still be useful...

"I'm a bit rusty now," I said, with what I hoped was polite finality. Shocking really, that I could remember so clearly how to curse but not how to converse in French.

"Ah," said Mrs. Barraclough, the disappointment in her voice implying that it was a great mistake to become rusty.

I had not done temp work since I had first entered the job market after leaving college ten years earlier but I had not forgotten its pros and cons. The main advantages were the feeling of being outside the system you were working for — unless one was very unlucky, a temporary assignment lasted only a matter of weeks, while the permanent employee was on holiday or off sick — and the other was that one need have absolutely no twinge of loyalty or responsibility. You were simply there to hold, one in each hand, lightly, temporarily and with questionable efficiency, two links of a chain which normally relied for its strength on the commitment and integrity of another who would soon return and clean up the mess. Such was the treachery of the temp.

Not that the agencies were beyond reproach. I had decided to register for permanent work while temping and one of my few stipulations regarding preferred permanent work environment had been that it not be in the world of finance. Figures were not my forte. The next day one of the agencies rang to say that a fabulous job had just come in, that it was just what I was looking for, the money was terrific, the location was great, it was an up-and-coming company, they wanted someone straight away, and when could the agency send me for an interview? When I asked for more details the breathy, excited voice at the other end of the phone said, "You'll be the personal assistant to one of the directors. They have brand new offices in Devonshire Square, very close to the Tube." It occurred to me to ask what the director did. After a small but significant pause, the voice said, "He's head of the Finance department." Such was the treachery of the employment agency.

"I'm working for a couple of blokes who spend all day trying to work out how much stuff they can fit into a container."

I said this to Bryn after my first day of temping. We were in the bar of the Strand Palace Hotel, drinking champagne cocktails, celebrating my success at averting insolvency.

"What sort of container?" asked Bryn.

"Those huge cargo containers that go on ships. You see them on the backs of lorries sometimes. They're like enormous metal boxes."

"Oh, yeah, right. That's what they do?"

"Have a guess what they were trying to fit in today."

"Bicycles," said Bryn, grinning, entering into the spirit of the thing.

"Pews," I said. "Some church in Belgium has bought all the pews of a church that's being pulled down in the east end and they have to be shipped over there in one load. You should have seen these two tearing their hair out, trying to work out how to get them all in."

I had ended up in the import and export business, which sounded very grand, but all I had done all day was type out shipping manifests and bills of lading. Still, from the office window I could see the Thames, and the endless coming and going of river traffic helped soothe my bored restlessness.

After lunch that first day I rang Bryn and suggested we meet after work. He was currently working in an insurance office somewhere in the City and was able to commute by car. I knew he would be more than ready for a drink after the working day and would be only too happy to drive me home.

Bryn, who was big on a sense of occasion, said he knew the perfect place, the cocktail bar of the Strand Palace Hotel.

"We'd better say half six," I said, after we had arranged where to meet. "I'm supposed to work nine to five but I didn't get here until ten."

One thing I had overlooked in my determination to live close to Bryn was the necessity of commuting into the centre of London. As far as the Underground was concerned, most of the activity was north of the river and I now lived firmly south of the river. The nearest tube station was Brixton, the southernmost stop on the Victoria line but still two miles away from Phil's flat. The nearest British Rail train station, though only ten minutes walk from Phil's, was, I discovered, simply a means of getting to the Brixton tube and this was the first stage of a journey which involved, as it turned out, three hectic changes. Catching a bus was out of the question. I had a horror of buses which I was unable to explain, even to myself, and anyway buses travelled in unpredictable packs and were notoriously slow. So, in spite of my attempt to be early on the first day of my new job, I misjudged the time it took to get there and rolled up just before ten.

No-one seemed to care much but I wasn't taking any chances and was prepared to work till six.

"Half six, then," said Bryn. "You can't miss it, it's opposite the Savoy Hotel."

I emerged from the Trafalgar Square tube station and walked briskly up the Strand, thrilled in spite of the noise and dirt and jostle to find myself one of the thousands of people who lived and worked in the great metropolis. I've arrived. *Je suis arrivée.* "I'm here," I whispered to myself as I marched smartly along. "I'm here, in London."

The foyer of the Strand Palace Hotel was thickly carpeted, hushed and intimidating. I felt self-conscious wearing clothes in which I had sat at a desk all day and carrying a rather shabby shoulderbag, especially when a very attractive woman, tall, slender and elegantly dressed, emerged from the lift, and swept past me like a burnished bird of paradise, trailing a waft of divine fragrance.

The clothes I wore to the office were not clothes I liked. There was work, then there was the rest of my life and these two worlds were separated by a bottomless chasm. Work — and the rest of my life. I made a mental note to go shopping that weekend, tucked my bag under my arm to cover the worn bits and walked into the bar.

"I feel underdressed," I said to Bryn, as I sat down next to him in the subdued light.

"Have a couple of these — that'll sort you out," said Bryn and he slid a drink over to me. The tall stemmed glass held a clear, very pale gold liquid and two Maraschino cherries speared on a cocktail stick. Clusters of tiny bubbles appeared, rose through the liquid, disappeared, then reappeared at the bottom of the cocktail. The exquisite colour of the drink reminded me of the shining hair of the bird of paradise who had passed me in the hotel foyer and suddenly I was overcome with feelings of inadequacy. Money — that was the thing that separated you from the world of the elegant and burnished — money, and I would probably never have enough of it, certainly not by typing out bills of lading all day. I started to tell Bryn about my job, trying to make a joke of it but my mood sank lower and lower until I became dejected and then argumentative. What was I doing working in an office anyway — a pound of flesh for money, that's all it was, with no reprieve in sight.

Some people turn to their parents, some to their grandparents, some to friends, and some tell themselves comforting lies, as they strain to develop from children into grown-ups... *Yes, you are talented, you are good-looking, you will succeed.* In order to survive the ordeal of emerging from the world of the child into the big ugly world of the adult, the one thing you need is emotional support and if you don't get it from those close to you, those expected to provide it, you turn to others who are willing to encourage you — "Y*our hair — it's great!*" — and you remain indebted to them for the rest of your life.

A steady drip of disapproval, mockery and sarcasm on a growing human being has a Bonsai effect, restricting growth, stunting desire and holding back ambition, so that the place one is supposed to call home becomes a place of torture, a place where you had always to be on your guard to avoid a new wound.

Far from providing the necessary encouragement, my parents never stopped finding ways to tear down even the smallest supporting structures I attempted to build for myself.

…"Why don't you ever bring your friends home?" my mother once asked — I was fourteen. I didn't answer. Not after the way she had reacted the previous year when I told her my periods had started. In an instant I understood why it was called "the curse". Embarrassment, shame, disapproval, that was just the beginning. Why would I want a friend to see that I lived like that? And, at the same time, "Be open," I was told. "Let people see who you really are, let down your guard."

The riddle of childhood — or the riddle of *my* childhood — was: What's left when you knock the corners off something that has no corners? Amazing that there was so little physical evidence when one considered the extent of the emotional on-slaught. Damaged goods, that's what I was….but until you got really close, the damage was invisible.

Bryn understood this, that's why he was so important to me. He could see beneath the surface. He knew why I sometimes behaved badly, why I sometimes became aggressive. He saw my struggle and accepted it. He understood my overwhelming need for something that I had not even properly identified….because it was his struggle also. We both understood the importance of using our brains to do something creative, to make something coherent and sustaining out of what was often incoherent and destructive.

Bryn raised his glass, took a swallow of his cocktail and said, "Look, if things don't work out, you can always come and live with me."

"What do you mean, if things don't work out?" I protested — hollowly — my longing for the thing being offered battling with my pride. "Why shouldn't things work out?"

We were on our second cocktail.

"Don't be like that. I'm just offering you the choice, that's all."

I fell silent, took a gulp of my drink, said, "Okay," then looked up and was stunned to see Nick walk in through the gilded doorway and sit at the bar. Of all people, Nick, the man I had been having an affair with when I was married to Ian.

It hadn't taken long to discover that the only time Ian wanted to make love was on a Saturday night when he was drunk. He was half-drunk most evenings of the week but on Saturday nights he indulged with abandon and I was expected to be part of this indulgence. Half the time he was too drunk to make love and I was left stranded but relieved in the middle of my feigned sexual arousal.

My affair with Nick had kept me sane during the deterioration of my marriage to Ian....or rather it had provided me with a kind of insanity that was more familiar, more acceptable. *People should always behave as though they are between planes*, who was it said that? And that was exactly what Nick and I had done. From the moment we met he and I were like two hitherto un-mixed chemicals....put them together and the results would be unpredictable and potentially dangerous but the temptation to perform the experiment was irresistible. With Nick I became aware that I truly existed and that life was worth living; we were the kind of people who thrived on uncertainty, a whiff of danger and a necessity to live absolutely in the present.

Just glancing at Nick's back gave me a frisson, reminding me of the moments we had snatched together and the fleeting pleasures of our affair, which was doubly doomed because we were both married....in almost every sense we were "between planes". When we were together, we created a world in which I seemed to be far more capable of living than the one to which I was obliged to return. *Nick!* I exclaimed to myself....*but what are you doing here?*

The hotel cocktail bar was large enough and dim enough that there was little chance of being noticed by Nick unless he moved away from the bar. This was unlikely — he was on his own so he would talk to the barman — and I had time to think about what I was going to do. It was an opportunity, of course, but for what?

"You know what we should do later?" said Bryn, busy with his own thoughts.

"What?" I asked, leaning back in my chair so I could study Nick.

"Go to The Hundred Club," said Bryn.

"The Hundred Club?"

"In Oxford Street. They have live jazz every night. It doesn't open until ten so we could have a meal before we go." He peered down at his watch. "We wouldn't have to rush. There's still plenty of time."

Cocktails at six-thirty, followed by an unhurried meal, followed by live jazz into the early hours of the next morning. And this was Monday...

"All right," I said.

There was work and there was the rest of my life — and I never had the smallest doubt which was more important.

"I'll go and give them a ring, find out who's on," said Bryn, rising from his chair.

No-one could ever accuse Bryn of not being a man of action. Something was no sooner thought of than it was done. That was one of the things I liked about him. One of the many things...

I started trembling with excitement as I watched Bryn walk out of the bar into the foyer because I suddenly knew what I was going to do.

Nick was chatting to the barman. A born salesman, he could strike up a conversation with anyone, quickly discover what wavelength they were on, and join them there, thus giving the impression that he was an unusually caring and concerned individual. He could shake his head about the price of groceries with pensioners, flirt outrageously with young unmarried women, bandy political chat and sexual innuendo with businessmen, analyse the objectionable noises that passed for music with nervous adolescents, grumble with foreign tourists about England's apparent lack of service, and — to their delight — scandalise middle-aged housewives with jokes about what salesmen got up to "on the road". Nick was friendly, impertinent, knowledgeable, and a conversational chamaeleon. And he was still crazy about me, I was quite sure of that.

I reached for my bag, found a scrap of paper and wrote *Ring me at work tomorrow* followed by the number, which I had to look up on another scrap of paper in my bag. Anything else would have ruined it. I had no idea why he was in London. He would have no idea why I was in London. The situation had a pleasing symmetry about it.

When Bryn came back and told me who was playing at The Hundred Club and that we shouldn't miss it, we agreed to leave immediately so that we'd have time to find a good restaurant near Oxford Street.

Suddenly it did not matter one iota that I was underdressed; my felt self — the one that Nick admired and desired — was an invisible protective layer that floated over the top of my clothes. As we left the bar, I told Bryn I had to go to the toilet and to wait for me outside the hotel, then I walked into the Ladies, counted steadily to twenty, walked out again, back into the cocktail bar and straight up to Nick who turned mid-sentence as I approached. Before he had time to register who I was, I kissed him on the mouth, put the note on the bar beside his drink, made a gesture of extreme regret, turned and left swiftly, taking with me the image of Nick's eyes alight with astonishment and the barman turning away, an amused, knowing smile on his face.

The Hundred Club was called that because its address was 100 Oxford Street and it was at the eastern end of that street, just beyond the main shopping area in the direction of the junction with Tottenham Court Road. When we got there at ten-thirty, having dropped into a nearby pub after the restaurant for a quick one — Bryn said drinks in the club were overpriced — the place was filling up rapidly and a trio was already playing.

Bryn plunged forward towards a table that was empty because the top of it was awash. Someone had spilled a drink that hadn't been mopped up and it was dripping off the sides. He told me to sit down and claim the table then made his way to the bar and came back with two short drinks on a tray and a pile of thick bar towels. *No sooner said than done...* He mopped up the mess, dumped the sodden bar towels on the tray, pushed it aside, picked up his drink: "Cheers!" he said, raising his drink a couple of inches before beginning to sip it.

"What are we drinking?" I asked.

"Whisky. Johnny Walker, Red Label. Black Label is better but they don't have it."

"Cheers," I said and sipped.

Does anyone actually like the potent, half-medicinal, half-herbal, primitive earthy taste of Scotch whisky the first time they try it? Perhaps it was the mystique surrounding the drink that kept people trying it and eventually, like anything else, it grew on them. I decided to reserve judgement until I had sampled the fabled Black Label. Meanwhile, intrigued by the sheer uniqueness and objectionableness of the taste, I continued to take tiny sips.

A young woman came to the table to take away the tray on which were piled the soaked bar towels: "Sorry about that," she said, smiling.

"Absolutely no problem," replied Bryn.

He turned to watch her shapely bottom for a few seconds as she went back to the bar and murmured, "Nice bum."

"Yes," I said. "Very nice." We could have been talking about the weather.

Then he turned to me: "So — what did you think of the Strand Palace?"

"The cocktail bar?"

"Yeah — nice place, isn't it?"

"Very," I agreed, warmly.

"Especially that bloke at the bar that you couldn't take your eyes off."

I blinked at Bryn: "The bloke at the bar?"

"The one you kept looking at," said Bryn, smiling his certainty.

My god, he doesn't miss much, I thought. Or had I been that obvious?

"It's o-*kay*," said Bryn, with extreme emphasis. "I'm not jealous — well, I am a bit, naturally, but I'd really like it if we brought that kind of thing out into the open. Look," he said, leaning in closer, "I don't own you and you don't own me. There'll be times when other people will — well....when we'll be drawn to other people— "

"Like that barmaid," I said, sharply.

"I didn't try and hide it, did I? Actually, that was sort of intentional. Her bum wasn't that great. I was trying to make a point, because you tried to hide the fact that you were looking at that bloke in the Strand Palace and — well, it never works."

"I was just *looking* at him," I protested, feeling uncomfortable because, even though it was the truth, it wasn't the whole truth.

"I know. It's all right. I was just *looking* at the barmaid." He put down his drink and reached out to take my hand. "I don't mean to make you feel bad. It just that — it seemed like a good opportunity."

"To do what?" I asked, more and more unnerved by the turn the conversation was taking.

He released my hand with a parting squeeze, before returning to his drink. "It's connected with that book I was telling you about."

"Which book?" I asked, even more baffled.

"Now is probably not the best moment to talk about it but.... that book you pulled off my book shelf, remember? *Open Marriage*?"

I recalled the book's cover, the title in white block capital letters, and below it the two red hearts side by side, overlapping, with an open door depicted in the overlap area. "I haven't really had a chance to— "

"I know, I know." He brought his face a little closer so I could have no doubt that he was in earnest: "Look, I don't want to ruin the evening with a heavy discussion now but I do want to talk about it — about the stuff in that book. I want to hear what you think. But let's talk about it some other time, yeah? Tomorrow evening?"

I nodded.

"Sure? Okay, good. Ah — here comes the great man himself."

A roaring cheer went up as Don Weller came on to the stage, his huge bulk dwarfing the tenor saxophone that hung around his neck. The golden sheen of the sax was dulled from use and looked more like a piece of machinery than a musical instrument, one that had been handled and even mistreated by sweating, not-entirely-clean hands. He wasn't a musician, he was a workman and his work was making music.

I persevered with the whisky. One thing about alcohol, you can rely on the fact that it will change the way you feel. The results are unpredictable but after a few drinks, one is more or less guaranteed to be in a different frame of mind.

And that was exactly what I wanted.

I had started out as a character in one play, thinking I knew my lines, my well-thumbed script now at the bottom of my rucksack, and had ended up in a completely different play with no script at all. I took a bigger swallow of my drink; there had never been a time when I had been more open to new experiences.

Next day I stood in the doorway of the coffee room, chatting to Melanie, the filing clerk who worked in the room opposite, while I waited for the kettle to boil to make another cup of instant because I had a hangover. All Melanie did every day was pull out files, make notations in them and also in a big ledger, and put them away again, and since it was tacitly acknowledged by the management that this was soul-destroying work, she was allowed to have a radio on as long as she did not play it too loudly. The station she listened to featured dated hits, the kind of music that was even more mind-numbing than the work but these rusting "golden oldies" seemed to keep Melanie happy.

She was putting labels on a newly opened box of files. Without looking up she asked, "Have you seen that handbag Mrs. Fellows has today?"

"No. Why?" Mrs. Fellows was one of the executives.

She raised her face and her eyes were enormous. "It's real alligator! Must have cost a fortune! I asked her was it new and she said she got it on the weekend. She said as soon as she saw it she had to have it. I bet she does all her shopping in Bond Street." With exquisite sarcasm, she added, "Must be nice not to have to look at the price of something before you buy it."

"I've never set foot inside any of the shops in Bond Street," I said, thinking that one day I might, though it wouldn't be to buy an alligator handbag.

"We're in the wrong jobs, you and me," laughed Melanie.

Suddenly, because my head was pounding, I resented being lumped together with her and her windowless room full of manilla folders and her files and her cheap transistor radio with its squawking prehistoric pop music — *"Oh, my old man's a dustman, 'e wears a dustman's 'at"* — resented being dragged down to the level of people like her, who disapprove of the extravagances the rich allow themselves — and not for any ethical reason but out of envy, pure and simple, because these extravagances are the trappings of a world to which they will never belong, because they know they don't belong to it. Well, that wasn't me. *One day*, I thought, *my life will have all the things in it that I want — and that does not include an alligator handbag. One day I will know why I am alive and I will know it from the inside out and not the other way around.* And I felt the way religious persons must feel, when they lean on their faith to keep going, although I could not have begun to describe the mystery that lay behind my conviction. Like them, I simply — believed.

I went back into the coffee room. As I poured boiling water over the little mound of white sugar and coarse brown powder in the cup, I heard Melanie start to sing softly along with the radio: *"The answer, my friend, is blowing in the wind, the answer is…"*

I returned to my desk and the phone rang. It was Nick. I could hardly believe it.

"You won't believe this, Loulou — but I've been looking for you," said the familiar voice at the other end of the phone....his voice....one of the things I liked best about him.

"You're right," I said, "I don't believe it."

Nick had always liked it when I provoked him a little; he said it made him feel alive. More alive. And from the beginning, he had refused to use my given name.

"Lowri? What kind of a name is that?" he had jokingly protested, when we first met.

There was nothing I liked better than an unorthodox approach to conversation so, delighted, I fired back: "It's Welsh, boyo. It's Laura in Welsh, isn't it?"

"No, no, I can't call you that," he insisted, ignoring my self-mockery.

He was like a puppy with a brand new slipper which delighted me even more. "Here, let me have a better look at you." He touched my shoulder so that we faced each other. For five seconds our eyes were locked together, then he said, in a voice softened by emotion, "You have really pretty eyes...." and I could see him melting, so I threw caution to the winds, leaned forward and kissed him. And the world, which had done nothing but whirl and tilt and shift uncomfortably since I had married Ian, stood still. And the best part was that he wasn't shocked. He took a deep breath, recovered, and said slowly:

"Loulou, that's what I'm going to call you. So — Loulou, shall we see if we can sneak away from all these people and find somewhere quiet?"

When was that? Four years ago? We were introduced to each other at a crowded party by Ian, who had then moved away to refill his glass — his first priority was keeping his beer topped up — and when Nick paid me the two unexpected compliments of being interested enough in me to want to rename me, and then telling me he liked the colour of my eyes....right then, I stepped out of Ian's disquieting world and into one of my own, where I began to recognise myself again.

I sat there at my office desk, staring out at the choppy metallic waters of the Thames, the phone pressed against my right ear, listening to Nick's voice. I'd have given an entire day of my life to go back and—

"Miss Williams?" said a brisk voice behind me.

I jerked around and saw Mrs. Fellows with a sheaf of papers in her hand. Recovering instantly, I said into the phone, in a completely different voice, "Would you hold on for a moment, please?" and put the receiver down on my IBM golfball typewriter.

Mrs. Fellows smiled: "I need this rather quickly and my secretary is taking an early lunch. Would you mind....?" That meant it was urgent and she needed it ASAP. She may have been one of the high-ups and able to afford an alligator handbag but she was also pretty damn nice.

"Yes, of course," I said.

"Thank you. You're a lifesaver. I'll be in Mr. Walker's office." Mr. Walker was the company director.

I waited till she was out of earshot and picked up the phone again: "Nick, I have to go. I've got something really urgent to do."

"Can we meet for lunch?"

"Okay, where?"

He gave an exasperated little exhalation because he knew he had to think fast: "Did you notice that pub opposite the Strand Palace Hotel? Victorian-looking place?"

"Not really, but I can find it."

"It's called The Coal Hole — charming name — you can't miss it, stand with your back to the Strand Palace and you'll see it on the other side. It's not exactly opposite, but you can't miss it."

He was talking quickly because he knew I had to get off the phone. Odd how something like that can make you long for a person.

"All right. What time?"

"One o'clock?"

I looked at my watch then at the document Mrs. Fellows had placed on the top of my stack of work, desperately trying to estimate how much typing was involved. "Better make it half past. Don't worry if I'm a bit late. Sometimes the tube takes longer than I expect. But I'll be there."

"And how will I recognise you?"

"Nick!" I exclaimed, and laughed out loud.

Mrs. Fellows walked past the office again and glanced over at me, this time unsmiling, and I hastily put the phone down and reached for her pile of papers.

I got home from work a little after six and as soon as I opened the front door of the flat I heard someone crying. For a few night-marish seconds I imagined it was me crying and I had a vision of myself, sprawled across a bed in a dimly-lit room, coat and shoes still on, shoulderbag flung on the floor, my face buried in the pillow, sobbing. I stood rooted to the spot for a few seconds more, blinking, until the image disappeared and I was once more simply standing, dry-eyed, in the hallway of Phil's flat.

Phil came out of his bedroom, saw me, and looking very sheepish, stuffed his hands in his pockets.

"Sorry about this," he said softly, jerking his head towards the closed bedroom door.

I assumed we were talking about Phil's girlfriend, Angie. "Is she all right?" I asked.

"She was a lot better before she discovered she was pregnant."

"Oh dear."

"She says there's no way she can have it. She still lives with her parents and she says they wouldn't hear of letting her have it. So she wants an abortion. I told her I'd pay for it, but she's still pretty worked up about it all. Apparently it's not the first one she's had and she thinks it may ruin her chances of….you know….later on… "

"Oh, I don't think that's true," I said, earnestly. "I think that's just something they say to scare us."

Phil squeezed his lips together and nodded, then he sighed: "It'll be okay. She only just did the test so she hasn't had time to— "

A quavering voice called out from the bedroom: "Phil?"

"Better go. Sorry you had to come home to this. I'll take her out in a minute, then you can have the place to yourself. She'll feel better after she's had a couple of drinks." He went back into his bedroom and closed the door.

Dislodged from my own emotional crevasse — I had not met Nick for lunch as arranged — I went into the kitchen instead of into my bedroom. I had been relishing the idea of coming home and indulging my disappointment with a flood of tears, but the thought of Angie curled up on Phil's bed, her face wet and shiny from crying after the unwelcome discovery, somehow prevented me from doing so. Two weeping women in the flat was too much to contemplate.

Instead I made a pot of tea, the way people are supposed to do in a trying situation. I was still furious with myself.

When I pressed my foot against the base of the pedal bin to throw away the tea bags, I saw, lying torn open on top of the muddle of bread wrappers, empty baked bean tins, crisp packets, egg cartons and newspapers, a small white box with the name of a pharmaceutical company on it. Angie's pregnancy test.

I went into the bathroom to wash my hands. On the sink next to the cold tap was an unfamiliar object. I looked closely at it. It was a pale blue plastic cube, about two inches across, with smoothed corners and one side hollowed out. At the bottom of this hollow was a circle of white cloth or perhaps absorbent white paper, slightly domed, with a pale blue cross in the middle, as if someone had taken a thin blue marker and drawn it there, lightly but very precisely, like a blueprint in reverse. Angie's pregnancy test result — positive. Astonishing how a mark on a piece of white cloth, something so small and seemingly insignificant had the power to make a frightening idea you had been carrying around in your head suddenly real — and throw your whole life into confusion.

I sat there, quietly swallowing mouthful after mouthful of the consoling tea, until I heard the sound of Phil's bedroom door opening.

"We're off out to the pub!" shouted Phil.

"Bye!" I called out and two seconds later the front door banged shut.

Now I could replay in my thoughts the events of the day. At a quarter to one, about halfway through Mrs. Fellows' typing, I realised with a sinking heart that I was not going to make it to The Coal Hole in time to meet Nick and the faster I tried to type the more mistakes I made. Mrs. Fellows walked past the office a couple of times but I pretended not to see her and went on typing. The third time I heard her say to a colleague, "Yes, it's on the way, it's being typed this minute."

At a quarter to two, twitching with agitation, having hastily scanned the typed document through and hoping I hadn't missed too many mistakes, I handed the whole thing over, accepted the inevitable effusion of thanks, shot out of the office, ran down the four flights of stairs and raced towards the tube station.

It would take at least fifteen minutes just to get to Charing Cross, the nearest tube station to the Strand. Two changes were necessary — Victoria and Embankment — and the tile-lined tunnels that connected one line with another were sometimes terribly congested so it took forever, or so it seemed, to make a connection. And once there, after emerging from the tube I'd still have to walk the length of the Strand....Nick would wait, but for over an hour? If I were very late he would perhaps call my place of work again and if I were to return there I would at least hear his voice again, we could arrange another meeting. Torn between going back and going forward, I became completely im-mobilised, and immobility is not something the city likes. I was pushed and shoved by passers-by, briefcases and bags bumped against my legs, I was jostled from all sides. The stern expres-sions on the faces of London's hardened tube travellers made it plain that standing still in the middle of a busy Underground sta-tion at lunch-time was definitely against the rules. I knew that even if I got to the Coal Hole and Nick was still there, I would not have time to linger before having to return to the office. I was close to tears. *I'm here, I've arrived....but now I'm not doing so well...* When a tall, pinstripe-suited gentleman, thrust against me by the flow of passengers, muttered an extremely annoyed "I do beg your pardon," I had abandoned the whole plan, turned round and started back to the office.

Nick did not phone again.

I slowly poured myself another cup of tea. I was furious with myself because it hadn't occurred to me to take a taxi. That just proved how much of a newcomer I was to the great metrollops. There was tomorrow, of course, and Nick at least had my work phone number now and, best of all, I had the flat to myself for the rest of the evening until the pubs closed.

Feeling my optimism slowly returning, I pulled out a record of Shostakovich's Fifth, placed it on the turntable, turned up the volume and stretched out on the sofa in the living-room. The commanding minor chords of the symphony's opening movement filled the room: this was Shostakovich's moment to fight back, in answer to criticism from the Russian government for the lack of patriotic feeling in his music, which he pretended to accept as justified. One instrument after another surged into the fray with the same message: *Life is brutish and frustrating, and your heart will be broken many times.* I began to cry — it was finally my turn — and once started found I could not stop. My feelings for all living creatures made to suffer great pain and indignity and forced to make difficult decisions were all mixed up with my own small disappointment and my heart felt near to bursting.

Then, appalled at my own self-indulgence, I stopped the record in the middle of the slow movement, threw on my coat, picked up my bag and, not caring if I found him in or not, briskly walked the half mile to Bryn's. Sometimes standing still is the only thing possible, sometimes moving forward is the greater imperative.

Bryn had a visitor, an old friend from university days.

"Jonathan has just turned up," said Bryn, after he introduced us, "He's over from the con-tee-non for a few days. I was about to come round and see if you were in. We are going out for a few drinks, then I'm treating Jonathan to a curry."

Because I had naively expected Bryn to be alone, perhaps reading or listening to Radio Three, I was caught off-balance by the situation and on being presented — out of breath, windswept and still in my work clothes — to Jonathan who was very good-looking, well-dressed and suave, I took an instant dislike to him and felt disturbed that Bryn's life included people like him. Jonathan lived in Madrid, Bryn said, where he worked as a translator and although he was British, born in Kent apparently, he oozed continental sangfroid. Simply by the way he smiled at me, I could tell that he regarded me as some kind of lesser creature, I could almost hear him saying it: *Not my type, actually....a bit below my usual standard....can't speak for Bryn....there's no accounting for taste...*

I sat in the back of Bryn's car on the way to the pub, listening to the two of them converse about Spain, politics, their careers, and about mutual friends from their university days, and I was consumed by a feeling of not belonging. And after two drinks on an empty stomach which intoxicated me beyond any reasonable expectations, I started to make flippant remarks to Bryn's guest, thinking he was the sort of person with whom one could carry on a bantering conversation that might pass for flirting and not really caring if he wasn't. If it was clear there was no chemistry whatsoever between us, I could at least still demonstrate my great wit and conversational agility. But it was the alcohol talking...

After ordering and paying for the third round, Bryn said "Excuse us a minute," to Jonathan, abruptly turned on me with an angry look on his face, pulled me aside and said, in a roaring whisper, "Stop being such a shit!"

Everything turned red and for a second I considered throwing my drink into Bryn's face but I could not bring myself to do it, because he had every reason to be angry. Out of the corner of my eye I saw Jonathan calmly extract a cigarette from a pack with a garishly coloured wrapping and light it. The flame from his lighter flared up like a miniature beacon, signalling danger. I put my untouched drink down on the bar, gathered up my coat and bag and silently left the pub. Bryn said something to Jonathan then followed me out. We stood on the pavement outside the pub entrance.

"What is the *matter* with you?" Bryn demanded.

"Why, what have I done?" I demanded back in a loud voice.

"You are being unbelievably rude. You've never met the guy before and you've done nothing but insult him all evening."

"Oh, leave me alone," I said, close to tears. "I've had a hor-rible day."

"Why? What happened?"

I pressed my lips together to stop myself from blurting out anything about Nick and stood there, staring defiantly over Bryn's shoulder. He shifted his weight to his other foot and ex-haled noisily as he tried to decide what to do next. At length, he said:

"All right, look, you don't have to tell me now....only I'm taking Jonathan for a curry in a minute and you can come if you like but you have to be a bit more civil to the guy."

"I don't want a curry. I shouldn't have come out with you. I'll just go on home."

Bryn took hold of my arm: "I'll drive you."

"You don't have to," I said, looking down at my feet so that he would not see the tears forming in my eyes.

Bryn's hand dropped away and he stared at me, making me look back at him, and in his eyes I saw as much genuine concern as anyone could possibly want from another human being. He said, "Are you sure you're all right? You know, you don't seem like yourself at all. Why don't you stay at my place tonight? I'll take Jonathan to his hotel after the meal and I should be back in a couple of hours. I'm not going in tomorrow so I'll drive you to work in the morning."

I mutely nodded my agreement.

After this little tête-à-tête, I let Bryn take me back to his house, a few minutes' drive away. Neither of us said a word. Once inside the house I slammed the front door hard to get rid of the hateful energy that had piled up inside me and stood completely still in the hall. Suddenly I wanted a cigarette more than anything in the world, my life seemed to depend on it. After an impatient search through all the pockets in the house produced nothing, I shamelessly rummaged through Jonathan's overnight bag and found two packs of cigarettes like the one he had produced in the pub, opened one, and took a cigarette, without a single qualm, as if to prove to myself that no amount of kindness could prevent me from being the thoroughly wicked person I really was.

Much later, when I was lying in bed listening to my pulse in the pillow and trying to make it slow down by breathing deeply, I heard the two men return, heard their footsteps come and go on the hard wooden floor of the hallway as they collected Jonathan's bag. I heard Bryn's car start up again and drive away, then heard nothing as I drifted into sleep, until I felt the bed shift as Bryn got in. I lay very still but Bryn wasn't fooled.

"Come here," he said, sliding his arm under my shoulder.

I rolled against him and we lay together without speaking. He didn't ask me to explain myself and I didn't offer any explanation. We lay in a profound silence which bound us more closely than any amount of verbal or sexual intercourse, so that I was soothed back into sleep.

When I awoke in the morning, Bryn was still asleep. I knew it was early because of the birdsong, the lack of traffic noise from the street, the night-time chill that still hung in the air. My eyes were open but my thoughts were still focussed inward and I stared without seeing at the ceiling, wondering if everything gets shuffled around in the night....the world is in turmoil, you are taken on terrifying unplanned journeys while you sleep, your dreams are inklings of this chaos, then, the instant before you wake, order is restored and all is as it was. The trees have not been uprooted, the houses stand intact, machinery hums, dogs bark. But do you know what happened while you slept?

To console myself I decided to think of last night's fiasco like that — it had all been a dream. And I had now woken up.

Bryn took me to Phil's flat to change clothes then — luxury of luxuries — drove me to work. Like a couple of chic Parisians we did not talk about the previous night's fracas; it was understood that sometimes these things happen — *mais bien sur, c'est la vie, n'est pas?* — and there was nothing to be gained from going over it again.

What we did talk about was Bryn's book; we had the conversation Bryn had said he wanted.

"So, you're saying," I replied, after a while, straightening my legs out to get the warmth from the engine to my feet, "that it's all right for people in a relationship — an intimate relationship — to go out with other people?"

Bryn said, "That's what the chap who wrote this book says, and the more I think about it the more I realise I agree with him. It's a pretty hefty test of trust though and the only way it can work is if the relationship is based on trust."

"But you trust the other person not to stray," I objected.

"No, that's not quite it. You have to trust the other person will come back to you."

I gave Bryn a wry look because I thought he was splitting hairs but as he was just then negotiating one of the nervewrackingly congested roundabouts that exist in central London, he kept his eyes on the road. Traffic flowed in a solid mass around a substantial patch of grassy ground with a statue of a man on a very lively horse in the middle of it.

"Isn't that the same thing?" I suggested, after he had safely attained his exit.

"Well, the rules have to be agreed upon — or rethought if you like. The way things are now, when someone is in a — let's call it a stable intimate relationship — and then gets involved with someone else and has sex with that person, it's called being unfaithful, which most people say is against the rules and which blows everything apart, to a greater or lesser degree, either temporarily or for good."

We came to a complete halt in a long queue at traffic lights.

"Y-e-s," I said, "which is understandable."

"Well, why should that be the case? There's no way to stop fancying other humans just because you've made a commitment to one of them."

I thought about Nick, about his smile and his smooth chest and the way a line of light brown hair trailed from his navel down his belly....I shook the image out of my head. "But the point of making the commitment," I said, "is that you promise not to act on any chance attraction."

How easy it is, I thought, to talk about these things in the abstract, as if they were mathematical equations, squiggles on paper, with brackets and fractions and those two little lines of the *equals* symbol, not events involving thinking, breathing human beings, beings riddled with all kinds of emotions and ambitions.

"People go back on decisions every day," protested Bryn, "it's human nature. What do you think divorce is for! No — that's neither here nor there. The only thing that holds people back half the time is fear of getting caught. What I think I'm saying is— "

"I understand what you're saying," I interrupted, "and I don't necessarily disagree with you. I'm just saying that it's not really — workable and therefore it will never catch on."

The traffic surged forward again.

Bryn went on, "This is the big difference between what actually goes on now and what I'm advocating. Let's say a man — or a woman," he added, giving me a swift, mollifying glance, "who is part of our hypothetical committed couple has to go away for a few days, to — to visit relatives, say. Okay, so on the train to — Lower Soddinghampton or wherever — the one who is going off on the visit gets talking to another passenger on the train, you know, the usual thing, the weather and other banal stuff, and then, without trying to make it happen, it becomes clear these two people are very attracted to each other. You with me so far?"

I nodded. I felt the brief jerk as Bryn changed from second gear into third.

"Well, the way things are now, if they take it any further and particularly if they end up taking it all the way into bed, it is described as cheating and the person cheating has to decide whether they are going to say anything to their long-term partner. And usually they don't because it's easier to say nothing, well, not easier, but it's safer. Because — let's say it's a man — he knows he'll get a total bollocking from his girlfriend or wife, probably get thrown out, etc., etc. Let's just say, it's ugly."

"And if it's a woman?"

"Same thing!" Bryn said. "She'll get a bollocking, she'll be made to feel like she's a slut and she'll probably get thrown out. End of story."

"So. What's the answer?"

"It's not really an answer, it's — well, the chap who wrote the book suggests a different approach, a different concept, a way to bring together the abstract and the actual. And I think I agree with him."

"Well, how does it work then?"

"Let's assume it's the woman making the trip, okay? She comes back from her visit to Aunty Mabel and tells her man that she met a bloke on the train, he seemed really nice, there was mutual attraction — to cut a long story short. they went to a hotel and had sex. It wasn't earth-shattering — well, perhaps it was, and needed to be — but it hasn't changed her feelings for him, it just satisfied something that....that needed satisfying. She's not in love with the bloke on the train and he's told her he's married anyway. But it's done and she does not regret it. She enjoyed it. But she still wants to be with bloke number one."

"Let's say the man she is telling is you," I suddenly blurted out.

"Exactly!" exclaimed Bryn. "That's what I'm getting at. That's the hard part. It's easy to look at it from your own selfish point of view, when you're not the one who has to be told, when you're the one who's had the — the bit on the side. Especially if you expect to be free to do exactly the same thing. I don't know what I'd do, I can only imagine, since I've never been married or in a long relationship. What I'd like to be *able* to do is say, umm….something like: I'm glad you're back, I'm glad you told me, I'm glad you found some pleasure, I'm glad we're still together. And mean it."

"But it would be sure to affect how you felt, wouldn't it? I mean, how both of you felt."

"Yes, but the idea is for it not to affect it for the worse. I reckon it could be a way of strengthening a relationship. Both people would know they were continuing to choose that one main person. And that would mean there was no reason to be jealous."

"Only if both people were in agreement about the whole arrangement," I said.

"Quite. And that," said Bryn, enunciating very precisely. "is the tricky part."

I looked over at Bryn as we crossed Blackfriars Bridge, as though I was absorbing what he had just said but what I was really absorbing was him. When you are talking to someone and they are doing something that requires concentration, like driving a car — especially along the congested arteries of a capital city — you are able to study them a little more closely than usual without making them self-conscious. There they are, busy concentrating on what they are doing because it requires some skill, even though they are exercising that particular skill without even thinking about it, so they do not have such a keen awareness of the attention of the other person involved in the conversation.

As Bryn and I talked, I watched him drive and couldn't help thinking, not for the first time, that there was something very graceful about his hands and their movements, about the way he made what he was doing look effortless: his left hand moved efficiently from steering wheel to gear lever and back again and his right hand took absolute control of the wheel when simultaneously changing gears and turning a corner became necessary.

And the whole time he was talking cogently on a subject that was not exactly everyday. What a work of art is a human being!

Hands... I remembered a comment I had once heard when I was walking along the street behind two young women in a town whose name I've now forgotten. I was seventeen at the time, they were both a few years older. I was sure neither was married, either from the way they were dressed or the way they walked or both perhaps; they wanted to appear — available. They didn't know I was listening or perhaps they didn't care that they might be overheard, for the one said to the other: "What's the most attractive part of a man?" The other young woman gave a coarse laugh and I held my breath, waiting for the crude response, or perhaps a jocular attempt at a euphemism. "His wallet," she replied, and bumped her shoulder against her companion, who said, "Oh, you're a right one, you are. No, listen. My mum says it's his *hands.*" "His hands?!" repeated the other one, her voice strident with disbelief. I did not hear any more of their conversation. I had stopped dead in the middle of the pavement, in order to let this piece of information sink in. *His hands...*

As Bryn slowed the car to a halt at the traffic lights in front of the Tate Gallery, I was seized by an insane idea and before I could stop myself, out it came: "I'm going to meet a man after work today, this chap I got talking to on the train yesterday, we really hit it off, "I jabbered, "so we'll probably go back to his place and have sex because it's obvious we fancy each other. Is that all right with you?"

"Is that true or are you just saying it?" asked Bryn, sharply, glancing at me with a severe expression on his face.

I backed down immediately: "I was pretending to test your theory."

"Well then, let's test it."

I laughed. "I was kidding!"

"No, what I mean is— "

"I just made it up!" I protested, still laughing.

"What I mean is… " persevered Bryn and I stopped laughing.

There was a long pause during which the lights changed to green and the line of waiting vehicles moved forward, then Bryn went on:

"…I want you to move in with me. I already know how I feel. It's how I've always felt. And I've never been more sure of it. I want to try this thing — this open marriage thing — and I want to try it with you. Because you're the only person I can imagine that it might work with."

The sudden serious turn in the conversation silenced me completely but my thoughts were flapping around in my head like startled birds.

I knew where it came from, of course, this drive not to be confined, not to feel trapped, restricted, not to have one's life circumscribed by convention. I realised it the moment I met Bryn's parents for the first time. No-one could have had parents — or at least a mother — more confining than Bryn's.

I'd been invited to Sunday tea because Bryn and I were "going out together".

On that Sunday, I left my parents' house just after three o'clock and started to walk the two miles to the village of Pentwynmawr where Bryn's parents lived. I went down the steep hill past the houses where some of my other school friends lived, across the railway line then further down into the valley. Here the river flowed under a short but wide span of steel bridge that allowed both pedestrians and vehicles to cross. I walked over the bridge, my footsteps making an echo-y clanging sound, then started up the other side, pacing easily alongside the broad, grey road that led to Pentwynmawr, Newbridge and places beyond. This road sloped gently upwards, past a couple of pubs — The Bird in Hand and The Greyhound — past the Catholic church and the local working-men's club. After that the built-up area gave way for the next half mile or so to farmland, green fields and thick hedgerows where unseen birds rustled and chirped, then the houses started up again.

At five minutes to four I turned into Fox Avenue, the street opposite The Three Horseshoes, Pentwynmawr's only pub, closed because it was Sunday, and knocked on the door of number 12, one in a long row of front doors that opened directly on to the street.

The house was cramped and narrow, with a shadowy, glacial, rarely-used front room that had faintly oppressive overtones of funerals. The adjoining living-room was warmer because of the open coal fire. Crammed in front of the fireplace were two armchairs and a large sofa, all covered in liver-coloured leatherette. This arrangement took up half the room; the other half was taken up by a highly polished sideboard, a dining table and four dining chairs which all seemed to struggle with the bulkier furniture for breathing space.

I had to keep up the pretence that it was the first time I had been to the house. The first time had been very different. Bryn's parents were away overnight and Bryn, after several drinks at a party, had cajoled me back to his house and then up to his bedroom, hoping for sex, which had not occurred: an apprehensive, fourteen-year-old virgin in a frigid bedroom with a male of the same age who was burning with lust had not been a formula for success. It was not difficult to pretend that this earlier visit to Bryn's house had never happened.

Edwin Morris, Bryn's father, had been in the Royal Navy and when I first saw him he struck me as a man for whom the word "jaunty" had been created. He had an energetic manner, a glint of boyish mischief in his light blue eyes and he held his head at an angle when he talked as if he expected to be challenged and was ready to goodnaturedly defend himself.

Bryn introduced us, mentioning Mr. Morris's naval background: "A girl in every port, eh Dad?" "That's right," replied his father, to which Bryn added with a snigger, "And a port in every girl." Mr. Morris laughed his full-bodied laugh but Mrs. Morris's mouth turned down at the corners and I felt the colour rise in my face because I knew that for a few seconds everyone's mind had been wiped clean of every thought except one.

Hetty Morris had been "in service" from the age of fifteen until the day she got married and no matter how you tried to gloss over it, that meant that for those ten formative years she had been a servant, a maid. And whether she had been born with the inclination to serve or had acquired it through practice, it was certainly in her blood now.

She sat, perched like a plump bird, on the edge of one of the hard, straight-backed dining chairs, watchful of my every movement, while I sat in the middle of the sofa in their cramped living-room, silent unless asked a question, afraid to move, because each time I did so, she enquired, in her high voice: "Can you manage? Do you need anything?" I had to fight off the feeling that she was connected to me by some unseen mechanism that meant any action of mine generated in her an automatic reaction. I was used to feeling inhibited by the presence of grown-ups but this was a more extreme form of imprisonment. The two males paid her no attention whatsoever — perhaps that accounted for her extreme behaviour — while I, sensitive to the nuances of a strange household and unnerved by her attentiveness and her drive to control what happened under her own roof, screamed inwardly.

During tea, she sat at the table for no more than ten seconds at a time, continually jumping up to get more bread and butter, more hot water, more milk, more cake, and when she did sit, her pale, flat, round face with its expressionless brown eyes and fixed half-smile ceaselessly scanned the table like radar.

"Sorry about my mum," Bryn said, as he walked me to the end of the street as the daylight was fading. "She's always like that, she doesn't know how to relax. I don't know how my dad puts up with it."

So if Bryn was more like his father than his mother, no-one could blame him. Better a rake than a slave…

Bryn dropped me at work without our talking any further about his "idea" and I spent all day with his words on the edge of my thoughts, waiting, as a dog waits for the whistle that precedes a walk, for an indication from something more powerful than myself to tell me which way the wind was blowing and what was going to happen next. ...*I want to try this thing and I want to try it with you...*

It did not occur to me to discuss my predicament with anyone else. My first attempt to do so — to confide in my mother — resulted in successfully severing forever the fragile conduit along which any such confidences might have flowed. At age thirteen, as I was dressing for school one morning, I discovered a brownish-red stain in the gusset of my white cotton school knickers. I knew what this signified but was unsure of the next step and unprepared for it. I took a clean handkerchief, dabbed at the area between my legs for further proof, and took it downstairs to show my mother. She was at the kitchen sink, washing up.

I held out the soiled piece of cloth but before I could say a word, my mother seemed to know exactly what had happened; her face contorted into an expression of utter disgust and she said, harshly, "Throw that on the fire!" and it was done. A door banged shut and stayed shut. I had committed the one truly unforgiveable sin — I had grown up.

So when faced with difficult situations, I knew I had to make up my own mind. And the way I did it was by pure instinct, as if the answers to my dilemmas were in the very air itself. I was like a primitive chemist, resorting to the most fundamental method of effecting change: I waited. And sometimes it worked beautifully...

That evening Phil and Angie sat at the kitchen table over cups of coffee, side by side and very close together, slowly turning the pages of the *Evening Standard.* I could tell by their silence and the way they touched heads from time to time that there was one thing only on their minds and that it would remain there — until Angie had her abortion.

Compared with the decision she'd had to make, my dilemma was insignificant....but I still had not decided: Should I or should I not — move in with Bryn? I rang and asked him to come round, telling him I wanted to talk to him, though I wasn't sure what I was going to say. I simply felt I should leave Phil and Angie alone with their thoughts.

Minutes later Bryn arrived at the flat — he must have rushed out and jumped into his car the instant he put the phone down. We stood in the hall after I let him in. He called out a greeting to Phil and Angie and there came a halfhearted reply.

"Let's go back to your place," I suggested in a low voice, "I think they'd rather be on their own."

Bryn nodded his understanding. "That's what I was going to suggest," he said. Then he raised his voice to address all three of us: "There's something really good on the box tonight — one of those Ken Russell things, about the life of a musician."

"Which musician?" Phil called out, hopefully.

"Elgar," replied Bryn.

"Oh," said Phil, clearly disappointed.

The camera took us slowly away from the pale silent bed, across the shadowed room, and out over the rooftops of Worcester, drifting like a cloud towards the hazy, distant spire of Worcester cathedral. The symbolism was clear and potent: Elgar's soul had finally been released from its earthly prison and had begun to soar. The scene would have been affecting to the accompaniment of any suitably sombre music but played as it was to a subdued rendition of *Nimrod*, the slowest and saddest of Elgar's *Enigma Variations*, it was heartbreaking and almost unbearable. No more pomp, no more circumstance, the "glorious war" was finally over.

Bryn and I sat in front of the television, a couple of feet apart in the two well-worn armchairs in his living-room, hypnotised by these final, moving moments in Russell's poetic portrayal of Elgar's life. The television screen darkened to black and the list of credits emerged from the lower edge and rolled slowly upwards. At last, almost blinded by the tears streaming down my face, I turned my head to look at Bryn and was astonished to see tears also streaming down his face. We blinked and smiled weakly but happily at each other. It was one of those rare moments when two people were able, without words, to acknowledge they were experiencing the same feeling, one of those clear, noble responses that come straight from the heart and make human beings believe that perhaps there is a god, who perhaps is good, and perhaps a little of this goodness really does reside in us all. Perhaps…

"That was — very beautiful…" said Bryn, softly, wiping his cheeks with his palms.

I nodded agreement and reached for my bag to find a tissue.

"…especially that bit where it showed him tramping across the Malvern hills and hearing music in his head. Tremendous stuff." He took a very deep breath and released it, as if to conclude this particular, unusually emotional moment in his life and ready himself for the next, which would be more rational, pushed himself up out of the chair, and said, in his normal voice: "And now I definitely need a drink! Shall I pop out to the offy and get something?"

For better or worse, I discovered I had made my decision. Or, rather, that my decision had been made and I'd scarcely played a part in making it. It had something to do with watching the television program and listening to the music….but it had more to do with Bryn's tears. When you see a man cry, really cry, the effect is profound; it changes you. I had waited and it had happened: the alchemy.

"I'll come with you," I said, "and I'm buying."

"Say no more," grinned Bryn, and he began to look around for his car keys.

In the off-licence I went straight to the refrigerated section where there was a small selection of sparkling wines and champagnes, pushing out of my mind the little voice that murmured its misgivings about my slender bank balance, and reached for a bottle of Moet et Chandon.

"Excellent choice," smiled the man working in the shop when I carefully placed the weighty, chilled black bottle with its gold-foiled neck on the counter in front of him.

"Are you sure that's what you want?" asked Bryn. He meant was I sure I wanted to spend that much money.

I nodded and pulled a tenner out of my purse.

On the short drive back to the house, I sat with the cold, tissue-wrapped bottle on my lap and neither of us said a word, because Bryn knew. We still had not discussed the subject of my moving in but he already knew — that was why he had not insisted on paying in the off-licence. Amazing, really, how much on the same wavelength we could be.

When we were back inside the house, Bryn remembered that he did not have proper champagne glasses. "I keep meaning to buy some," he said. Undeterred, I poured the fizzing liquid into whisky tumblers, handed one to Bryn, gripped the other, held it aloft and said loudly, "A toast!"

"My lords, ladies and gentlemen," intoned Bryn. "Will you kindly raise your glasses. The toast is..." and he turned to look at me.

"Elgar, music, and great artists like Ken Russell."

"Yesss," hissed Bryn, raising his glass.

"And..." I paused, looking him straight in the eyes: "And to the acceptance by the second party of the offer earlier made by the first party."

He was silent for two seconds, then his face broke into a sunny grin, "Hear, hear!" he declared, gulped down the entire contents of his glass, gave a subdued belch, waited silently while I swallowed a few mouthfuls out of mine, then took me in his arms. "The first party is very happy," he said, with feeling, then, in a less serious voice: "Are you hungry?"

"I believe I am," I replied.

He grabbed the champagne bottle and topped up our glasses. "Davy's," he said. "It's time I took you to Davy's."

I was suddenly full of an unfamiliar audacious energy that demanded to be let loose.

"Well, I should think it is!" I said, loudly. And we both laughed because I had no idea what or where Davy's was.

As we drove there, Bryn told me a little about Davy's history. A longstanding wine wholesaler's in Greenwich, it had been transformed into a wine bar. Unlike the interiors of most of the wine bars that were beginning to sprout in London districts, Davy's interior, with its sloping sawdust-strewn floor, the age-blackened oak barrels and the almost claustrophobic gloom, was completely authentic. Those barrels, now empty, standing on end and being used as tables, had once been rolled into that same semi-darkness down that same sloping surface to be stored deep in the wine vault.

The drink was excellent, Bryn told me, but the best thing about Davy's was the food: deep-fried whitebait, smoked mackerel, roast beef and gammon, thinly sliced straight off the bone, crusty bread and farm butter, plus desserts that carried a faint echo of the Middle Ages, like syllabub and gooseberry fool.

We drank Buck's Fizz and ate smoked mackerel. It came with horseradish and thin slices of cucumber, was something I had never tasted in my life before and was instantly converted to. As we worked our way through the succulent smoked fish, Bryn pointed to a large glass bowl, full of layers, that stood majestically on the food table behind the carved meats and the small white bowls that held curls of butter.

"Guess what that is," he said. Before I could reply, he supplied the answer himself, "Sherry trifle. You think you've tasted trifle before but you haven't, not until you've had Davy's sherry trifle. They make it with their own amontillado. You have got to try it."

"Yes please," I said.

We watched as the waiter dug into the trifle with a huge silver serving spoon and piled helpings of the dessert into two glass bowls.

The sponge in the trifle was drenched with sherry and with the juice from the fresh raspberries and peaches. It was like spooning up nectar....topped with cold custard and thick whipped cream. The word hasn't been invented to describe such deliciousness.

Next morning I told Phil that I'd be moving out. He seemed relieved, said he was thinking of asking Angie to move in and was also considering trying to persuade her not to have an abortion.

And the following weekend I packed up my belongings ready for the move to Bryn's house.

Bryn's address was 52 Sylvester Road, SE 22. This part of south-east London was officially East Dulwich but he liked to say he lived in Peckham, because it sounded more working-class. In this way he liked to indulge his penchant for inverted snobbery.

Sylvester Road was a long straight grey street and on either side of it modest, plain-fronted two-storey houses — originally built to accommodate factory workers, navvies, shop assistants, bus drivers, hairdressers, cooks, cleaners, librarians, civil servants, the whole vast human workforce on which cities rely for their day-to-day existence — stretched all the way from beginning to end like two rows of giant near-identical Lego pieces. Not many parked cars, this was not an affluent part of the city.

The houses were in sets of two with a few feet between one set and the next. Each set shared a front door and a short hallway that separated two dwellings contained under the same roof. Each dwelling had a kitchen, living-room and primitive bathroom on the ground floor and two bedrooms on the floor above. A window on each level faced the street. The only visible variations along the street were the curtains at these windows and the colours of the front doors.

Bryn shared his half of the set with Mr. and Mrs. Corbett, a retired couple who, by his account, led a subdued life which meant half the time he was unaware he even had neighbours. Occasionally, however, Mr. Corbett would make Bryn aware that he and Mrs. Corbett had been disturbed by the volume of Bryn's music. They were "nice people — but a bit of a nuisance sometimes." And no doubt they thoroughly disapproved of the garden at the back of Bryn's half — completely overgrown with untended shrubs, a couple of stunted trees and a dense uneven floor of coarse clumpy grass. A wilderness.

It took only a matter of hours to remove my belongings from Phil's flat to Bryn's house and no time at all to feel as if I belonged there. I had my own bedroom. It was accepted without question or discussion that I needed my own space but — also without question or discussion — it was understood there would be a significant amount of traffic between Bryn's bedroom and mine.

After we had moved everything, I lay on the bed, my boxed possessions on the floor around me, looking at the macramé lampshade and felt that a whole new era was beginning in my life.

The following week I was assigned by the temp agency to work for an Indian couple, Mr. and Mrs. Ravindara Peshwari, who had an office in their three-storey residence in Chelsea. They had two sons, black-eyed, black-haired, spoilt little maharajas, aged five and seven, who were looked after by a Dutch au pair. She was smitten with them both and it was not difficult to understand why: the black pools of their enormous eyes and the sound of their mischievous giggles were enough to melt anyone's heart.

As with the first place I'd been sent to work, the Peshwaris dealt in import and export though of what I was never quite sure. Once again, all I did was type, mostly generic letters of enquiry and acceptance....though I once saw an invoice that showed five thousand Hong Kong dollars had been paid for a string of black pearls and my mouth fell open at that.

The office was in the basement of their house in Redesdale Street, situated off the King's Road, Chelsea. It became a recurring phone motif — the voice on the other end of the phone asking, "Would you spell that, please?" and my reply, "R-e-d-e…"

Sometimes the smell of curry permeated the whole house, causing my mouth to water painfully but I was never invited to eat with the family.

At lunchtime I would emerge from my baffling basement duties in the world of commerce out into the bright September sunlight of fashionable West One. The thing I already liked best about London was being anonymous amid the great swirl and bustle of activity. Life was going on, even if my life and, I suspected, that of half of the people around me was confused, uncertain and aimless. The invisible barriers around each harried individual were restrictive but also protective. We were all involved in a conspiracy of running away from our own dissatisfaction and simmering ambitions — and it was an exhausting, never-ending race.

But now I had a base, a place to hang up my togs, and I suddenly felt I had the best of both worlds, the uncertain and the certain. And as I walked along, I thought, Perhaps I shall be torn for the rest of my life between the desire for the familiar and the desire for the unfamiliar, the known and the unknown…and wondered if I would ever find an answer for the biggest question of all: What do you really want? Or if I would spend the rest of my life feeling incapable of answering it.

That morning I'd had to stand all the way from Brixton to Victoria on the packed tube. When it stopped at Stockwell the doors slid open and, standing as I was, wedged up against the doorway, I found myself looking straight into the face of a young woman who was waiting on the platform only a couple of feet away. She was about the same age I was, had been reading a book and when she looked up, our eyes met and I recognised myself — the innocence, the stoicism, the optimism, the uncertainty, the yearning for a life that was meaningful — all kept under wraps yet glimpsed in a single glance. I wanted to step out of the tube, walk up to her, speak to her, say something — anything — but of course I did not move. The great anonymity of city life kept me silent. We both looked away, the way city people do, the tube doors banged shut and I finished my journey with the unspoken words rolling round inside my head....*I know how you feel....I feel the same way....one day we may be allowed to fulfill our enormous potential. But when? And how?*

As I walked along the King's Road, trying to decide where to go for lunch, my thoughts turned to Nick. When Nick and I kissed, the world stopped, all difficulties evaporated, and I was filled with a desire completely missing from my marriage to Ian....and I was introduced to the importance not only of being wanted, but of wanting. It's funny, really, how you find out what you're missing. And once you find out, a line is crossed and there is no going back. After my first taste of that kind of desire, I began to live for it and thought I would never again be able to live without it.

With Bryn, this feeling appeared in flashes but it didn't matter; what Bryn was providing was a place in which to experiment, with him....and perhaps with others. *Plenty more fish in the sea...*

I meant my marriage vows when I said them. It was Ian who pushed open the door that led to my breaking them: he drank too much, hated silence, drove too fast, tried to control me and denied me the affection I craved. In the big book of betrayal, these were minor transgressions apparently, but the thing that unequivocally tipped the scales was his relationship with his mother. He was tied to his mother as surely and securely as if the cord had never been cut and it became clear that no other woman could ever displace her. They were two of a kind: both were only children, both had a drinking problem and each encouraged the other shamelessly.

My thoughts were jumping all over the place. No sooner had I thought about Ian's mother than I was completely absorbed by the sight and sound of a well-heeled couple emerging from a restaurant, obviously in the middle of a conversation:

"Yes, I quite agree," said the man, "but the truth is, she is utterly incapable of taking on that kind of responsibility."

"But she's never been given the chance to prove herself," said the woman.

"But you don't *wait* until you're given the chance," protested the man, "you have to seize it!"

They could have been talking about me.

As I walked along, the people in the street continued to hurl themselves at me. Two punks swaggered past, their torn black and tartan clothing held together with zip-like rows of safety pins and their hair in defiant purple spikes; an elderly woman proudly paraded a gurgling infant — her grandchild? — in a pushchair; businessmen in pinstriped suits, complete with bowlers and tightly furled umbrellas in spite of the cloudless day, trod smartly along the pavement to appointments with other men in suits; young clerks with aspirations hurried along scowling. And, of course, there were lots and lots of young women, alone or in twos and threes, who stopped every dozen yards to look at the displays in the boutiques, their eyes filled with the heat of the hunt as they searched for something that would separate them from all others — that one special outfit or accessory that would declare their individuality to the world and make them truly happy. Dreams....money....happiness....forever fatally connected.

Nearly all the shop windows carried variations on the same themes — crocheted tops, flared peasant skirts over flounced white petticoats, mountainous platform-soled shoes, abbreviated skirts over tights patterned with Op Art designs, long white patent boots, patchwork bell-bottoms and denim jeans that started to flare out in the middle of the thigh and didn't stop until they reached an outlandish bagginess at the ankle — so that each young woman would end up with an only slightly different version of these looks.

And then I thought about the gorgeous female I had seen in the Strand Palace Hotel the day I saw Nick, and about what makes a woman beautiful, and what separates the merely good-looking from the stunning, the unforgettable, and what was behind the whole concept of being captivating — and once again I felt myself yearning for the protection and opportunity afforded by wealth. *Money isn't everything, but it's a good friend....* this was something my mother liked to say.

My thoughts jumped again, this time to the idea of fragrance, because that was what had lingered after that woman had disappeared from view — not her clothes or her hair or her flawless skin, but her heavenly fragrance.

Bryn had made it clear he had no expectations of a financial contribution from me for living with him and I realised with an ecstatic jolt that I would be able to do what I liked with the money I'd been forking out on rent. I vowed right there that I would go that weekend to a perfume shop I had seen in Knightsbridge and buy myself a new scent.

I had been walking along the King's Road for fifteen minutes, my stomach was rumbling with hunger and my mind was in turmoil from the visual onslaught of the street scenery and my own tangled thoughts. When I saw the *Coffee Shop* sign above the entrance to a Habitat store, sighing with gratitude I launched myself towards it.

I ordered a simple lunch of French bread, cheese and chutney, with a glass of white wine, seated myself at one of the small, round, blond wood café tables and waited for my food to arrive.

Much as I liked being an anonymous speck in the great swirl of human dust out on London's streets, eating alone in a crowded interior was altogether a different matter. One of the difficulties was the painful self-consciousness I experienced — a feeling instantly and involuntarily conjured up by my own mind when I found myself in such a situation: a lamp was rubbed and the same annoying genie plumed out. Other solitaries had their own ways of dealing with this problem, but I was not a smoker and I never had a newspaper with me — the two most common solutions — so I dug into my shoulderbag for the little red notebook I carried around. It was a diary for that year, 1977 but there were so many pages without entries, particularly after July 17, the day I had told Ian I was leaving him, that I had started to use it as a journal and now, without even glancing at the date printed in heavy black letters on every page, I scribbled in it as if the pages were completely blank.

My lunch was brought to the table by a young man in a long white apron that crackled when he walked and threatened to trip him up.

"Ploughman's with a white wine?" he enquired, his manner a combination of the timid and the professional....*I have a job to do and I want to do it well and impress you, but I may make a mistake. If I make a mistake, you won't laugh at me or say anything to hurt me, will you?...*

"Yes, thank you," I said, smiling with manufactured bonhomie and in my manner was the same ambivalent approach to communicating with another human being who was a complete stranger but with whom I was forced to have contact....*I may make a mistake....you won't hurt me, will you?* We could have been founder members of the Society for Doormats and Underdogs.

I tore into the hunk of bread, scattering crust crumbs like shrapnel, dotted it with lumps of cold butter and devoured a few mouthfuls. I then sliced into the cheese, a pale, crumbling Cheshire, and added small forkfuls of fruity Branston pickle before popping the pieces into my mouth. How quickly I forgot that eating was one of the cardinal rules of existence, the opposite of starving; to keep living, one must eat. Why was that connection so tenuous with me? After a few minutes the desperation went out of my hunger and I looked at the diary entries:

Sunday July 17: A dismal, rainy day. Told Ian I am leaving. He was inconsolable.

Wednesday July 20: Went out for a drink in the evening, ended up arguing. Now convinced I am doing the right thing.

Friday July 22: Stopped working at the ice-cream factory.

Saturday July 23: Moved out.

My ballpoint pen hovered over the next available blank page. I wanted more than anything else to give some kind of shape to the significance of those moments, those intensely personal moments when life had been such a struggle, such an effort — I was sure no-one else in the whole world could possibly know how I had felt when Ian and I separated — and it was therefore extremely important to describe them. I was being changed by my new life, sometimes from one moment to the next, and I wanted to tell the world how that felt — no, that wasn't it....what I wanted was to be able to describe those moments so well that the world would feel them too. And the first step was to write down exactly what had happened. The sculpting of events into memorable moments —perhaps into a story — would come later.

I was suddenly seized with a familiar exhilarating focus, everything else fell away and I was left with only one task — to record the events of my own life. I downed the glass of wine as if it were water, then looped the strap of my shoulderbag over my arm and still clutching my pen in my right hand and my little red diary in my left, went to the café counter for another glass. The person behind the counter was a flushed, fleshy woman in a long, shapeless dress woven out of some sort of brown fustian who looked as though her whole life revolved around wholemeal flour. She was friendly enough but her manner and movements were slow and measured, downright ponderous in fact and I watched, amazed and incredulous, as she took a good five minutes to do something that would have taken a more energetic individual no more than thirty seconds. The woman in front of me who was currently being served at this glacial pace turned to face me: "Earth Mother," she said and rolled her eyes.

When I finally turned to go back to my table I saw that the young waiter in his floor-length apron, apparently having assumed that I, absent for so long, had left the café, was now clearing away my meal, the remaining cheese, the torn French bread, dirty knife, scrap of lettuce, half-used pat of butter. When he glanced up and saw me returning to the table, an appalled expression appeared on his face and I watched a swift backward replay of his clearing-up as he replaced the knife, replaced the bread, unwrapped the cheese, and so on. I gave a little laugh because I felt so sorry for him and I tried to think of something to say, something to put him at his ease, but all I could do was grin. Blushing furiously, he scurried away and I was left with my good intentions hanging in the air, the grin frozen on my face. It occurred to me that he probably thought I was laughing at him and my heart squeezed painfully....*I made a mistake, you laughed at me....you're just like all the others after all.*

Annoyed with myself, I sat back down at my table, sipped the second glass of wine and returned to my diary. The urge to immortalise my life had passed and I leafed through the pages aimlessly. That was another thing about alcohol, it stirred up strong feelings but then left you alone in a haze with them. Determined to write something and prevent the downward spiral of my feelings, I tore a blank page out of the book and started a letter to Nick, mentally noting that I would have to send it to his business address.

"You have really nice breasts," observed Bryn, one evening, as we were undressing next to his bed.

"Not too small?" I said, angling for another compliment.

"Neither too small nor too big. And in such nice condition. A nice firm handful," insisted Bryn. "God, you should see some women's breasts, great pendulous things." He blew a swift explosive stream of air out through his teeth: "Julia's are like that."

...So he's had Julia, the owner of the voice at the other end of the telephone, that first weekend I came to visit...(*"Julia plays trumpet in the big band....Don't look so worried"*...)

"And I love your fanny," Bryn went on, shocking me with a word I had not heard spoken aloud in this context before. "It's so— " he gave a little low growl of exasperation, "so secretive, so hidden away. It excites me."

We got into bed.

"Mmm, you smell terrific," he murmured, nuzzling my neck.

I was wearing my new perfume. *Vol De Nuit* by Guerlain. *Night Flight: For the woman who is rare, daring, enigmatic.* Oh yes, that's me….given the chance. (*"But you don't wait until you're giv-en the chance….you have to seize it."*)

I wanted to ask about Julia, just the simple facts, but while I was willing to accept that I was not about to be displaced in Bryn's attentions just then, I was not willing to bring another female into the bed, not even in the abstract.

After our initial caresses, Bryn said, "Here, you get on top. I can control things better that way."

And he did. His compliments had loosened up my emotions, causing my positive feelings for him and our life together to blossom into desire. I felt myself being teased, entered and slowly filled, until the ache of arousal, which had waxed and waned indecisively, turned into a quiver of hopeful expectation, which still threatened to disappear. Bryn, sensing this, placed his hands firmly on the sides of my waist and kept absolutely still. Frowning with determination, holding his breath momentarily, he stopped moving for a few agonising seconds. At last my mind was able to appreciate the thrilling intensity of his presence inside me and suddenly I felt the swift surge of satisfaction, like a sob in the pit of my stomach followed by the answering spasm of Bryn's climax.

I rolled off him and we lay on our backs in silence while our breathing subsided.

"That was terrific," said Bryn. He breathed deeply for a few seconds, then said, "I wonder what happened to Alan Jenkins. You remember Alan Jenkins?"

I was surprised at the abrupt change of subject but glad of the diversion because my thoughts were slipping backwards.... *What was it like with Julia?*

"Uh....yes," I answered, laughing gently. The three of us had been in the same year in grammar school.

Bryn rolled over to look at me, grinning, "Sorry, my mind jumps around after sex. My blood runs backwards or something." He pulled me into his arms and kissed me.

"That's okay," I said, touched by his explanation. "Yes, of course I remember him."

He shifted on to his back again and returned his gaze to the ceiling. "All those records of unknown American singers he used to come and play for us, d'you remember? The Crystals....The Marvelettes... The Beatles did cover versions of all those songs and everybody thought they were originals."

"'*Wait, oh yeah, wait a minute, Mr. Postman*', " I sang softly.

"Yes! And that Tamla Motown concert he took us to, in Cardiff, remember?"

"We were the only white people in the audience," I said, laughing.

"I know! And that amazing all-star line-up... "

"Everybody who was anybody on the Motown label."

He raced down the list: The Four Tops, Martha and the Vandellas, The Supremes, Mary Wells, Smokey Robinson and the Miracles, The Temptations..."

"And Stevie Wonder!" I said. "Don't forget Stevie Wonder."

"*Little* Stevie Wonder he was then — he was just a kid!"

"Thirteen," I said.

I could still see him.... a skinny little black kid, blind, he had to be led on to the stage, harmonica in his hand and he stood there, grinning, quivering with musical energy.

Bryn's voice was filled with the warmth of happy reminiscence. "What was that song he sang that really got the crowd going?"

"Fingertips!"

"That's it — unbelievable."

There was a long pause. I turned my head to look at him. He was still staring at the ceiling, a gentle smile on his face. "Alan Jenkins," he repeated as if in his mind he was meeting Alan again after all this time, smiling at him. "I wonder what he's doing now... "

And how long ago was that? How old were we, the three of us — fifteen? sixteen? — when we stood over Alan's pale blue Dansette record-player and he slid the shining black LP out of its sleeve and said, "Listen to this," and for the first time I heard the high, hard, tuneful voice of Arthur Alexander singing, *The Night Has A Thousand Eyes*.

"That boy was way ahead of his time," said Bryn, still thinking about Alan and all the music he introduced us to. "He really knew what was good and what was going to be big. He was a bit of a genius like that. I wish I hadn't lost touch with him."

I was liking Bryn more and more as he went on talking because, yet again, he was demonstrating his gift for appreciation, which was something that I lacked — people were guilty till proven innocent, to pay someone a compliment was alien behaviour — and because I was thinking, *We go back a long way,*

Bryn and I. We have a history. And because I realised, with a sense of being singled out for good luck, that I had something — a very particular something — that Julia did not have — nor any other woman for that matter. I had a shared past with Bryn, and Bryn was the kind of person to whom this meant a great deal. We had grown up together and here we were, together again. No matter what our history actually was, we *had* a history and nothing could change that. Nothing.

And what was our history? The pursuer and the pursued? Not quite. From the very beginning, when we met as young teenagers, Bryn took enormous pleasure in who I was and how I behaved and when you're an adolescent, anyone who gives you that kind of approbation means everything to you.

The summer of 1964 — we were both sixteen — he watched, beaming, as I turned cartwheels all the way across the school playground after learning that I had passed all eight of my 'O' level exams. He ran after me, laughing, and shouted, "How do you do that?"

That was when my life seemed charmed and I felt I was invincible. I had soaked up everything that my teachers had to tell me about those subjects and sailed through the exam papers with scarcely a day's revising. My highest marks were in physics and mathematics. If I liked something I did well in it and I loved those two subjects. Algebra was recreation. When I sat down to do my algebra homework my father, who had also been good at mathematics in school, would come and sit beside me, copy out the problems for himself and we solved them together, usually getting to the solution within seconds of each other, both grinning triumphantly.

There was no such thing as the future then. The future was — days that hadn't been lived and why think about them until they arrived? And I did not have the dream that most of my girlfriends had, the one a girl was expected to have, of a husband, a house and babies. There was a signpost at the entrance to that particular avenue that said, clearly and unequivocally: *Dead End.*

As a teenager I once said to my mother: "I'm never getting married."

"Aren't you, love?" she replied, airily, as if she knew better, and her tone alone shook and undermined my conviction.

I was conveniently ignoring the fact that marriage — an unusual kind of marriage, admittedly — was now what Bryn was suggesting. As far as I was concerned, we were together and that was enough. We had both wanted to escape from our roots, from the insularity and confinement of our backgrounds, we had both wanted to fly away from Wales....while still holding Wales like a warm secret in our hearts. It was a good place to be *from.* The difference between us was that Bryn had always wanted to make good his escape with me by his side....while I had always wanted to escape alone.

And we had escaped. But Wales had been sluiced out of my heart by subsequent events and by my fear of being criticised or — worse — laughed at. So the warm secret had languished and grown cold from lack of reinforcement. Perhaps, for me, my being with Bryn again now was nothing more than a need to restore Wales into my history and my heart...

Next day I travelled to work elated. Two letters had come for me in the morning post, one of them from Nick. When I saw the familiar jagged writing on the envelope I felt my mouth stretch into a smile.

"You're very popular today," said Bryn, as he extracted the two envelopes from the rest of the post which was all bills judging by the business-sized manilla envelopes with their small clear address windows. He added, "And I get all the chaff, do I?" And perhaps I only imagined the slight edge in his voice when he said this.

I waited until I was on the train to read Nick's letter.

Dear Loulou,

I was thrilled to finally hear from you. Ever since you appeared out of nowhere and stole that kiss from me in the Strand Palace Hotel I've been bubbling over to talk to you. I completely understand about your not making it to that pub with the very unromantic name! I waited for an hour and then I had to leave. But I was disappointed, so much so that I got a bit plastered and drove like a maniac up the M1. I didn't get nabbed — fortunately — this company does not take kindly to people who get speeding tickets while driving company cars!

There is little point in going on about the "shock-horror" of your leaving Ian. Suffice to say I was pretty impressed that you were able to do it, I mean, make a decision which is the right one but so traumatic initially. I rang Ian (the week after you left actually) all casual, just to say hello and he told me. He didn't sound particularly cut up, in fact he mentioned a new lady friend named Vicky. Yes, men are rats.

What I'd like to know now are your intentions. You have so many options open to you. You could be a bachelor girl, have a career and use men in ways that Cosmo readers would love to hear about. Or you could go on Le Grand Tour - you parley Frog and sprechen a bit Kraut so you'll never be stuck. You could even get yourself a nice fella, settle down and be "normal" — please don't!

Whatever you do, <u>do not lose touch with me</u>. It's bad enough not being able to be with you but not to know where you are would be unbearable. "So!" you are saying, "if he likes me so much what the hell is he doing up in Manchester with his little wife and his company car?" Don't ask me that question cos I don't really know the answer. I'll tell you what though. Your leaving Ian has done wonders for my sex life with Marilyn. She used to "enjoy" sex only under sufferance. Through my sweating eyes I used to watch her evaluating the state of the ceiling paint. In fact, there were occasions when I had come back from seeing you, utterly satiated and, because Marilyn wasn't fussed and I was too full of you, we didn't

— well, you know, for weeks and weeks. But now - ka-pow! I think she saw a warning light and is now attempting to make up for lost ground.

When can I come and see you? I have to come down to London about once every two months. Just tell me when and where and I'll be there. But I'm warning you my intentions won't be honorable. First I'll sweep you into my arms and give you the most passionate kiss of all time then I'll pull your sweater off over your head then I'll reach down into your jeans and place one hand firmly on your — oh heck, no more space.

Love you. Nick xxx

I pressed the letter against the front of my coat and looked around the crowded carriage at the other morning commuters. Some were reading newspapers, some had their noses in books, some were leafing through business papers in open briefcases on their laps. Others were chatting to companions and some, more asleep than awake, were staring blindly like dismayed moles through the train windows at the backs of the decaying Victorian houses lining the railway cutting or at the misty cityscape beyond. And I had to smile again, because I knew that no-one had what I had in my hand at that moment — a love letter.

I pulled out a *Daily Mail* that someone had wedged between the seats, straightened it out and turned the pages, idly scanning the news. When I got to the Woman's Page I read a little more closely. There was an article by the chief buyer for Miss Selfridge, one of the super-trendy boutiques in Oxford Street, London's shopping mecca. In it she described how, masquerading as a customer, she sometimes went into the communal changing rooms at Miss Selfridge — with clothing to try on, of course, she did not want to look suspicious or make the customers think she was staring at them — because, she explained, "I like to see how people approach the clothes." After one such visit she returned to her office and said to her assistant, "I don't know why we're trying to sell them pretty underwear, you should see what they're really wearing....so we filled the changing-room walls with huge blow-ups of models in attractive underclothes. There's nothing as devastating as seeing yourself in your tired underwear in a mirror, with a lovely girl wearing glamorous undies reflected in the same mirror. You're suddenly aware of a bra that should be pensioned off or the value of a good simple petticoat."

I felt utterly betrayed.

Wasn't it bad enough, disrobing alongside complete strangers in noisy, garish surroundings that smelled heavily of cheap perfume and sweat, the whole time being deafened by inane pounding pop music, feeling horribly vulnerable because of the amount of bare skin one was showing, hoping one's bra and knickers were not too awfully grubby, struggling into ill-fitting, over-priced clothes, breathing in hugely to do up zips and finally trying to evaluate the overall effect and not look like an egomaniac because something actually worked or weep because it didn't, without pictures of women with perfect figures in glamorous déshabillé looming over one? I was outraged.

Fuming, I closed the paper and stuffed it untidily back between the seats. A man sitting opposite looked at me disapprovingly and I suddenly felt as if I were pushing an enormous weight up a hill so I leaned my head back, closed my eyes and pretended to sleep.

The Indian household was in silence when I let myself in. Down in the basement office, rolled into the typewriter, was a note: "We have all gone to Hampton Court for the day. Please type the letters in the manilla folder for me to sign. R.P."

I pictured them, the two handsome little Indian boys, dashing through the densely hedged corridors of the Hampton Court maze, their mother smiling and walking calmly beside her husband around the perimeter, while the au pair chased after their giggling offspring.

An hour later the task was done; the letters were typed, proofread twice and replaced in the folder. I sat staring at the wall for a while, not sure whether I was annoyed or relieved that the phone was not ringing. I had no idea what I should do next or how to fill the rest of my time. It was impossible to embark on some kind of project, like filing or alphabetising, because so much of Mr. Peshwari's business was kept hidden from me.

The silence was oppressive and in no time at all, I had reached the point where I was completely at the mercy of my situation. I chastised myself: I was no better than a piece of tinder; I could flare up or sink down in an instant depending on whether I was given something to do or not. And I was reminded of the two letters of reference I had come across at my first job.

I had been sent to collect a file from the personnel department and as no-one was in the office when I got there I decided simply to get the file myself. When I opened the drawer labelled Surname S-W, I saw my own name on a file — WILLIAMS, Lowri M. — so I pulled it out and looked at the contents. There were two references, one from my mother's employer: "I have known Miss Williams and her family for many years. While I know nothing of her ability in her work, I am quite satisfied as to her integrity, loyalty and desire to take up a worthwhile career..." and the other from my college supervisor: "When Miss Williams finds her employment interesting and challenging she is capable of extremely good work." ...*And when she does not, she is capable of almost any mischief.*

It was very clever, I mused, the way people were able to convey something without actually saying it. What was more impressive was the fact that she was absolutely right about me. I pushed that thought away and drifted upstairs to explore.

On the ground floor were the kitchen, dining-room and a large living-room, beautifully furnished, all of which I had seen before, if only briefly. In the bay window which overlooked the street was a tall blue glass vase that looked fantastically elegant and in it an exuberant display of lillies and gladioli. I went up two more short flights of stairs to the top floor of the house, where there were two large bedrooms, a small bedroom — the au pair's — a box room and a bathroom. There was a faint smell of roses — Mrs. Peshwari liked to use rosewater. I went into the bathroom and looked at myself in the mirror. A semi-circle of tiny jagged sunbursts sparkled in the top left-hand corner of my field of vision — the beginning of a migraine, which meant an incapacitating headache was not far behind.

I opened the bathroom cabinet, hoping to find some Paracetamol or Anadin. The shelves were laden with some of the aids available to ease the stresses of modern life: in addition to the ubiquitous Alka-Seltzer there were two kinds of laxative, indigestion tablets, a prescription medicine for high blood pressure, a tube of Savlon, plus the products indispensable to the upholding of feminine allure: Café au Lait matte foundation, Paprika Spice lipstick, eyeliner, mascara, eyeshadow, a Dior powder compact and a Dior perfume, plus cottonwool, makeup remover, astringent and a Dior night cream. Mrs. Peshwari was a loyal customer.

On the narrow top shelf was a wafer-thin white box about the size of a playing card with the name of a pharmaceutical company printed across it in light purple letters. It contained, nestling in small clear plastic indentations backed with foil, a dozen round white pills, each with the word *Calmpose* on it in tiny letters of the same pale purple. So that was her secret, the always cool, calm and collected Mrs. P. — she took tranquillizers.

The sparkling sunbursts had subsided and the inevitable, subsequent, all-too-familiar dull pain was just starting in my temples. I took down the thin white box, stared at it for a second then, utterly devoid of circumspection, pressed one of the small round tablets through the foil and swallowed it. What was the worst that could happen? I'd have a headache but at least I'd be calm about having it. My bravado soothed me — it was the perfect antidote to the mind-numbing experience of being confined in the silent house and having nothing to do. I went back down to the basement to wait for the effect.

Next to the basement office was a small peaceful sitting-room where Mr. Peshwari liked to lounge on a sofa covered in thick soft leather the colour of sage and have long telephone conversations in Hindi. These were punctuated with "achha", which meant "okay" and the occasional English word which stood out incongruously as words in one's native tongue always do in the middle of a foreign language, except that a 'w' came out as a 'v' because of his accent: *babble-babble-babble-achha!-babble-babble-babble-babble-British Airvays-babble-babble-achha!-babble…*

On a low, glass-topped table in front of the sofa was a pile of glossy magazines. I picked up the copy of *Cosmopolitan*, remembered the article I had read in the Daily Mail and felt unusually sceptical. What other shifty behind-the-scenes activities were there to discover? What other betrayals? On the cover, arranged in a bower around the stunning model whose unsmiling face with its scornful expression had the perfect smooth skin of an infant, were clusters of short phrases, the tempting morsels of the wonders within: *Is he The One? Take our quiz to find out*; *Catwalk Looks at Kittenish Prices*; *Conquer Your Fear of Flying High.* With detached amusement I realised I was reading every phrase on the cover of the magazine over and over again. I seemed to be physically incapable of turning the page to look inside. Finally, with a concerted effort I forced myself to turn to the page with the quiz and reached for a pen. My brain now felt as if it had been wrapped in warm silken clouds, softening the edges of all external stimuli. Overcome by lethargy again, I dropped the pen and lay back with my face against the expensive leather, like a baby settling into its mother's arms.

...There was the one who drove me home after a party, came into my room and made love to me, like a rabbit — *hnh-hnh-hnh-hnh-hnh-hnh-hnh-hnh-hnh* — then with a groan he came, making me feel like a slot machine. Afterwards we had a tedious philosophical debate about who was more at fault....because his girlfriend was a pal of mine. Not The One.

And there was the one who, frustrated by my black moods, one Friday morning thrust a five-pound note into my hand and said, "Here, go and see your mother for the weekend." And the instant I got on the train to Wales I realised that the trouble lay not with me but with him and his way of solving problems by throwing money at them, and knew I had to extricate myself. When I returned and told him it was all over between us he pro-tested, through tears, that he wanted to marry me, had saved enough money for a deposit on a house, and I had to look down to make sure my feet were still on the ground. Also not The One.

And the one who told me he had perfect pitch....we were on the sofa, listening to a Joni Mitchell song. "What key is this in?"

I asked. "E minor," he said, in a dismissive voice as he slid his hand down inside the front of my dress. Not The One.

Then there was the one — how could I ever forget him? — who blew a loud raspberry in my ear because I was lying so passively on the bed, completely unmoved by his inept advances. Definitely not The One.

I felt my face burning against the soft leather of the sofa so I rolled on to my back and put my arm over my eyes so I could see this horrible man better. I should have slapped him for that disgusting noise he made into my ear; after all, what had he done but turn his pain into my pain. But no, the point of the sword broke off and stayed embedded in my flesh and became part of me, never to be removed.

I was becoming sleepy. The leather sofa was incredibly comfortable.

…That's what happens….when you're soft inside….no matter how high your defences, how tough your exterior….someone gets a cruel thrust in and it stays in and there's no avoiding it. You want to fight back. You want to say, *No, I don't like that, stop.* But you don't….because another part of you is saying, *What does it matter?* That's when you discover all sorts of cracks in your armour….and it's only later that you discover it did matter and it still matters….but by now it's too late, the damage is done.

And that's what you become. Damaged goods. You try to contain all the blackness that you are holding in but it starts to seep out and there is nothing you can do about it. *Be open,* they say, *let people see who you really are, let down your guard.* What they don't understand is that you didn't start out with your guard up;

you went out into the world completely unprotected, glaringly vulnerable, and you quickly learned that if you wanted to survive — and sometimes you weren't entirely convinced that you did — you needed some kind of armour in order to protect all that softness inside yourself....and your armour had to be very strong. So strong that the weight and thickness of it were sometimes insupportable. It weighed you down and sometimes you wondered how you were able to bear the burden of it.

It occurred to me to wonder what might happen if I took all Mrs. Peshwari's little white pills. I would perhaps expire right here on the luxurious sage-coloured leather with my memories spread out in my head like a full hand in a card game. And there would be no more of those who were Not The One. No more need for armour. No more pain.

I shifted into an even more comfortable position on the sofa and sighed. There *had* been one, perhaps The One....but there wasn't any more.

His name was Miles. I was living in his sister's house when we first met. Her name was Vanessa and her husband's name was Timothy.

Bryn and I had eventually broken up after I decided I didn't want to get married to him but I had stayed in Southampton and, after temping for over a year, I finally accepted a full-time position that appealed to me, as a secretary in the Entertainments and Publicity Department of Southampton City Council. On hearing I was looking for somewhere to live that was close to the Ents and Pubs office, Timothy, one of the senior clerks, offered a room in his place.

It was a large house, four bedrooms, and Vanessa did not work so they took in lodgers to help pay the mortgage. There were two of us lodging, myself and a young man called Raymond. We each paid a set amount per week, had our own bedroom and were treated like members of the family, with dinner provided every weekday evening.

Vanessa and Timothy were in their early thirties, old enough to command respect from us but young enough not to seem completely "past it", the ultimate insult.

I was twenty-three and had no idea that in a couple of years I would be married — though not to Miles. He came over for dinner one evening and Vanessa introduced us:

"This is my brother, Miles," she said and we gave each other a shy smile.

At the end of the meal, as everyone helped to clear the table, Miles and I found ourselves alone together in the kitchen and he asked if I would like to go to the cinema the following evening and I said yes. We both knew that something was happening between us.

All the next day I felt I was walking on air.

I shifted slightly again on the leather sofa and felt myself drifting towards sleep. Now my whole body felt as though it was melting away. I was more relaxed and carefree than I'd ever been in my life.

…They say women always remember what they wore….I had on a rose-pink angora sweater with short sleeves and a scoop neck, very flattering because it fitted so well, a short gored leather skirt the colour of caramel and sling-back shoes with rounded toes in the same caramel colour. Around my neck was a long wafty silk georgette scarf the exact shade of the sweater. It's true that people look their best when they're comfortable and everything I had on felt like a second skin.

We went to see *Midnight Cowboy* at the cinema opposite Tyrrell and Green. The film had just started when we got there. We went in, climbed the shallow densely carpeted stairs up to the balcony and stood there, holding hands, peering around for a seat. The place was almost full. The rolling carefree theme song was playing — *Everybody's talkin' at me* — and for the first time in my life, standing there in the darkness, with the film unfolding on the screen and the music playing, next to a person who was too good to be true, I knew pure joy. He was handsome, soft-spoken, gentle. And young.

Too young. I was twenty-three and he was eighteen. *Everybody's talkin' at me, I can't hear a word they're sayin'…*

I was awoken by an ambulance siren in the street outside and for one blazing moment I thought it must be coming for me but the shrieking clangs swept past the house and on towards the far end of Redesdale Street and out of earshot. I looked at my watch — ten past five. I had slept for over three hours. I listened for a few moments. The house was still silent. Feeling somewhat disoriented, I gathered up my things and left. My mouth was very dry but the migraine was gone.

On the way to the train station I went into Boots the chemist and bought a do-it-yourself pregnancy test. I was taking the pill and didn't feel pregnant, even though I had no idea what being pregnant felt like, but I was so late. When I asked for the kit, the shop assistant, a woman in her fifties with flamboyantly dyed hair, leaned over the counter and said, with a witch-like leer, "What'll you do if you are — get rid of it?" My stomach turned over and I looked down into my purse so that I wouldn't have to look at her revolting expression.

Then I got on the wrong train at Victoria station. When it didn't stop at Herne Hill, that was when I discovered my mistake. After flying through Herne Hill, the train went on a fantastic, non-stop journey out of central London, through the suburbs and off into the wilds of Kent. Station after station fled from the train: West Dulwich, Sydenham Hill, Penge East, Kent House, Beckenham Junction, Bromley South, Bickley, Short-lands, St. Mary Cray, Farningham Road, Meopham, Sole Street, and finally Rochester, where at last it stopped.

Dozens of fuming passengers dismounted, trundled over to the other track and climbed into a train back to Victoria. A hollow tinny voice over the Rochester station PA loudspeakers apologised for the mix-up. So it hadn't been my mistake after all.

All the way back on the stuffy disgruntled train I listened to an American girl tell her travelling companion about a friend who ran away from a health farm where she had gone to lose weight.

"She couldn' stendit — they di'n't give her inny hot food addawl! She di'n' dare go back for her suitcase. She sent some-one else to giddit."

Someone thin, presumably.

All the way back to Victoria we went, non-stop again, thank god, shooting through all those peculiarly-named stations for the second time and by the time we got to Victoria, I had decided I'd had enough of trains, perhaps for the rest of my life. I rang Bryn from the station concourse, explained what had happened, and he agreed to come and pick me up.

It would take Bryn at least twenty minutes to get to Victoria so I went into the station café and ordered a cup of Rombouts coffee. While I waited for the steaming water to drain through the filter into the thick white cup with the shield insignia on the side, I looked in my bag and there was Nick's letter — what a long time it had been since I'd read it on the train that morning — and there was the other letter, which I had forgotten about. It had a Belgian postmark so I knew it was from Rowena.

Dear Lowri,

You'll have to forgive teh mistakes that follow — have just started work at NATO and been confronted with an electroc typewriter and in my day matey we only used manoals so this is all a bit of a challengw for a simple girl like me. Anyhow, regardless of typing errors, I shall attempt to reply to your very nice letter…

Rowena was married to Malcolm, who had worked with Ian in northern Germany. Both men were employed by the Ministry of Defence and had been posted to Germany within a few months of each other, to be followed by their wives (and children, if applicable) who — whether they liked it or not — followed on after their menfolk.

I met Rowena and Malcolm at the same party at which I'd met Nick, the first party for ex-pats that Ian and I gave after our move. Rowena smiled warmly, and her eyebrows gave a lift of interest when Ian said, "This is my wife, Lowri." I, in turn, was impressed by her firm handshake and piercing green eyes. I soon got to like her for her brutal honesty. Though she and Malcolm had two young children, Sarah and Lucy, Rowena wasn't afraid to admit that she wasn't sure she even liked kids that much. She seemed to be only one step on the other side of the door marked "parent" and wasn't entirely sold on parenthood. I think she was one of the few people who, given the chance, actually might have "sent them back" and I often wondered if this brand of honesty was an advantage or a disadvantage to her growing daughters. Her love for them was obvious; so was her absolute refusal to indulge them. No doubt they grew up with the inevitable ambivalent feelings daughters have towards their mothers.

At the end of a three-year stint, MoD employees were moved on somewhere else to work — a new posting it was called. Ian and I came back to England, to sleepy Gloucester, Rowena and Malcolm went to Brussels. In her letter Rowena invited me to visit. I read the letter all the way through twice, finished my coffee and walked outside the station to wait for Bryn. By the time I saw his car approaching in the line of traffic coming along Wilton Road, I had made up my mind: I would go and visit Rowena in Brussels.

The traffic slowed to a halt at a red light and I dashed out into the polluted air between the thrumming vehicles and dropped into the passenger seat beside Bryn.

In front of Bryn's car was a man on a motorbike with a large clipboard fixed to the handlebars, positioned so that he could glance at it without taking his eyes more than a few inches off the road ahead. Consumed by curiosity, I asked Bryn,

"What's he doing?"

"The Knowledge," replied Bryn. "That's what they have to do, to be a taxi-driver — you know, the ones in the black cabs. They have to know the streets inside out."

The lights turned green, Bryn eased over into the adjoining lane and we drew level with the man on the motorbike so I had a better look at his set-up. There was a page of text and a large-scale street map folded down to the same size, side by side, both firmly clamped to the clipboard with two of the biggest Bulldog clips I had ever seen.

"How long does it take?" I asked Bryn.

"A couple of years, I think. Than they have to sit an exam. Pretty stiff too or so I've heard."

A couple of years....I was just starting to get to know London's streets and it was thrilling to think of being so familiar with them that if someone were to flag down my taxi, lean towards my open window and say, for example, "Sydney Street, please" I'd know immediately to come at it from the south because Sydney Street was one-way going north. I'd be one of those efficient — though taciturn — taxi-drivers, weaving smartly in and out of slower traffic, nipping around buses and lorries, turning on a sixpence in the middle of the street when necessary, and negotiating the capital's clogged arteries with only one aim — to get my passenger from A to B in the shortest possible time and with the least possible effort.... *When Miss Williams finds her employment interesting and challenging she is capable of extremely good work*"...

I was in the middle of this splendid new career when Bryn brought me back to reality: "Fancy a hamburger? There's a Great American Disaster round here somewhere."

There was a space inside me that had been filled with a whole string of things: desire, boredom, nihilism, nostalgia, travel lust, ambition, regret — but not food. "That sounds great," I said. "I'm starving."

Bryn turned off in the direction of Knightsbridge and we picked up speed. "Well, I just got informed today that I have to go to Bristol for a few days, week after next."

"Oh yeah?" I said.

"The powers-that-be have decided to have the annual conference down there and head office wants a couple of us from the London branch to go and talk to the chaps in the sticks, tell them how we do it in the metrollops. Pretty bloody condescending if you ask me, but hey ho, it's all paid for. You can come if you like, I'll be staying in a nice hotel. I'll be driving down on Thursday and coming back Sunday evening."

Bristol....Brussels...

"Actually, I've been invited to Brussels," I said.

It was Bryn's turn to say, "Oh yeah?"

"One of the letters I got this morning."

"Anyone I know?" asked Bryn.

"No, I don't think I've ever mentioned them. Rowena and Malcolm. I got to know them in Germany when I was married to Ian. He and Malcolm worked together. Out there the wives automatically get thrown together so Rowena and I got to know each other. We don't have that much in common — they have a couple of kids and she watches TV and sews — but we liked each other so we kept in touch. Malcolm got posted to Brussels about the same time Ian got posted to Gloucester."

"Well,' said Bryn. "Brussels sounds a lot more exciting than Bristol."

We were driving along Brompton Road and I looked out of the car window as we passed the vast dusty-pink, several-storey gothic edifice on the left side of the street that was Harrod's, the department store where you could purchase anything from an envelope to an elephant. Then Bryn abruptly turned left into Beauchamp Place and there was The Great American Disaster.

The place was packed. The clash of dishes and glasses and cutlery, the scrape of chairs and tables being shifted around, the piped rock music, lively dinner conversation, and the frequent commands of the kitchen and waiting staff piercing the uproar made the place like bedlam. Our waiter had a sign pinned to the back of his shirt with *Running in* scrawled across it, so the whole restaurant knew he was a trainee. His face was flushed and tense, he was practically trotting from table to table. I couldn't help thinking that a malicious fellow worker had put the sign there surreptitiously. My heart went out to him — I made a mental note to give him a big tip.

After we had ordered, Bryn said, "So when are you going — to Brussels?"

"I haven't decided."

"You know, you can get the tube all the way to the airport now. The Piccadilly line goes all the way out to Heathrow. Takes about forty minutes. Fantastic service."

Then I thought of Nick and the possibility of being alone with him in Bryn's house and suddenly my priorities shifted: "Perhaps I'll wait," I said, "until after you've come back from Bristol. It might be nice to have the house to myself for a few days while you're away."

"Nah, why wait?" admonished Bryn. "Just go. Then perhaps you'll decide you want to come to Bristol as well."

I lived for that kind of enthusiasm and spontaneous planning. It was something that had been entirely lacking from my childhood. I gave a little laugh: "All right, I might just do that."

"You'll get a permanent job one of these days and then it won't be so easy to take a day off to go anywhere. Take advantage of what you've got right now."

The Running-in waiter brought the bottle of wine we had ordered, opened it and was about to pour a sample into Bryn's glass when Bryn raised his hand and gestured across the table, directing the waiter's attention to my glass.

"You taste it," he said to me. "You know as much about wine as I do."

The waiter poured a few centimetres of the wine into my glass.

I suddenly felt a surge of confidence, because of Bryn's comforting presence and the compliment, so casually thrown out, and knowing the waiter was anxious to please….and because of the invitation to Brussels, and the thought of seeing Nick and not really having to feel guilty about it and of the whole idea of personal freedom and the power of encouragement. Bryn had the exact combination of being casual and committed that suited me and I wanted to sing. Instead, I raised my glass, swirled the wine around for a second, sniffed it, took a mouthful, noted the typical, pleasing, light but rounded flavours of the zinfandel and thought, *It's true, I can have it all.*

"Parfait," I said, to the waiter who looked petrified so I quickly translated: "Perfect," and the three of us beamed at one another.

Bryn and I were in excellent spirits by the time we left the restaurant.

After the perfect wine, the super-fresh salad made with a type of very pale but very crisp lettuce I had never encountered before called Iceberg — popular in the USA apparently — and the smoky, completely lean hamburger — this I had risked with the addition of blue cheese, bitten into with narrowed eyes then almost swooned with pleasure when the combination of flavours hit my taste buds — we rolled out of the Great American Disaster as if reluctantly leaving a really good party.

Marvellous how a full stomach makes one's doubts and anxieties recede. Now there was only sitting next to Bryn in his car, watching the incessant activity of London's evening streets as we drove by, and a profound sense of satisfaction.

When we reached Bryn's house it was only eight o'clock but the events and emotions of the day stretched out behind me like an entire lifetime and I was suddenly exhausted. Bryn said he would stay up for a while longer and went into the living-room to watch television while I prepared for bed.

I went into my own bedroom so as not to be disturbed when Bryn finally came to bed. I heard him go out again, probably to the off-licence, which probably meant he would up for at least another couple of hours. I remembered the pregnancy test and went into the bathroom to do it. Negative. Relieved and, by now, almost unconscious with exhaustion, I fell into bed so I had no idea what time it was when Bryn eventually returned.

I woke at dawn, having had far more than my usual quota of sleep, so I got up, went into the other bedroom and slid in next to Bryn without waking him.

After a while I drifted off again and had one of those vivid, disturbing morning dreams when one slumbers only a fraction of a level below consciousness and the dream is like life with the veneer stripped away, more real than life itself. I awoke with a violent start and sat up, hot, sweaty and disoriented, as if I had been scorched.

Bryn stirred, rolled over towards me, put his hand on my back and mumbled sleepily: "You all right?"

"I had a bad dream. I dreamt that Ian's father died."

"It was just a dream. Come here."

I lay down again, put my cheek against Bryn's warm shoulder, replaying the dream in my mind because it had been so real, and waited for my breathing to slow back to normal. Bryn put both his arms around me. Then, perhaps in an attempt to help calm me down, he started to tell me about a dream he had once had. He had been sleeping with a woman and had awoken abruptly and feverish in the middle of the night. The woman asked him if he was all right because he had been tossing and turning and crying out in his sleep and he told her that in his dream he had been wrestling with Raquel Welch and had finally overpowered her and had sex with her.

"And this woman threw a bloody fit," said Bryn, his voice a high-pitched whisper that conveyed his lingering indignation and incredulity. "She stormed out in the middle of the night, refused to talk to me on the phone and I never saw her again!"

It was getting lighter, someone started a car out in the street, it was almost time to get up.

"Was she — well endowed?" I asked.

"What? Who?"

"Your lady friend."

"What a peculiar question. No, actually she was built like a boy and I rather liked that — for a change."

"Well, there's your answer," I said.

"Rubbish!" protested Bryn. "What has that got to do with anything?"

And I thought, even the most understanding of men would need ten lifetimes in which to appreciate the extent of women's insecurities. And then, in a rare moment of insight perhaps precipitated by the dream, I thought that, on the other hand, women had not even begun to make allowances for the insecurities of men.

Two days later, Ian rang, to say his father had died, killed in a traffic accident. I froze with the phone against my ear. I did not mention my dream. When you tell people something like that, especially some individuals, men mostly — who seem to think that being hardheaded about the intangible is some kind of virtue — they don't believe you, they think you are making it up, showing off, trying to get attention. But I knew things like that actually happened.

My father had three brothers, of whom only one — Gwilym, the unmarried one — used to write letters to my parents, though these missives were very sporadic. A few times a year, as she was laying the table for breakfast, my mother would announce, "I dreamed about Gwilym last night. We'll get a letter from him soon." And either that day or the next, without fail, a letter would arrive.

Ian, I could tell, had a great need to talk to someone who had known his father — a gentle, tolerant, smiling man — and would therefore be readily sympathetic.

"Mamum's in shoak, she's drinking too much," he said, thereby informing me obliquely that he was too.

It had been very sudden. Mr. McKay had been crossing a street in Glasgow late on a black rainy night after a local council meeting and a drunk in a van had ploughed into him, killing him instantly. Ian gave me a few more details about the incident, then asked, tentatively, "Yurr no goin' to be down this weh anytime soon, arr ye?"

And I knew he wanted to see me and I felt a surge of pity, the feeling that is so tied up with love, to the extent that it is sometimes mistaken for love, and I could not help myself. I agreed to go down to Gloucester that weekend. Bristol could wait. Brussels would have to wait.

"I have to go to Gloucester — to talk to Ian....about — about the divorce."

"Right," said Bryn, with forced equanimity.

We both knew I was not being entirely truthful.

"I'm not looking forward to it," I said, straining towards honesty.

"What will you do — go down on the train?"

"I suppose so....perhaps I'll take Friday off and go straight after work on Thursday."

"I'll give you a lift to Paddington."

I was sure that Bryn, though aware that Ian had rung, had forgotten about the dream I'd had. And I did not remind him. For some reason I was not able to tell him that I still had the impulse to comfort Ian.

The 125 from Paddington to Gloucester was crowded and I ended up sharing the cramped space of the enclosed area that was at the end of each carriage with two teenage punks, one of whom had a small, round, black badge pinned to his tartan jacket with a slogan printed on it in white block letters: MODS STINK.

The first-class compartments were almost empty, as usual.

We all staggered slightly as the train pulled out of the station and for the rest of the journey we were rocked aggressively from side to side as the train sped west.

After a few minutes, Punk One demanded of Punk Two:

"Why's 'iss train called the One Two Five then?"

"Iss 'cause iss fahst, innit."

"Wot — you mean, like, it can go 'undred twenny-five miles an hour?"

"Yeah, tha's right."

There was a short pause followed by the incredulous hushed reply: "F-a-c-k."

Every time we passed a train coming the other way on the adjoining track there was a noise like that of a colossal, leather-bound book being violently slammed shut — a terrifying sound

— and a sense that the air in that small space bulged for a second then shrank back. And each time this happened, the two punks, as if on cue, shouted, "Fack!" and then laughed like maniacs.

For the whole journey they ignored me completely.

The train swept west through Berkshire and across a corner of Wiltshire, as if searching blindly and haphazardly for the source of the river Thames which is in the village of Coates, between Swindon and Stroud. Somewhere east of Swindon, however, the train, after giving a swift, distracted glance at the surrounding countryside, instantly abandoned its search and veered north, continuing its rushing onward journey, now with the grander aim in mind of Gloucester with its half-timbered buildings and Norman-built cathedral.

Ian was at the station to meet me. *Handsome.* That was the word that rose above all the others that crowded into my mind when I saw him. He had grown a beard in the last few months and the next impression was one of lots of very dark brown hair which only made the whites of his eyes look whiter and his cheekbones more sculpted....hazel eyes, an interesting mouth, a serious expression.

Two years ago, when we went back to Wales together for my father's funeral, Ian wore a black suit and black tie with a spotless white shirt, an outfit which made him look even more handsome. One of my uncles stared hard at him for a few seconds, then said, "You'd think Ian was a laird, with those looks."

So what happened? What went wrong? (...*drinks too much, tells the same jokes over and over, only wants sex when he's had a few and then it's over in minutes....I could go on...*)

"Guid jurrney?" he asked, after we had kissed briefly and drawn apart. I was immediately charmed anew by his Scottish accent and felt an emotional echo of the first time we had met.

"I had to stand all the way," I said.

"Ye'll be exhausted, then."

"No, really I'm fine."

It was as if, on the surface, we were still friends. There had been a falling out, we had said and done some inexcusable things, tensions had run high, but now — now all that was history. Or, rather, *we* were history….because when I looked at him more closely, his eyes said, *How could you have left me? For better or worse, that's what you said.*

"So sorry about your father," I said.

"Aye, it was a real shoak. Mamum is having a difficult time wuth it." That confirmed how concerned he was that she was drinking too much.

And yet….I still wanted him to like me, to want me….what kind of madness was this? Had I removed myself from the situation only to keep dragging all my confused feelings around with me, like extra luggage? It's easy enough to leave a foundering relationship — physically. You just uproot yourself, like an ailing plant, and let the weeds take over. Emotional departure….that's another matter.

"When is the funeral?"

"Mundee. Arr ye shur yur no tired?" His lovely, lovely accent…

"No, really, I'm fine. Nothing that a couple of drinks won't fix." I made myself smile.

So that evening, an hour after I stepped off the train, Ian took me to a party, a small affair in the house of one of his colleagues. He said he'd accepted the invitation a couple of weeks earlier and had decided not to cancel because he thought it would be a good distraction. "Ye cannae drink alone fur long," he said, and I was surprised at the serious tone of his voice. For once, he was not joking. Shocking how effective the crucible of grief was at reshaping human beings.

There were two Americans at the party who had fought in Vietnam. Ian introduced me. When I shook hands with the burly one, I registered something amiss with his right hand, as if the usual framework of the bones was disturbingly incomplete, and I felt my smile solidify on my face. After we moved away to get a drink, Ian told me this man had lost half his hand and both his legs in the Vietnam war. This piece of information made me initially pensive — was it bravery or bravado to offer a ravaged hand in a handshake, knowing the contact would instantly force an unsuspecting stranger to struggle with their shocked reaction….but my pensiveness was replaced by something more fatalistic. I decided that all that mattered was living for the moment, pushed the question about the injured GI out of my mind, and joined Ian in drinking the night away. For once I couldn't have cared less how much Ian drank.

When we got back, very late, to the house in Dimore Close, the house that still belonged, inconveniently, to both of us, Ian took me in his arms and we fell into bed.

But, to my relief, after the lager, wine, and champagne, sleep soon overtook him. Ian's sex drive had always been easily derailed by too much alcohol.

In the morning, I listened as Ian bounded out of bed and bustled about, washing and dressing and grooming himself, turning on the radio in the bathroom to listen to the news, turning it off, then going downstairs to make coffee in the kitchen and turning on the radio down there. Familiar sounds. I was suddenly overcome by emotion, as if the connection between us had not been broken, merely tested, and now I had returned, the marriage was still intact, we could start again, couldn't we? And yet I knew I would not be able to talk to Ian about this. My innermost feelings were a secret that I must never share — I'd learned how important it was to keep my guard up. And I thought, Why do I never tell people how I feel and what I'm thinking? Why am I so secretive?...

My mother said, "No need to cry. Nothing to cry about."

And once again I was torn, between instinct and obedience, between the force of my emotions and the pressure to obey. Obey....no, that's too strong a word, when you're only nine. No-one ever used the word 'obey' — you just did what you were told. Do what you're told, that's how they said it. You must do what you're told...

It was Sunday, a pleasant Sunday afternoon in September, not hot, not cold, not sunny but not entirely overcast either. Soothing weather. My mother and I were on the landing at the top of the stairs, staring out through the window that overlooked our back garden. The door to my brother's bedroom was a few feet to our left and the door to the bedroom I shared with my sister was to the right. The door to my parents' bedroom was across the landing, behind us, their window overlooked the street in front of the house. All the doors were wide open and in each room the same things were visible — floral wallpaper, the corner of a high bed, dull wooden floorboards and the edge of a patterned rug. Under my parents' bed a white chamberpot, a sight that filled me with shame.

We stood there, looking out at the back garden, at the rows of vegetables, the greenhouse, the big rectangular lawn, recently mown and rolled, the corrugated iron roof of the garage, and at my father who was at the far end of the garden near the fence.

My dog, Treacle, had been missing for three days and that morning my father had said to me, "Come on, we'll drive around in the car, see if we can find her."

He reversed the car briskly out into the street and pulled up by the front garden gate. I dashed out after him and jumped into the passenger seat. But just before we drove off, my mother came to the front door and called my father's name, as if he'd forgotten something, so he went back into the house while I sat there — patiently, now that I knew we were going to find my dog.

I'd had Treacle since she was eight weeks old. My father brought her home in a canvas bag, took her out and placed her on the sofa from where she promptly tumbled on to the floor. She lay there, stunned for a few moments, then she saw me kneeling beside her, jumped up and licked my chin, and I knew we were going to be friends. She was a mongrel mix but she had the pale golden-brown coat of a retriever, the same colour as the thick golden treacle that I stirred into my porridge every morning. So that was what I called her. Treacle. I'd had her for nearly two years now.

My father seemed to be taking a long time so I ran back inside the house which seemed to be deserted.

I called out: "Dad?"

No answer.

I ran up the stairs and stood on the landing, looking out through the window. From the front garden gate to that landing was a straight line and one of the first things I taught Treacle was to stay at the gate while I trotted up the long garden path and into the hall, where, a moment before racing up the stairs, I would turn and shout, "Come!" and she would fly from her spot at the gate, invariably passing me halfway up the stairs so she always reached the top before me, and when I got to her I would congratulate her and make a huge fuss of her. Neither of us ever tired of playing this game.

I called out again: "Dad?" Still no answer.

I heard a door close and my mother came up the stairs. But before she reached the top stair, I saw him. He was at the far end of the garden, near the fence, talking to our neighbour, Mr. Price, whose back garden adjoined ours but, in complete contrast, was a jungle of weeds and coarse overgrown grass. They were both shaking their heads and looking down at the garden path near my father's feet, where there was an inert pale golden-brown heap. I felt a lump in my chest, as if my heart had suddenly grown too big and was trying to escape up through my throat and I could feel the prickles behind my eyes that meant I was going to cry. My mother came and stood next to me and I thought, Mam will put her arm around me and everything will be all right. She must put her arm around me and hold me, that was the only thing that would allow me to keep living. Instead, she folded her arms and said, brusquely, "There now, no need to cry. There's nothing to cry about," as if the most important thing was to move me to a place where emotions were not given free rein, where they were held in check because it was for the best....and after she spoke, I found myself caught in a struggle between following instinct and doing as I was told. I tried to will my heart back into place, to get rid of the lump in the back of my throat, but it stuck there and I was unable to talk or cry....and my conflicted emotions at that moment became carved, as if in marble:

I am alone, I am so sad I feel I may die….but I must not show these feelings.

Whenever I got into an argument on the phone with my mother, Ian took her side. That hadn't helped marital harmony. I made contact with her infrequently and when I did — scribbling an airy greeting on a picture postcard or sending a casually chosen Christmas card — it was more out of a sense of duty than anything else. So months would go by until, not having heard from me by mail, my mother would phone. I would go out into the hall, pick up the receiver and at the other end of the line would be the familiar voice, shrivelled by distance and longing: "I haven't heard from you for ages. Have you fallen off the end of the earth?" Instantly on the defensive I would answer rudely, "Yes."

And this would set the tone for the ensuing conversation, in the course of which my mother used any means she could to try and get the thing she most wanted from me — a declaration of affection — while I in turn used every means at my disposal to defend myself against the onslaught, which amounted to nothing more than emotional blackmail.

And, overhearing my curt replies and my tone of voice, oblivious of my extreme inner turmoil, Ian would hiss at me from the adjoining living-room, "Be *nice*."

Seething inside, I would listen to her criticisms and complaints about my behaviour while I glared down at the brown cork tiles on the hall floor, tiles I had laid there myself so that this lifeless unheated area would be a little warmer when one answered the phone on a chilly day.

A little warmth....sometimes that is the only difference between happiness and unhappiness...

What my mother did not know — and would have been incapable of understanding — was that the most potent weapon in her arsenal had been successfully launched and found its target long before, perhaps at my birth, when her need for my affection, for my love, my approval, had been driven into me like shrapnel, embedding itself deep into my flesh. The resulting injury manifested itself throughout my life as a tragic answering dependence on her affection, her love, her approval....which were never forthcoming. Because they were conditional. Conducting her crusade under the flag of Parental Love my mother had made an effective and permanent conquest. That was the superb, crushing irony of it....I had been riddled with lead....but was expected to fly.

I could hear Ian downstairs in the kitchen, the news had finished and there was music on the radio now. I shifted into a more comfortable position, not yet willing to get out of bed, unsure how to behave with the man I had recently deserted, was still married to and had just slept with — platonically. Any minute now he was going to call up to me. By nature a morning person, he had always disliked my fondness for lying in bed after I had awoken.

The phone was on a low shelf in the hallway of our suburban three-bedroomed house in Gloucester — this house. It was the same phone that, every couple of months, I would answer around mid-morning, after Ian had gone to work, and hear Nick's voice ask: "Are you alone?" If by chance I was not, this was my signal to reply, "Sorry, you must have the wrong number," and put the phone down.

But by some miracle I always was alone and after a simple, "Yes" — the same word but spoken with the complete antithesis of the tone I used with my mother — I would luxuriate in the sound of Nick's voice as he told me how much time we would be able to spend together and asked me where we could meet. That felt like love.

And it was on the same phone, in the same hallway, with the same mud-coloured cork tiles on the floor that Ian would talk to his mother, at least three times a week. In a cruel twist of the Oedipus complex, Ian did not have to challenge his father for his mother's affection; it was his and he was constantly reassured of it. Ian's relationship with his mother was another source of disagreement between us, though for completely different reasons. When his mother phoned, they talked to each other like lovers....in a way in which he never talked to me.

She always rang late in the evening, after coming home from whichever pub she and Ian's father had patronised. As soon as I heard Ian's, "Hullo Mum!" I'd go straight upstairs and get ready for bed. And ten or fifteen minutes later, as I lay there wide awake, I'd hear Ian wishing her goodnight: "I love ye. Yes, I do, ye knoaw I do. Guidnight, then. Y-e-s, I love ye, too." And I'd think, who's he married to, me or her?

Perhaps I should have known....that first time that Ian took me home to meet his parents. We slept in separate bedrooms for the sake of appearances and in the morning I heard Ian calling, "Mum?....M-u-m!" This was followed by footsteps running up the stairs and Mrs. McKay's voice asking, "Yes, love?" followed by Ian's voice saying, "Tea, Mum," followed by another "Yes, love." At the time I found it touching....no doubt about it, just another of the many faces of love.

Another time, a friend who happened to be with us when Ian's parents visited, later remarked that Mr. McKay was like an amiable ghost, always in the background, smiling, not causing any trouble. He was the one who cooked her meals, made sure she did not make a complete fool of herself in the local pubs and put her to bed when she'd had too much to drink. Now that really was love...

Well, I thought, turning my head on the pillow and watching the leaves of the huge chestnut tree outside the window shiver in the wind, he really is a ghost now and Mrs. McKay has lost her protector. No wonder Ian is so worried.

What is love anyway? Oh, that question, which has a thousand answers. All I wanted was the impossible — a harmonious relationship which someone whom I saw every day, or almost every day. Oh, that's a good one. Good luck with that one.... the eternal rubbing together of two different personalities. The constant smoothing down of all the little spikes and crevices and mounds and lumps and hollows and cracks and corners of the ego. And for what? To be left one day, bereft, deserted, by accident or design, and plunged into despair — the despair of loss.... how wonderful it all was... But was it?

In the front garden of the house was an enormous horse chestnut and lying there in bed I could see its branches and their big bright green leaves, like huge hands. *Aesculum hippocastanum*, the only tree whose Latin name I knew. I loved that tree, it was like a friend. It was that tree that had made me want to buy the house because it reminded me of my childhood. At the end of every summer the tree would push out its fruit, shiny copper-coloured nuts encased in bright green prickly overcoats. As children we used to coax them out, thread them on lengths of thin string and play simple but very competitive games with them. We called them conkers.

When our marriage was falling apart, Ian said, "You never smile now," and I suddenly realised he was absolutely right and it was no use trying to deny it any longer. But where had the love gone?

Ian shouted up the stairs, "Arr ye getting up?" and although the familiar sharp edge in his voice was absent — he was making a special effort — I was immediately thrown back into the relationship I had been so anxious to leave and once again I could not wait to get out of it.

Yes, I should have known but I was blinded by love at first....and then the love disappeared....but where had it gone? And was it really love? How do you know? How can you tell? All the way back from Gloucester to Paddington, the wheels of the train seemed to mock me with their monotonous rhythmic litany: *How-do-you-know How-can-you-tell How-do-you-know How-can-you-tell...*

There was one time when I did know....sometimes you *can* tell...

Miles was a virgin when we met. He told me quite early on. Perhaps he mentioned it as we were driving to the cinema, that first time we went out, the day after we met in his sister's house. Or was it as we were leaving the cinema...?

I was used to the prospect of being greeted by the interior of a pub at the conclusion of any evening but as we drifted out with the crowd at the end of *Midnight Cowboy*, Miles said, "Let's drive out and see the Fawley flame." Yes, that was when he told me — that night, in the car, on the drive back from Fawley.

We stood, shivering slightly though it was a warm evening, on the pebbled shore beside the Solent and looked out across the estuary. Night and day, a plume of orange flame twisted and curled and fluttered like a flag at the top of an immensely tall grey pipe on the edge of the refinery. When the wind was strong, the flame broke into glittering orange pieces and reassembled itself, over and over again, and was endlessly fascinating to watch, especially at night.

As we stood there about a foot apart looking at the restless flame, Miles said, rather sheepishly, "I suppose you'll want me to kiss you now."

My whole body was charged with a hunger to feel his lips on mine, but "No," I said, mildly, because I knew I could wait, I was so sure it would happen. When I was sure of something my patience was boundless.

As we drove back into town, Miles said, "I should probably tell you — I've — um — well, I've never actually slept with a woman."

It sounded like an apology and I could not think of anything suitably consoling to say, so I simply turned and leaned towards him in the thrumming shadows of the car interior and kissed him lightly on the cheek....and the silence between us was full of anticipation.

The house was empty when I got back from Paddington. I dropped my overnight bag on the floor in the hall, went into the living-room, flopped down in an armchair and stared at the wall opposite, turning over the events of the previous two days. Whatever I had expected from meeting Ian again, nothing had happened to indicate a reconciliation. In my imagination, I was signing the divorce papers and sliding them across a desk to someone in a business suit.

Ian had tried to kiss me when he saw me off at the train station that morning but I had pulled away. There was a different chemistry now, or rather, there was a complete lack of chemistry. It was at that moment we both knew it was really over, that our marriage had now become just another phase of our individual histories.

I heard the front door open and close, then Bryn came into the room, holding a small shallow cardboard box containing vegetables, a loaf of brown bread and a jar with an unfamiliar label.

"I've been to Forest Hill," he said. "I went to the market and bought a Hovis loaf and some tahini."

One of the joys of living with Bryn was the way we had — without even discussing it — dispensed with the usual expected banal greetings, the 'Hi' and 'Hello' whose repetition starts to irritate like sand when you see the same person every day.

He went into the kitchen, there were sounds of cutlery against china, the clunk of the toaster, then, a few minutes later, he re-emerged. Tucked under his arm was the mysterious jar and in each hand he held a clear Pyrex dinner plate on which lay a knife, two slices of brown toast and one small fresh tomato, cut into quarters and juicily red-ripe. He opened the jar and we spread an oily beige paste on the toast and ate the tomato with our fingers.

"How did it go with Ian?" asked Bryn.

"Just the paperwork left," I said, improvising madly. "You know — a load of boring forms to sign."

"Then you'll be footloose and fancy-free again?" chuckled Bryn.

"I most certainly will," I replied, in the same lighthearted tone, spreading the paste on to the second slice. "What is this stuff, exactly?"

"Pulverised sesame seeds."

"It's good, " I said. Then, just making conversation, I asked, "What were you doing in Forest Hill?"

"I spent the night with Simone."

My solar plexus recoiled at these words, as if all the air had suddenly and violently been driven out of me....*spent the night with*....that could mean only one thing.

"I went to The Clock for a couple of pints last night and bumped into her at the bar. It's no big deal. Simone and I have known each other for a long time."

I was so stunned by this casually given piece of information that Bryn seemed to interpret my silence as a cool, disinterested reception of the facts.

He went on: "I suppose you could say we use each other. She knows I don't love her — and anyway she's still in love with Rob. She's told me that more than once — she's never going to get over him. So we were just — fulfilling a need really. We both know what the score is. It's not the first time. Anyway, she's a heavy breather, it gets on my nerves. Let me put it this way — it doesn't mean a thing."

Bryn finished his toast. "This bread is good, isn't it? Do you want some more? I'm having another slice."

"All right," I said, automatically.

While Bryn was out of the room, I calmly evaluated my feelings, trying to decide if I could take him at his word. Sometimes it's the truth that is hardest to believe....*doesn't mean a thing.... not the first time....*nor would it be the last, I thought.

By the time Bryn returned, the disturbance created inside me had subsided and I realised I didn't care. *It's working*, I thought. *He's told me, I don't care, it must be working. This is it — an open relationship.*

But you should care, a tiny voice inside me said. *Why don't you care? Don't you remember how much you cared when—*

Bryn placed two more slices of buttered toast on my plate.

...fulfilling a need... "It's just like being hungry, needing to eat," someone once said, about wanting sex. "It's an itch you have to scratch. Why suppress it?"

"I didn't sleep with Ian," I said, flatly, not wanting to elaborate on the weekend but also not wanting to lose the opportunity to attempt the kind of revelation Bryn had made.

"You didn't?"

"Well, I did *sleep* with him but we didn't — you know."

For a few long seconds we both chewed in silence, then Bryn said: "That must have been a bit strange. The two of you in bed together but no how's-your-father."

"Well, that wasn't so unusual really."

"Oh."

Bryn was being very delicate, mutely acknowledging that since it was he who had introduced the topic of our respective "away" games, he must now allow himself to be drawn into an area which did not concern him and obviously did not interest him, simply to allow me to talk about it.

I could not help thinking that, had we been in a pub, after dark, with a few drinks inside us, talking about the same thing, with the usual pub noise and bustle around us, the conversation would have taken a metaphysical twist and we would have become animated, as we dissected and examined the subject at hand — in the abstract. That was another thing I liked so much about Bryn — his fondness for intellectual argument and abstraction. It kept things in proportion....or perhaps all it did was keep things at bay.

But here, on an overcast Sunday afternoon, in a quiet shabby room, over toast, tahini and tomatoes, we were forced to be more down-to-earth and deal with the details of these new developments. Not that I wanted any further details from Bryn about his recent encounter.

"It was probably the best thing that could have happened," I said. "Getting that close together again and being faced with — a closed door."

"A closed door?" Bryn enquired, a little too politely.

"I mean — oh, you don't want to talk about this — I mean my feelings for Ian. There was really nothing there any more. What I'm trying to say is — it's over. This weekend just helped me prove it to myself." I put my plate down and placed my hands on the arms of the chair with finality. "Why don't I go and make some tea?"

"I have a better idea," said Bryn. He looked at his watch, at me and then with an oddly aloof expression on his face, enunciating outrageously he said: "Whay don't we gew end hev tea et the Ritz?"

And I could have hugged him for his quick thinking and perfect timing.

Bryn parked outside the ICA on Pall Mall so that we could walk across Green Park to Piccadilly where the Ritz Hotel dominated the north-east corner of the park. To walk through one of London's parks — especially on a Sunday — was to understand how Londoners stayed sane. They lounged in deckchairs, sprawled on plaid rugs, threw balls for dogs, sauntered the narrow grey paths that skirted the grass and, if near water, fed the ducks and ordered cups of tea in the cafés. In other words, they slowed down, relaxed, and renewed a very necessary connection with things natural. The pervading air of a London park was one of tranquillity and one entered these metropolitan oases with a strong feeling of relief at reclaiming one's sanity.

"I can see how this place got its name," I said, looking around and smiling as we walked across the beautifully maintained grass of Green Park.

"Apparently there's an underground stream, that's why it stays so green."

"And no flowers," I observed. "Rather effective, that. Makes it seem greener."

We walked out through the ornate black-and-gold-painted park gates on to Piccadilly and turned right in the direction of the Ritz. Impossible to walk through such an imposing gateway and not hold oneself a little more erect.

And impossible to walk into the hushed, cool, pastel-painted foyer of the Ritz and not feel a little overawed. It was Bryn's way to shift into a higher gear when faced with situations like this, situations that demanded a certain style which he perhaps thought he did not have, so his approach was pre-emptive and he wasted no time in mustering as much panache as he possibly could, and it worked. And only someone who knew him well would be able to note the uncharacteristic edge of stiffness that came into his manner.

He went straight up to the pale, willowy, impeccably-dressed hostess — no doubt chosen for her ability to blend into her surroundings — who hovered at the entrance to the tea-room, clasped his hands behind his back and stated, in a charming clipped voice, "Good afternoon. We'd like to take tea."

Take tea?....he was laying it on a bit thick.

I stared, enchanted, into the room behind her, at the chintz curtains and the white table linen, the delicate chintz-covered chairs, the teapots dipping their spouts over the bone china cups in their matching saucers, the triangular sandwiches and fancy cakes on tiered dishes and the smattering of hats which were like bigger fancier cakes.

"Do you have a reservation, sir?"

"I'm afraid not."

"I'm very sorry, sir, but we are completely booked for today."

And that was that. She turned her attention to another couple and we were left standing there, confused and adrift for a moment. Bryn recovered immediately: "I know somewhere else we can try. Come on."

We went to the Orangerie in Kensington Gardens, where the interior was all white with white Grecian statuary. Bryn ordered a scone with his Earl Grey and I had a piece of their Jolly Rich Fruit Cake with my Darjeeling. The waitress finished writing on her pad and held out her hand for the menus. "And a bottle of the Sauvignon Blanc," added Bryn, almost as an after-thought. Turning to me as he relinquished his menu, he said, smiling, "To go with the surroundings."

And after two glasses of wine each we ended up having the conversation I had imagined earlier, where we dissected and analysed and intellectualised the dichotomy between love and lust. At one point Bryn said things would be okay in a conventional relationship if it weren't for his lust. And the anxiety which I had expected — but had not experienced — when he told me about Simone, finally rose up in me, uncontrollably, making me quake inside because I knew that this lust of his was something that was never going to go away.

I suppose I wanted him to say, Yes, it's you and only you I want, for ever and ever, and I'll never look at another woman again....but I knew it was asking too much.

So I let Bryn do most of the talking while I tried to come to terms with what I thought I'd already come to terms with — that he was always going to want to go to bed with other women, and sometimes he would act on this wanting. And would then tell me about it.

And presumably he would be willing for me to do the same thing — have other lovers. But would I want to talk about it?

As we were leaving The Orangerie, Bryn reminded me of his upcoming business trip to Bristol.

"I know you haven't decided whether to come or not, but the invitation still stands," said Bryn. "I'll be in meetings during the day so you'll be free to do whatever you want."

I had collected myself somewhat after our serious discussion over afternoon tea and now felt calmer and more accepting. At Bryn's words, my own lust — for travel and a change of scenery — swelled in my thoughts. After a minute's deliberation I replied, "You know, I think I would like to come. I can go to Brussels at a later date." Then reality elbowed its way in: "But I'm not sure I should take any more time off work....I already took the day off last Friday. The agency will start to think I don't want to work full-time."

"Come down on Saturday then, on the train."

The train again....my favourite way to travel....the small leather overnight bag containing a change of clothing for evening, a toothbrush, hairbrush, all my make-up. I took enormous pleasure and pride in travelling light. And this time I would be going to a destination that was not weighed down with unpleasant associations and bad memories, as was Gloucester. In fact, Bristol was a place imbued with good memories, pleasant associations — the bistro, my brother's wedding, the famous mother-of-pearl ring...

"All right, I will come," I said and then in a burst of spontaneity, like someone choosing a certain horse in a race purely on the strength of an inexplicable optimism, I added, "Let's go and buy me a ticket this instant."

"Yes?" Bryn hovered on the brink of his own enthusiasm.

"Yes!"

"Excellent!" declared Bryn.

We drove straight to Paddington and there I was, once more standing at the Advanced Tickets window, confidently asking for a single to Bristol for that Saturday.

But in the car on the way back to Bryn's I felt my heart sinking, the way it sometimes did after I had behaved impulsively and I heard my mother's voice....*You shouldn't rush into things....*and thought perhaps I had not considered my choice carefully enough. After all, there was Nick — *Just tell me where and when* — and the opportunity of being alone with him in Bryn's house. How long had it been since I had last seen him? A month? Five weeks?

That evening I took a long hot bath, holding a silent dialogue with myself, a replay of the conversation about love and lust, and all the misgivings came flooding back. In confusion I went into the living-room where Bryn was watching television and told him I had changed my mind, I would not be going to Bristol.

"But you've already bought your ticket!" he protested.

I simply pulled a face, pretending I didn't care about the ticket, it was just a piece of paper, just money spent, the whole thing a completely reversible decision and announced I was going to bed. But Bryn's obvious disappointment weighed on me so heavily that after a couple of minutes, lying naked and alone between the cool sheets, I felt lost. I put on a thin slip and went back downstairs, to ask Bryn if he was coming to bed soon. He was sitting at the kitchen table, staring into space, a dejected expression on his face. When he saw me, he immediately came over, put his arms around me and hugged me tightly. We stood there, I in my thin slip, him in his brogues and fully clothed, until I was overcome by a feeling of vulnerability and began to cry. No sobs, no heaves, just silent weeping. After that we went to bed together and made love. Love. Not lust. And I fell asleep in his arms.

On the Thursday Bryn got up early to leave for his trip. He came upstairs just before he left and gave me a kiss on the fore-head, saying, "See you Saturday."

An hour later I walked to the tube station to go to work as usual, still arguing it all out with myself what I should think and what I should do and still not able to decide. As usual, I fell back on something outside myself to settle things. On the short walk between the tube and the office I devised a plan: I would try and call Nick at his office in Manchester — something I had never done before — and if I managed to speak to him and he was able to come down to London at such short notice, I would throw everything else aside to be with him.

Once through the entrance of my office building, instead of waiting the usual minute or two for the lift, I ran up the stairs to the fourth floor, taking the dirty-white concrete steps two at a time, energised by my own decisiveness.

In Bristol, while Bryn was at his Saturday meeting, I sat on the terrace of a café in Park Street, drinking espresso and glancing at a very pretty female who had more hair than I had ever seen on one human head: long, supernaturally thick, wavy, tawny-brown locks with subtle golden highlights surrounded a pale, heart-shaped face, a face with a smattering of freckles but without a trace of make-up. Her hair hung loose down to her shoulderblades, like a lion's mane, untamed by a ribbon, ornament or controlling cut — and all I could think about was how anxious this would make me were Bryn here. Because her hair made this woman beautiful, impossible to ignore, desirable.

Later in the day, I sat on a tall stool in a department store, looking at dress patterns in a thick book, and afterwards at the cool plump bales of material, stroking and fingering the exquisite silks and cottons and lace purely for the pleasure of it. As I strolled through the haberdashery department a woman shopper came up to me and shyly asked me if the store stocked a certain type of cotton she was looking for. When I told her I wasn't a shop assistant, she apologised and reddened with embarrassment. People in shops often mistook me for an assistant;

I had come to the conclusion it had something to do with the aloof expression I adopted when I was looking at merchandise I had no intention of buying.

"Excuse me, could you tell me where I could find…"

"I'm sorry but I don't work here."

"Oh, I do beg your pardon."

"It's quite all right," and I'd give the kindest, most understanding smile I could but they would invariably scuttle off, having committed a small but very embarrassing crime.

Bristol had changed a good bit but I could still find my way around and remembered where certain places were, like the antique shops that lined Christmas Steps near the Colston Hall and the bistro where I went with my brother and his fiancée a week before they got married in — when was it? 1966? 1965?

We all ordered *coq au vin*, drank too much, and Liz and I laughed helplessly at my brother's shaggy dog stories. Back at their flat, they showed me a garish vase given them by their landlady as an engagement present. Though they both disliked it, they could not bring themselves to throw it away so it stood conspicuously on the mantlepiece in case she dropped in for a chat — something she was apparently in the habit of doing.

"But you don't like it!" I protested.

"I know," said my brother, "but she's a nice old thing and we don't want to offend her."

It was to Christmas Steps that my brother took me to choose a piece of jewellery, a gift for being their bridesmaid. In shop after shop I pored over tray after tray lined with black velvet until, in a cramped, Dickensian shop halfway up Christmas Steps, the asthmatic owner gently wheezing as he hovered patiently over me, I chose a ring with an enormous round slice of mother-of-pearl set in silver. My dustbin lid, I called it. I adored that ring.... and the following year I lost it. I was visiting an old college friend in Nottingham and we went shopping together. In one of the big department stores we both needed to go to the toilet so we went to the one in the store. We emerged from the stalls at the same time and as we stood at the sinks, chatting and laughing, I took the ring off, without thinking, as I did at home when I washed my hands, and forgot to put it on again. Fifteen minutes later, having left the store and walked a little way down the street, I suddenly realised what I had done and we rushed back to the store but of course it had gone and, for a while, I was inconsolable.

You lose the things you like and have to force yourself to keep the things you don't.

I sat on a bench in the pedestrian precinct, opposite a cinema that was showing the latest James Bond film, ate an orange and smoked a cigarette. I hadn't been able to get in touch with Nick at his office. A colleague of his had told me that he was in Bolton for the day. So that had settled it. Brussels, Bolton, Bristol.

The sun appeared from behind the clouds, making every-thing hot and glaring. Luckily the bench where I was sitting was in the dappled shade of a tall plane tree and I felt calm and utterly content, as you do when floating on your back in water or when someone brushes your hair. I had done the right thing, coming to Bristol.

Afterwards I went to meet Bryn at a designated spot on the other side of the precinct. I was sauntering along in my own little private piece of universe, when a voice said, "Hullo!" and there was Bryn, coming out of a bank and smiling in the sunlight. His meeting had finished early. We walked along, his arm around my waist and mine around his, and told each other how funny that we should have met accidentally like that. And I forgot the feeling of detachment that had carried me through the day; I had had my quiet break, eating an orange and smoking under the trees near a cinema showing *Moonraker*, and was in the mood to prefer walking and talking. Everything was perfect.

That evening Bryn and I ordered veal and spent the entire meal feeling guilty as we recalled a TV programme we had recently watched showing fattened calves imprisoned in their stalls, so overfed that, without enclosing walls around them, their legs would not support them. We kept recalling and reminding each other of the gruesome details.

"Okay, that's it," said Bryn, after we had chastised ourselves for minutes on end. "I've decided. This is the last time I'm eating veal."

"Me too," I immediately agreed. "Let's make a pact. No more veal."

And with serious expressions on our faces, we shook hands across the table.

The ride back from Bristol to London in the car next day was warm and, for me, pleasantly soporific. I had not slept much the night before — I had lain awake while Bryn snored gently beside me — but I was happy. Things were still close to perfect. I reclined the passenger seat and stretched out my legs, thinking about the things that made me happy....sunlight, music, nice clothes, travelling....being with someone who has lots of confidence...

The previous evening, when we got back to the hotel just after midnight, we were accosted by a clerk who came out from behind the reception desk and demanded to know if Bryn's room was for double occupancy. I had on a red dress slit up the side and a red rose pinned in my hair and it occurred to me that this clerk might have thought I was a prostitute especially since, as Bryn and I stood waiting for the lift in the hotel foyer, I put my arms around Bryn's neck and passionately kissed the side of his face.

"Is the room for double occupancy?" demanded this silly little martinet.

"Oh — yes, yes it is," said Bryn, completely uninterested, looking at me and not at the clerk.

"Then we will have to charge you for double occupancy," came the stern reply.

"Fine," replied Bryn, in a nonchalant tone of voice that indicated he couldn't have cared less and was above any further discussion on the subject.

Then, right there in front of the quivering hotel clerk he kissed me full on the mouth, to show me how important I was, how much more important than paying a little extra for double occupancy and being publicly forced to do so by a fastidious weasel. Squashed and defeated, the clerk stuck his nose in the air and paddled petulantly back to the reception desk where he very pointedly made some notes in a large black book on the desk. Another small, potentially embarrassing crime....except that Bryn had not been embarrassed.

As we drove out of Bristol towards the motorway, I told Bryn about the brown bread ice cream I had seen on a restaurant menu and Bryn pointed out some gas storage tanks near the motorway that had some relevance to his meetings. He waved an arm in the direction of an enormous tangle of industrial pipes.

"Look at that," he said. "That's the Parkway plant....beautiful," and when he said the word 'beautiful' I thought about the girl with the mane of tawny hair whom I had forgotten about and my happiness evaporated.

I glanced over at the huge industrial plant he was indicating, then looked away, trying not to think about what it was like.... when I had not had to worry about other women...

Miles never looked at another woman when he was with me. I was his whole world because I was his first love — and his first lover. He was as interested in my thoughts and opinions as he was in my body. We talked for hours sometimes. And when we went to bed he never pawed or grabbed at me, was never rough. Kissing him was like sinking into the softest bed imaginable, and when he caressed me and gently grazed my nipples with his fingers I almost fainted with pleasure.

His sister Vanessa did not approve of my going out with her "little boy" as she referred to him. After a few weeks she started dropping big hints and making pointed remarks. "Miles only goes home for a clean shirt these days," she said, one morning after overhearing Miles — who had stayed the night again — saying *Goodbye* and *See you later* to me at the front door, and there was acid in her voice. I suppose you couldn't blame her, with the difference in our ages; she thought it was just infatuation on his part and manipulation on mine.

But it wasn't, it was love. I felt it with every atom of my being. I adored him and he adored me and when we were apart, we ached to see each other. And the opportunity soon presented itself for Miles to prove just how much I meant to him....but the irony was that this was how I got thrown out of his sister's house.

One evening, a few weeks after the first Christmas I spent at Vanessa and Timothy's, Miles and I were alone in the house. Tim was away visiting his elderly parents, Raymond was at his girlfriend's place for the weekend, and Vanessa had gone to a show in town with a friend. As Tim had taken the car, Miles was to collect Vanessa and her friend after their night out. Miles had an old banger, a Ford Cortina, one of those indestructible wrecks that looked as if it might fall apart at any moment but just kept on going.

"I'm to listen for the phone," said Miles, as we undressed going up the stairs to my bedroom.

But when the phone rang, his mouth was on mine and the heat of our bodies was setting the room on fire so he ignored the persistent ringing. "They can get a taxi," said Miles, softly. "I'd rather stay here with you than be a chauffeur for Nessa."

The weather had turned ugly, rain was bucketing out of a black sky, as if to provide a poignant backdrop to our lovemaking. The niggle of guilt I felt about the two women trying to find a taxi in the rain was gone as soon as he stopped speaking and started kissing me again.

An hour later we were back downstairs watching television when Miles said, casually, "I wonder where they are?" No sooner had he said this than the phone rang and he went out into the hall to answer it. I heard a few indistinct words followed by a long silence, a few more unclear words, and then, very clearly, "I said I was sorry!"

When he came back into the room Miles' face was flushed but he said nothing, just stood there in silence — an angry silence — until I asked him what was going on.

"That was Nessa. She's at the Royal South Hants. She and Linda got a taxi after the show but a car skidded and ran into them because of the bad weather and Linda is in the hospital Emergency Department — she has a broken nose."

My hand flew to my mouth: "Oh Christ," I said in a whisper.

Miles shrugged: "Nessa was giving me hell — for not answering the phone. I told her the same thing could have happened if I'd been driving. She wanted me to feel guilty and she got pissed off that I wasn't." Right there, Miles, though younger than I, gave me my first lesson in the meaning of personal priorities, and the price one might have to pay for sticking to them.

Relations between Miles' sister and me soured rapidly after that. For Christmas she had knitted me a woollen scarf. A month later she was telling me to get out.

We were at dinner, Raymond, Timothy, Vanessa and myself. She let Tim tell me.

Dinner was toad-in-the-hole, one of my favourite meals. I had just dug out, from the large oblong Pyrex dish in which it was cooked, a hunk of nicely browned batter with a plump sausage in the middle of it. My mouth was watering. Then Tim said, "I think you had better find somewhere else to live," and suddenly my appetite had gone. Raymond went on eating silently, a few seconds ticked by.

"How soon do you want me to go?" I asked.

"By the end of the month," said Vanessa, icily.

The room stood still, they turned into cardboard figures. I started eating but the food tasted of nothing. No-one had the least doubt why this was happening, we all knew, all four of us: Nessa was determined to wrest Miles out of my grip.

…But if you think that will stop us seeing each other you have another thing coming. He loves me and nothing you can do will make him give me up, <u>nothing</u>. He loves me and I love him and there's nothing you can do about that, not a thing.

"All right," I said.

It didn't take me long to find another place. The next day I rang the landlord of the flat I'd had in Howard Road and asked him if he had anything available.

"Well, fancy you ringing me up!" he said, sounding very cheerful, "I was going to put an ad in the Evening Echo this afternoon. The place at the back is about to become vacant, the garden flat, you remember it? The girl in there is moving out at the end of the month. It has a double bed so the rent's a bit more but not much. That do you?"

So I moved into the garden flat, which was self-contained except that I had to go into the main house to take a bath or use the telephone callbox. When Spring came I would leave the door open to let in the breeze and the leafy-earthy smell of the garden.

A tabby cat adopted me. She just walked in one day with her tail straight up, looked around and then up at me with amber eyes, as if to say, "I'll take it."

I would lie on my back on the big bed, happily indolent, waiting for someone to come along the path that ran from the house to the garden flat to say I was wanted on the telephone. The cat, whom I'd named Felicity, would be stretched out on my stomach, purring. And I would lift her, still purring, gently on to the floor, get up and go to the phone and it would always be Miles.

"What are you doing?"

"Nothing — stroking the cat."

"I'll be there in about half an hour."

And I would go back to lying on the bed, thinking it was the best thing in the world, that little half hour before Miles arrived, when I knew exactly what to look forward to, the softest kisses imaginable, the palms of his hands on my body, the exquisite expressions of love.

Somewhere between Reading and Windsor, Bryn took his left hand off the steering wheel and reached over to hold my hand: "I'm really glad you came to Bristol," he said. "I'm much happier when you're around."

"Are you really?" I replied.

"Don't you believe me?"

I suppose I ought not to have sounded surprised but I was. It wasn't that I doubted him, I was taken aback that he had actually said it. It was not the kind of revelation I was used to hearing, it was not the kind of thing anyone in my family would have dreamed of saying: the expression of personal feelings and emotions was actively discouraged and any attempt to discuss such things was beyond the pale, a sign of perversion almost. And actually to pay someone a compliment? Absurd. So my delight at Bryn's unexpected comment was complicated by something approaching shame — an unwritten rule had been broken — leaving me tongue-tied.

"Yep," continued Bryn. "You looked really great last night, by the way, in that red dress." He paused, still holding my hand.

"And I'll tell you something else, while I'm at it. I'll always take care of you."

*....I'll take care of you....*that was what he had promised the first time. No-one else had ever said anything like that to me before. In fact, if I was convinced of anything when I finally realised I could not go on living at home, it was that no-one was going to take care of me even though this was the thing I needed most. The first time Bryn had said these words, they were like a life-belt thrown to someone floundering in open water and in danger of drowning.

And now here he was, saying it again. Oh, the things I'd been offered by men... Bryn represented security, deep affection, and a shared history, Nick generated my desire, which was never satisfied. Ian had been a necessary mistake. And Miles — Miles was the one who broke my heart. He introduced me to the phenomenon of needing another human being so badly I felt I had been living only half a life before him. We were twins who had been separated at birth and did not even know it until we were restored to each other. When he told me he no longer loved me I was sure I would die...

However, there was also the growing question of culture, intellectual stimulation, appreciation of the arts....and I had no doubts about who was offering these pleasures.

"I haven't heard any decent music all week," complained Bryn, as we were coming over the Hammersmith flyover. "I seem to remember there's something on at the Albert Hall tonight." And without waiting for a response from me, instead of turning right towards Battersea Bridge to cross the river, he turned left and carried on driving towards Hyde Park and Kensington.

As it was Sunday, Bryn managed to find a place to park on Kensington Gore close to the Royal Albert Hall and I stayed in the car while he went to the box office. I opened the window and sat there, with the glossy black-painted iron railings of Hyde Park on my left and, over on the right, the Albert Hall, the elegant, red brick rotunda with its high windows and beige frieze of Roman figures. The traffic on Kensington Gore was much lighter than it would have been on any other day of the week. I could count the seconds between the swish of the passing cars.

Bryn was practically jumping up and down when he returned: "I was right!" he exclaimed. "You'll never guess what's on tonight."

"Then I won't even try. Come on, what?" I said, smiling, infected by his enthusiasm.

"*La Grande Messe des Morts*," intoned Bryn, relishing the French words.

"The Berlioz?"

"Yes-s-s-s," hissed Bryn.

"But do they have any seats left?"

Bryn squeezed his lips together, raised his eyebrows and waved a pair of tickets in front of my face: "Front row centre — they had a cancellation ten minutes ago."

"You jammy bugger!" I said.

"The luck of the devil," beamed Bryn.

"Do we have time to go back to the house first?"

Bryn consulted his watch: "Barely....nah, let's have something to eat round here. There's a pizza place a bit further up the road."

In the nearby Pizza on the Park we chose an American Hot — it took us only minutes to agree on the delicious combination of salami, garlic, chili peppers and mozzarella cheese — after which I freshened up in the marble-floored Ladies room and we were back at the Albert Hall an hour later, queuing up against the great curving exterior wall of the place, waiting for the doors to open.

There were almost as many performers on stage as people in the audience, the sight of the double choir — the sheer number of singers — massed behind the orchestra gave me gooseflesh. And when their combined voices hit the first dramatic *fortissimo* note of the requiem mass, I could scarcely control my emotions. I had a vivid blinding image of my father, trapped in heaven listening fiercely to this impassioned celestial music, wishing he were part of it, and I had to squeeze my eyes shut and cling to the armrests of my seat so as not to cry, because I knew that once started I'd never stop. Music that powerful was a force to be reckoned with, a storm to be weathered.

Bryn sat absolutely still through the whole thing but at the end, as the final chord resounded throughout the hall and the conductor, frozen in place for two seconds, turned to face the audience, Bryn applauded noisily along with everyone else and shouted, "Bravo! Bravo!" After a few seconds he suddenly stopped clapping, hugged me tightly and shouted over the din:

"I want a bigger house!!" then rejoined the thunderous applause all around us. I looked at him quizzically.

Still facing forward, clapping his palms together loudly, he yelled, "I want to be able to play music like that and not think about the neighbours!"

And, as usual with Bryn, it was — almost — no sooner said than done.

The next day at work, I received a phone call from the Alfred Marks Bureau telling me they had been contacted by a company who wanted to interview me for a permanent position, personal secretary to the company's marketing executive. Was I available? I said I was.

Five minutes later I had a phone call from the interested company's personnel department and after a brief conversation with someone trained to give absolutely nothing away about a prospective interviewee's chances, an appointment was made for me to be seen the following day.

The following morning I awoke, wracked by indecision about what to wear, wishing I had not let myself be pressured into being seen so promptly. I was still savouring some of the choicer moments from my stay in Bristol.

Pulling one thing after another out of the ancient mahogany wardrobe, making the thin metal coat-hangers clash and swing violently, I dragged each garment on and immediately wrenched it off again. Why was I so indecisive? At last I had an interview for a permanent job that sounded extremely promising, good firm, good location, probably good money. Exactly what I had been looking for, and I was pretty sure that if I performed well at the interview I'd be offered the job, but what to wear?...

The answer was staring back at me every time I looked in the long watery mirror affixed to the wardrobe door: I would only ever be half-suited to the kind of work I was looking for, which was secretarial employment. Each outfit I chose was a sartorial battlefield on which the conservative fought with the outlandish. There were the clothes I liked....and there were the clothes "for the office", clothes I had grudgingly accepted I should possess and which I resisted wearing if at all possible. While half of me craved the stability, the status, the perks of permanent employment, not to mention the regular and substantial injection of money into my bank account every month, the other half dreaded the thought of the daily nine-to-five grind, with the same faces, the same desk, the same work and the same commute, stretching out into the future, dreaded the inevitable feeling of being stuck, of being shackled to a situation that had lost its appeal. No matter how stimulating a job was initially, after a few months, having easily mastered its intricacies, I became bored, then discontented, then downright mutinous.

After forty minutes the bed was strewn with all the clothes I owned, the thin metal hangers were clanging to a standstill in the coffin of a wardrobe and still I had not decided. I glanced at the clock. Twenty minutes to put myself together and get out of the house. Forcing myself to keep moving and not panic, I snatched up my bag of cosmetics and swept off to the bathroom where the light was best for putting on make-up. I would start with my face.

As I stroked tobacco-brown eyeliner along the lid of my left eye, I started mentally to put together an outfit: my tobacco-brown calf-length straight skirt which fitted so well, the ivory silk blouse with pearl buttons down the front and slender sleeves that came to a point precisely in the centre of the back of the hand, my chestnut-brown leather shoes with stacked heels and — I had to have my little rebellion — the antique snakeskin shoulderbag that I had bought from a stall in Petticoat Lane for a quid. It was slightly battered but retained its air of decadent glory. The day was warm enough to go without a coat but I rolled up a thin ivory-coloured cardigan and put it in the snakeskin bag, just in case the weather turned cool.

On the tube to Victoria, as I sat hastily rehearsing some shorthand outlines in a small notebook in case I was tested, I noticed that my bland understated outfit was drawing the occasional admiring glance from both men and women, so I knew I had gauged it right.

The interview was on the sixth floor of a tall modern office block on the north side of Vauxhall Bridge and the job was that of secretary/personal assistant to the manager of the Marketing Division of Rank Hovis MacDougall — RHM, a huge food company, the one that made Hovis, my favourite bread. *Don't say brown, say Hovis!* A small but significant connection which I found encouraging.

And when I was introduced to the man for whom I half-hoped to work, my smile was genuine: he was well dressed, well spoken, obviously intelligent, brisk but not cold, and exactly the same height I was, which removed all trace of my nervousness.

After we shook hands, I sat in the offered chair and he retreated behind a large light grey desk. He had black hair, a Roman nose like Brando's, and eyes the same colour as his desk. He wore a grey suit, a striped tie and had a thick gold ring on his wedding finger.

"I see from your resumé that you have had plenty of similar experience," he said, looking down at my CV, while I studied the stripes on his tie. Then he looked up, not smiling, so I was able to see what he really looked like: "And you are a fast typist."

"Yes," I replied. "Perhaps it has something to do with the fact that I play the piano." I was always prepared for this to be taken seriously or as a joke. Neither was the case here.

"Ah," he said, dismissively. "And you take shorthand....I should tell you that I do very little dictating, I prefer to write drafts in longhand and have them typed, so....lots of typing but not much call for shorthand, I'm afraid. I hope that isn't a disappointment to you?" His voice rose very slightly at the end of the sentence to indicate a certain concern but also a gentle warning of what would be expected of me.

"Not at all," I said, in a neutral voice, cheering inwardly. While I loathed taking shorthand, I was happy to type until the ruminants wound their way back to the farmyard.

After that I did what I always did at interviews, I adopted an attitude as if I, too, were considering him for a vacant position in my life — for which there were other contenders — and I answered his subsequent questions with a combination of interest and reserve. And something told me that he liked this. He needed a secretary but he was not looking for someone who would simply follow orders, waiting to do as she was told and no more. He was looking for someone with the kind of initiative and re-sourcefulness that he valued and exercised in himself. And he was looking at her….we both sensed it.

As I rose from the chair to leave, he came round from behind his desk and shook my hand again, thanked me for my time, then added, smiling, "That's a marvellous handbag, by the way. Very unusual. Well, goodbye. We'll be in touch very soon."

It's mine, I thought. *The job's mine.*

Back down on the ground floor, I pushed open the heavy spotless plate-glass door to leave the building and stepped out into the street. The incessant angry roar of London's traffic assailed my ears but my spirit was light, happy, ready to celebrate. And, the person I wanted most to celebrate with was Nick.

"Nick Thornton," said the familiar cheerful voice.

I said, very quickly, "Nick, it's Loulou, can you talk?"

There was a two-second pause, then: "Uh — oh, yes, I've been expecting your call. Hold on a moment, please..." and I heard him say to someone in the room with him, "I'll see you for lunch then, twelve noon in The Cricketers." Another short pause, then he was back on the phone again: "That was close. Marilyn was standing next to me when I answered the phone."

"Oh god, sorry."

"It's okay, she's gone now. I'm all yours. It must be something pret-ty serious for you to be ringing me here."

But I could tell by the tone of his voice that he was ready for anything, ready to drop everything for me, which was what I was about to ask him to do.

"I'm dying to see you," I said.

"That's very flattering. You know I'm always dying to see you. Where are you? Slouched over your typewriter staring at the Thames?" He pronounced it exactly the way it was written, the way a foreigner would who didn't know any better: *Thayms.* Damned silly English language.

"Actually….I'm outside the station," I said.

"Station?"

"Manchester Piccadilly."

"The train station?" He gave a sexy little groan: "Okay, I can fix things here. I'll get there as fast as I can. You know what I'm going to do, don't you, the instant I see you? "

"I hope so."

"Just stay where you are. Give me fifteen minutes, twenty at the most."

I looked at my watch and pictured Nick looking at his watch. It was half past eleven.

"What about your lunch date?" I asked.

"I'll tell Marilyn I got held up here. Oh blast, I have no way of getting in touch with her now… "

So that was how I ended up taking a taxi from Manchester Piccadilly railway station to The Cricketers in Fanshawe Street, sitting silently in an obscured corner of the lounge bar, peering furtively around the tall back of the settle that hid me, while Nick and his wife sat at the bar, drinking gin and tonic and eating scampi and chips out of baskets. I heard Nick order everything.

Marilyn had neat, shiny, chin-length blond hair and smart clothes but she was plump and prissy and plain. She taught history in a secondary school, instructing sullen thirteen-year-olds about the Battle of Hastings, King John and the signing of the Magna Carta, and the Wars of the Roses, but she had *wife* written all over her. No cutlery was provided with their lunch and Nick waved his food around when he talked while she ate daintily, her little fingers curled like fern fronds.

At one point Nick slid down off his bar stool and started walking towards the Gents, but then veered off in my direction and, with one eye on his wife's back, slid into the seat alongside me, planted a kiss on my mouth and whispered, "Not long now."

And that was why I was there: for his clandestine kisses and his desire, which ignited my desire and filled out the corners of my whole being, making me feel potent and unstoppable, for the danger and the sense of living life at a heightened pitch, like a spy; I was there for the whole damned illicit thrill of it.

I had phoned the Alfred Marks bureau immediately after the interview.

It went well, I'm going home, I'll come into the agency tomorrow. Just like that. After all, they'd get the equivalent of a month's salary if I was offered the job and I was convinced I would be. And immediately after that I had phoned Bryn: *It went well, I think I've got the job. I'm going to jump on a train and go to Kingston market to do some shopping to celebrate.* Sometimes my audacity and mendaciousness shocked even me. But once I had decided I wanted to see Nick it would have taken an army to stop me. It was the kind of energy and singlemindedness that moves mountains and wins wars.

...Like that time I decided I had to see Miles, when I was living in Southampton and he was at university in York, over two hundred miles away and I had no car and only a few pounds in the whole world. He usually drove down on the weekends to see me but had sent me a note to say his car was acting up and he would not be able to get down that coming weekend.

I stood in the middle of Southampton High Street on a Friday afternoon, aching to be with Miles and knowing I had no money for the train fare but with my mind racing through possibilities. Refusing to be deterred. I hurried home, snatched up my exquisite gold wishbone ring and my beautiful solid silver bracelet off the top of my chest of drawers and walked all the way to Northam Road where the secondhand junk shops and antique shops were located, one after another, down the street. All I got was nine pounds from the first shop I went into and the ring alone had cost over twenty pounds new, but it was enough..... except that when I got to York everything went wrong.

Nick and Marilyn finally came to the end of their lunch. "Can I give you a lift back to the office?" I heard her ask, and Nick replied, "No thanks, love, I'm going round the corner to get a newspaper then I'll walk back. It'll do me good."

I pictured the scene I was unable to observe: her slipping her arm through the handle of her sensible Marks and Sparks handbag and both of them leaving the pub, her giving him a wifely peck on the lips outside on the pavement, and him, closing the car door for her and smiling brightly, because he was about to take off all his clothes and make love to another woman, one who excited him far more than she did.

We walk briskly back to Nick's office. Nick wants to hold my hand and I am afraid we will be seen by someone who knows him, knows his wife, but if he is willing to take the risk... We don't talk. I wait outside his office building while he goes in and makes his excuses and the necessary arrangements. I have no idea what they are and I don't care. I am waiting for our mouths to meet. His car is in a multi-storey in the next street, on the third level, he says. There is a lift just inside the entrance but the sight of the silent cars in their narrow gloomy spaces makes me want to run instead. I take off at high speed, surprising Nick, who gives chase after a few seconds. A car comes squealing round a corner and I move over to let it go by, hugging my snakeskin shoulderbag tight against the side of my chest. The driver slows down and looks at me uncertainly as he passes but I grin, give an impudent wave and keep running. Nick catches up with me. We are both out of breath, laughing like possessed teenagers. I drop my bag on the concrete floor and bend over at the waist, getting my breath back.

"Struth," Nick pants, his hands on his waist, his chest heaving, "my heart is going like the clappers. There's the old jalopy over there."

Inside the car his hands are all over me. Kissing him is the best thing in the world.

"Where can we go?" I ask.

"Home, of course," he says.

"Your house!"

"Why not? Marilyn is teaching all afternoon."

This just makes it more exciting. "All right," I reply, "if you say so."

"You know, sometimes I think I wouldn't care if she came home and found us, then she'd kick me out and I'd be free." He turns and looks at me, only half-joking.

This statement shocks me so much I am lost for words. *Free....*

We do not go up to their bedroom. There is a big sofa downstairs, lace curtains over the windows. We remove our clothing and suddenly all I am aware of is skin, warm skin, his smooth firm chest against my breasts, his thighs against my thighs, his erection against my stomach, his hands sliding down my back. And all the time we are kissing he is making little wriggling noises of pleasure in the back of his throat....and I am thinking, *This is what I want, this is all I want, this is heaven.* Then there is the sudden leap to the animal part of it, the joining of our two bodies into one entity, and my own narcissism carries me along....because sex with Nick is not that great. I never come. But it doesn't matter. That is not what I am looking for with him. What he gives me is the continual reassurance that I am attractive, sexy, desirable — alive. He knows how to light the blue touchpaper even if the flame does not consume me. He admires me openly, desires me openly, kisses me passionately, fucks me unashamedly. He makes me believe in myself, in my power as a woman, and this is sweet sustenance to me, irresistible and utterly indispensable.

...It's quite surprising, the things that can make up for not having an orgasm...

My elegant silk blouse and sleek dark skirt were limp containers into which I re-inserted my drained limbs. While I repaired my make-up and tidied my hair, Nick made me a cup of coffee. Afterwards he drove me back to the station, to catch the three-thirty to Euston. Before I got out of the car we kissed fervently.

"It was really great to see you," said Nick. "A fabulous surprise. And that little session will keep me going for — oh — hours."

I gave a sly laugh. "Ring me when you're next in London?" I said.

"Wild horses couldn't stop me," smiled Nick.

I had twenty minutes to kill before my train and remembering what I had said to Bryn about going shopping, I went into a boutique near the station that had cheap girly stuff and bought a tee-shirt with a tropical beach scene on the front, two pairs of lace knickers and a necklace made from dozens of tiny seashells which made a pleasing light pebbly sound when the strands moved against one another. I ignored the little voice that laughed at me for being such a hypocrite.

As the train gathered speed I pulled out my purchases from the boutique's neon pink carrier bag, scrutinised them briefly, put them back and began to think about Bryn, about what I was going to say to him when I was back in London. I thought back to what he had said about open marriage that day as we drove past the Tate Gallery — "The person cheating has to decide whether they are going to say anything to their long-term partner. And usually they don't."

Bryn had told me about his night with Simone, had made it clear it was not the first time and probably would not be the last. He had put his words into action, had put the theory to the test. And after the initial jolt of the revelation, how had I felt? Had it made any difference? Couldn't I do the same thing? Wasn't this the opportunity I'd been waiting for?

I mentally shied away from the answers to these questions because they required me to be more honest with myself than I cared to be, and my heart sank when I realised I could add one more item to the growing list of opposites between which I would vacillate for the rest of my life....this time the dilemma between dishonesty and honesty...

..."Well, it's about time!" exclaimed Bryn.

I stared at him in silence, taken aback by his enthusiastic response.

"I was beginning to wonder how long it would be."

"How long what would be?"

"Before you took advantage of the freedom you have."

"I don't think of it like that," I protested.

"I know!" exclaimed Bryn. "That's how it is with practically everybody, haven't you noticed? They're walking round with a bloody ball and chain on one ankle and they're so used to it they think *not* having it is abnormal."

"Including me."

"Yes! Most people don't want freedom because they wouldn't know what to do with it if they had it."

"So....you don't mind?"

"Of course not."

—No, it wouldn't be like that....I sat and stared out of the train window, feeling the regular jolting rhythm of the wheels on the tracks, my mind full of journeys and encounters, both imagined and remembered....the one in the immediate future with Bryn....and that one in the past....the one that changed everything...

…"What are you doing here?" asked Miles, amazed, when I materialised in the open doorway of his shabby university bedsit, flushed, having walked the half mile from York station. I hadn't phoned, I hadn't wanted to break the spell. He had two books open on the desk in front of him, they looked like textbooks, with a writing pad beside them.

"I had to see you," I replied, smiling to cover my uncertainty. I nervously felt for my gold wishbone ring, third finger, right hand, was reminded with a jolt that I had sold it earlier in the day for a fraction of what it was worth. Suddenly I wanted to cry.

"How did you— " he began.

"I came up on the train." Why wasn't he coming over to hold me? I looked down at the floor then back up at him. "Aren't you pleased to see me?"

"I'm a bit — shocked, that's all." He gave a small awkward smile.

I had pictured us rushing into each other's arms, hugging fiercely, silently, everything else fading away. At last, he stood up and came over to me, put his arms around me but he did not kiss me. Trembling with apprehension and regret, I pulled his face towards mine…

I looked out at the sprawling suburbs of Manchester as they began to thin out, not taking anything in, and thought about that other return train journey from north to south, from York back to Southampton, after going to see Miles.

Then I held one of my silent dialogues with myself, tried to argue it out, asking myself all the usual questions, useless questions:

Why is it such an effort for you, pushing into the future? Why do you live in the past so much?

I can't help it. I remember things. It's as if they are branded into my memory.

But you can't change anything. Why not forget it? Forget it and move on?

I do move on, I have no choice. But I can't forget. I wish I could but I can't.

Everyone makes mistakes, bad choices, everyone. Why should you be an exception?

I don't want to be an exception. I'm not an exception.

Well, why do you linger on your mistakes so much? Why don't you forgive yourself and just put it down to experience?

Because I wanted everything to be — wonderful....and it wasn't...

Sitting there, staring out through the train window, I felt the weight of the past dragging me down....I had wanted everything to go on being wonderful....was that a crime?

A man and woman boarded the train at Milton Keynes, the only stop between Manchester and Euston, and sat facing each other in the seats across the aisle from me. She was all colour — curly ginger hair, emerald green dress with apple-green edging, bright red lipstick and red shoes; he was monochrome — white, black and shades of grey. They were in their forties and were friends but not, I thought, lovers. There was an invisible barrier between them — they liked each other, but not enough, or rather, he liked her, but for her something was missing. He was too polite, too considerate perhaps. Too calm and colourless. She wanted someone a little more — vivid. However, if she was unwilling to share her body with him, it soon became clear that she had no such misgivings about sharing her thoughts.

When they got into the carriage they were obviously in the middle of some weighty discussion and she was doing most of the talking:

"Look," she said, with enormous finality, as if she was about to reveal at last the secret of the universe: "All people have agendas. The ones who don't are either utterly lost or they're just covering up."

Her companion nodded: "I see." He was unconvinced but was giving her his full attention, being agreeable because he still hoped she might change her mind, about going to bed with him.

She went on, "If a woman is looking for a mate — and if she's not why would she get involved physically or emotionally? — then from the time the thing starts, there's an inner countdown. The man is either going down the same road as she is or he isn't."

"Is that right?" Now that she was revealing the inner workings of the female mind he was more interested.

"Yes!"

Like him I was waiting frantically for her next utterance. She sounded so sure, so absolutely sure of what she was saying.

Please go on, tell us more, we need to know…

"A woman watches for signs of love," she continued, "for signs of a real bond. If she thinks it isn't there, then she has to create a break of some kind, to see what he'll do if it looks like she might disappear."

Her companion thought about this for a minute: "So it's a kind of test for the man?"

"Exactly. It's a test. And if he fails, she'll start looking elsewhere."

A test….but a test of what? Love? Need? Control? Fidelity? Loyalty?

Then I stopped listening because my mind had shifted unpleasantly to a moment during my visit to Miles in York, a moment which smouldered deep in my memory….*His arms are around me but I am rigid with fear. If I don't move it will be all right, it won't have happened. Nothing will have changed. I'll be like a stone, round which water swirls and rushes, and everything will be wonderful again.* I threw the memory back into its dark hole.

In a sweetened version of the criminal returning to the scene of the crime, when I got to Euston I decided to go and have another look at the building in which I was sure I would be working after sailing through the interview that morning with Mr. — what was his name? — Tree, that was it. Oliver Tree. No middle initial. Unusual name....perhaps he was distantly related to that Victorian theatre impresario. Had it been only that morning that we had shaken hands and he had briefly admired my handbag? I felt as if a larger chunk of my existence had passed than merely hours.

The high office block that housed Rank Hovis MacDougall stood on Millbank, at the north end of Vauxhall Bridge where the two lanes coming across the bridge from the south flared out into three lanes in order to allow traffic to turn left towards Chelsea or right towards Westminster as well as continue on towards Victoria. That was another thing about the job — there would be a fine view from the sixth floor over the rooftops of Pimlico and Victoria and across the Thames, the kind of view that, like the city's green spaces, kept human beings sane.

It was almost seven o'clock and lights blazed in almost all the windows of the twelve-storey building, making the interiors of the individual offices glow like the rooms of an enormous doll's house. I was satisfied. It had not been a dream. A pair of dark-suited men, both tall, with serious expressions on their faces, carrying briefcases, left the building as I stood and watched. I did not linger to see if Mr. Tree would exit the building. It was possible he had already left. I turned and walked back across Bessborough Gardens towards the tube station.

It was a fine dry breezy evening, one of those evenings when it is almost an act of sacrilege to descend into the hot stuffy tunnels of London's Underground system. I stood at the top of the steps down into Pimlico tube station trying not to breathe in the stale, body-warmed air fanning up from below, not wanting to descend, and thought about the alternatives. Then I had the bright idea of walking all the way back to Bryn's house, a distance of perhaps three miles. I'd follow the route Bryn took when he drove, along Camberwell New Road, turning right at Lordship Lane. It would not be difficult, the exercise would be good for me and who cared how long it took. So I started to walk. I crossed the river along Vauxhall bridge, glancing down at the choppy, metallic-looking water that was starting to darken as daylight shifted into twilight.

I paced steadily along Camberwell New Road, remembering the couple on the train and what the ginger-haired, emerald-dressed woman had said about people and their agendas. Applying this to myself I concluded that I must be one of the utterly lost because I had no agenda, no plan. As I had just perfectly demonstrated, I conducted myself according to instinct and to my many whims and hunches, and simply waited for the fall-out. On the strength of a single sentence I was capable of throwing my whole existence into disarray. *What's eating you? Plenty more fish in the sea. Try that on for size. What's on your agenda?*

The process of walking was the closest I ever got to stilling both mind and body. When I walked I could mentally digest and understand — if not always accept — the things that happened to me. My body walked automatically, left, right, left, right, one arm lightly holding the strap of my shoulderbag, the other arm swinging by my side like a pendulum, while I sifted and sorted through my thoughts. My brain was the domineering cerebral invalid who never stopped chewing over the events in my life while my body was the loyal servant charged with carrying it around, never happier than when required to move, when required to *do* something.

Like all big cities, after dark London changed. It was no longer the charming, quaint, slightly threadbare, almost avuncular place it was in daylight, full of tourists hung with cameras, and red double-decker buses, office workers hurrying out for a lunch-time sandwich, shoppers with their harvests of name-brand carrier bags, and noisy groups of friends, who came to the city "for the day" leaving their responsibilities and inhibitions behind in the small towns and villages where they lived. After dark the city turned its back on wholesomeness, shed its child-like innocence and became a place for adults. Neon lights cast things in a more and more lurid glow and shadows which were purple and blue in daylight became blacker than black.

After I'd been walking for about fifteen minutes, I saw a man in work overalls on a bench near a bus-stop directly under a street light about twenty yards ahead. He was sitting comfortably, taking advantage of the rest after his day's work, a work-box beside him and one arm stretched out along the back of the bench. He looked harmless. Nevertheless, I prepared myself to walk past him with composure, attempting the impossible task of not giving off any sexual signals — at that moment I'd have

given one of my little fingers to be wearing an enveloping bur-
ka. I drew level with this man. He stared at me, grinned and
said, "Cheer up, love, it might never 'appen," and, with a stab of
pain, I knew that, even though I was trying to look calm and collected, my face must have looked drawn and sad under the harsh
light. Burning with indignation and with the painful awareness
of how ill-equipped I was to deflect such comments, I began to
regret my decision to walk.

As I passed the entrance to a pub in Stockwell Road, a drunk
emerged, staggering slightly, bringing the sour smokey pub atmosphere out with him, and although I tried to avoid him, he
lost his balance and bumped into me. "Shorry, love," he burbled
and hastily attempted to straighten himself before moving off
unsteadily along the pavement.

I sank even lower....low enough so that, stealthily, like
a ghost that knows it is not welcome but is emboldened by its
seedy, disreputable surroundings and by the renewed feelings
of pain and confusion whirling round inside me, the memory
crawled back out from its black hole.

...We had made love, slowly, luxuriously, as always, and
were lying entwined in Miles' single bed. The two books were
still open on his desk a couple of feet away but now they were
just shapes in the gloom. Miles was usually satiated into silence
after sex but this time his silence had a loaded quality. Instead of
feeling utterly peaceful I had an inescapable sense of foreboding.

"Are you — all right?" I asked, carefully.

"They're throwing me out," said Miles, his voice barely above a whisper.

"Oh no — you have to find new digs?"

"No, not this place. The university."

I listened to him breathing for a few seconds.

"But... " I began. I really had no idea what question to ask. *How? Why? When?*

He went on: "I can't keep up. They gave me a warning at the end of last term. And now it's the end of this term and I haven't been able to….improve. I can't seem to concentrate…"

"Have you told your parents?"

"My parents? My parents….oh yes. They weren't that upset. I don't think they wanted me to go to university in the first place, especially all the way up here in York. "

Then, to my surprise, Miles started talking about his sister: "Nessa is furious. She blames you, which is idiotic — it has nothing to do with you. If anyone is to blame, it's her….but of course she'll never accept that."

"I don't care what she thinks," I said. "She should stop treating you like a little boy."

"She can't help it. It's understandable really. You don't know the whole story."

I said nothing. I knew he was going to try and explain his sister's possessiveness, her disapproval that I was years older than Miles and had obviously had experience with the opposite sex, while he obviously had not. She probably knew that he had been a virgin before I came along. I thought it touching that he was able to stand up to her, as he had the night of the accident, but that he also felt he had to support her in her opinions. It was a form of sibling affection that I was familiar with — in spite of our perpetual bickering, I adored my brother, would gladly have died for him — if absolutely necessary.

"I haven't told anyone this before," continued Miles, uncertainly, "I've spent most of my life pushing it away... "

Wait a minute, what is he saying?

"Our father is basically no good."

"Your father?"

"Yes. Our father, who raped Vanessa..." It sounded like a parody of the first line of the Lord's Prayer: *Our Father, who art in heaven...*

"When she was twelve..." *Thy Kingdom come...*

I squeezed my eyes tight shut to try and keep it out.

My throat closed up: *Why is he telling me this? Why is he trying to hurt me?*

I knew the answer: he needs to offload the hurt on to me because it has become more than he can bear. Now he has someone who can share his burden. Because we love each other. He has lived with the knowledge that his father is a complete bastard, now it is my turn to know it. And this is where I get hurt. It was quite logical really.

"Miles, I— " I began, but he started speaking again.

"You see....Nessa is not actually my sister."

Not his sister — adopted then, therefore not incest but still...

"That's why she's like she is about me. When I come back to Southampton she is insisting that I stop seeing you."

"What? She can't do that. How dare she?"

"She can't help it....she's — because — because she's — Nessa is not my sister. She's my mother."

It was like a dream, a very bad dream, and in the dream I had started to fall....just like that time in the funfair. I started to fall and the darkness swallowed me up.

...It was daylight so the noise and activity were less overwhelming, but I was still glad to have Dad's hand to hold on to. It was when night came and the sky was black that the funfair was absolutely terrifying, the look of it and the sound of it. That was when I had to hang on extra-tight to Dad's hand and also the corner of his coat. Big, leering faces, made even more horrible by the ghastly cheap overhead lighting, hung out high above me at every stall, their mouths opening and closing like gashes as they yelled at passers-by: "Step right up, every one a winner! Have a go, ladies and gents! Right this way, sir! Win a lovely prize for the little lady!" All around us was pandaemonium — jangling bells, squawks, screams and the swoosh and thump and rattle of the funfair rides with their hellish warbling accompaniment of snatches of loud pop music. Dad gave some coins to a scrawny woman in a cramped wooden booth and we climbed a shadowy staircase inside a tall wooden structure that seemed to me as high and narrow as a lighthouse. From somewhere inside came the grinding and clunking of machinery repeating its ponderous movements over and over again like an enormous, bad-tempered beast, well-trained and resigned to its labours. Shrieks of excitement and pleasure rose from another part of the structure. What made grown women scream like that? At the top of the wooden staircase Dad and I felt our way along a short

platform and sat side by side in the gloom on a bench that seemed to be made of lots and lots of thin, horizontal steel tubes, I felt the hard cold sour-smelling metal under my hand but before I had time to look closer, everything went black and suddenly I was thrown backwards, the bench somehow straightened out, upending itself and us, and I felt myself falling and I was no longer holding Dad's hand. There was no bench, no floor, no Dad, there was only falling through blackness in a paroxysm of terror, bumping against the hard cold tubing that fell with us…

I began to sob.

"I'm sorry," said Miles and I could tell by the way he held me so tightly that he was getting ready to say goodbye.

"There you are!" exclaimed Bryn, when I finally arrived back at the house in night air, drained, footsore and thirsty. "I was beginning to get worried."

"So was I," I said, sharply, thrown by his concern. Suddenly he was a parent and his concern was disturbing, intrusive. There was an almost imperceptible pause which was his way of acknowledging my lack of explanation. Then he said, pointing at the pink carrier bag: "Buy anything nice?"

"I wasn't sure at the time," I replied with leaden sarcasm, turning the bag upside down so that its contents slid indecorously on to the carpet and lay there like a pale collection of small dead animals: "Now I'm absolutely convinced of it — yes, *very* nice."

Still displaying almost superhuman forbearance, Bryn ignored this and asked, "So — you think you have the job?"

"Well....yes, I think so, oh, I don't know, stop asking me questions."

Why was it so difficult to communicate with another human being? Say one thing, mean another....I was exhausted from walking the garish, threatening London streets reliving my memories and utterly relieved to be home, but unable to show him any of it, unable to bring myself to ask him to hold me, which was all I wanted. It was all I ever wanted. (*Hold me.... make me feel safe...*) But sometimes the armour I'd grown was so strong that nothing could pierce it, not even Bryn.

Bryn, understandably, had come to the end of his tolerance. I could tell by the way he simply shifted his weight from one foot to the other. Sometimes human beings communicate all too well without words. "I was about to go to the kebab place in Herne Hill and get a take-away."

That was something else about Bryn — he never pushed me for an explanation. In fact he refused to be provoked by my unwillingness to talk, refused to respond to my obtuse proddings to try and get him to ask for an explanation. He just — moved on. And it worked: while he quietly got on with his own life, which included maintaining some semblance of civility between us, at least on his side, I gradually let go of the overriding idea I had, at times like this, that everyone in the whole world was having an easier time existing than I was. Bryn understood this better than I did myself. He turned to leave.

"I'll come with you," I said, hastily. The last thing I wanted just then was to be left alone.

"Come on then." And he started walking towards the door.

"Give me a minute to put some jeans on."

"I, too, have news," said Bryn, as he pulled away from the kerb, shifting briskly up through the gears.

"Oh," I said, softly, my voice betraying me — I had completely overlooked the fact that Bryn too had an existence.

"I think I've found another house!" he exclaimed, no longer able to contain his excitement, which in turn seemed to neutralise the antagonism that I had created between us.

"You have? Today?!"

He nodded vigorously.

"Whereabouts? You must show me where it is, right now, immediately, at once and without delay." Now I was appealing to his liking for a certain excess. And we turned and looked straight at each other finally, and smiled.

"All right," he said, relieved he had succeeded in lightening the atmosphere.

Ten minutes later Bryn drew to a gentle halt outside an imposing three-storey Victorian house in a street called Gubyon Avenue. All the houses in the street were detached but because they were large and had been built very close together, any sense of isolation was mitigated by a suggestion of community. There was a narrow flagstone pavement on either side of the road. We stopped outside number thirty-two. In front of the house was a low stone wall topped with iron railings to about shoulder height with a thicket of privet hedge hugging the other side of it and together they held the street at bay and obscured the small front garden.

The ground floor and first floor of the house were in darkness while the windows of the top floor were filled with the dim brownish-yellow glow created by low wattage tungsten bulbs. Bryn leaned over from the driving seat and we both looked up through the window on my side of the car. Bryn's head was touching my shoulder.

...Shall I or shall I not?....tell him...

"Two old ladies are living there at the moment," said Bryn, "with their poodles. The living-room is on the top floor, that's why the lights are on up there. What d'you think?"

I didn't care. It had walls, windows, a roof, doors, and inside there would be more walls, a staircase, somewhere to sleep and somewhere to bathe. "It's — huge," I said.

"Yes, it is rather large," said Bryn, pretending to be embarrassed. "I'll have a much bigger mortgage but I've got a rise in salary coming soon so... "

"When can we move in?"

Bryn turned and smiled at me. I had said "we".

...Why was I holding back? Didn't I owe it to him? Was it healthy to be capable of functioning on two different levels like this? What a foolish question....as if one has a choice about such things.

"Quite soon," replied Bryn. "The two old biddies are pretty frail and don't have any family to take care of them so they're going into an old folks home. I think they were relieved to have a buyer so quickly and they liked the look of me. They weren't greedy, they accepted my offer on the spot and even told me what needed attention. It was quite touching. Apparently the chimney has a leak, but I'll get Beetle to do it."

"Who?"

"Beetle. John Beadleholme. He's a builder. There isn't much he can't handle on a house. So — as soon as all the papers are signed and hands have been shaken, *Robert est votre oncle.*"

Bryn loved to translate the peculiar idioms of English into even more peculiar-sounding French, something he had started doing in school and which never ceased to make me laugh:

Bob's your uncle — *Robert est votre oncle.*

It's a piece of cake — *C'est un morceau de gateau.*

Then it came to me, pure and simple: what I wanted was to have more than one life, to live in more than one world. One would never be enough. The boredom, the demands, the sheer repetition that drove me from one would make the other more appealing, fresher, less used and vice versa. And this was what Bryn wanted too. We were actually in agreement about the most important thing. *We both wanted to stay together and still live as full a life as possible.* And the moment I had this revelation, I suddenly heard myself saying it, telling him.

"Bryn, I didn't go to Kingston today, I went to see a guy I know in — well never mind where. And — we — we had sex. He's someone I've known for a long time."

There was an explosion of total silence inside the car.

At length Bryn said, "Y-e-s..." softly and with enormous caution, so as not to frighten me off, because he wanted me to say more.

"I went to bed with him, at his house. He's married — his wife was at work. And — well — it's already history. How did you put it — when we were talking about it the other day? — the ideal response....on being told something like that?"

"It's done and she does not regret it," supplied Bryn, and then, with a great effort, he added: "She — enjoyed it."

I said nothing, because I could see he was struggling to absorb what I had just told him and that being confined by the unlit cramped space inside the car was not helping.

"And did she?" he asked, his voice colourless.

"What?"

"Enjoy it."

I could only sigh, hoping he would understand how much I did not want to reply.

Then Bryn said, "Well, I'll say this, your timing is — stunning."

*It's done, she does regret it.…*telling him, that is.

After another few seconds of silence, Bryn took a really big breath. His chest rose and fell like a huge bellows filling completely and then emptying. In.…out… "I'm glad you told me," he said, finally. "I just have to — take it on board now, that's all. Christ — that's easier said than done. I don't suppose it's anyone I know?"

I shook my head.

"I — umm — I hope you don't mind my asking but — well — would you care to tell me anything else about — about — this mysterious *him*? Just for the record, as they say. I'm curious, that's all. Actually," and he blew a little gust of air out through his nose, "I'm really bloody angry — but I know I have absolutely no right to be."

There was a long pause as we both struggled with our emotions.

The stained glass fanlight over the front door of the house that was almost Bryn's was suddenly illuminated from within by a light in the hall and the door cautiously opened, revealing a shrunken, stooped female figure wrapped in a shawl with two trembling white miniature poodles at her ankles.

Bryn turned to look: "That's Miss Marsh. She's probably wondering who we are and what we're doing out here. They're a couple of very nervous old girls."

"Let's go, then," I said.

Bryn started the car and we drove away. I watched his usual proficient handling of the steering wheel and could not help thinking he was glad to have something to do with his hands.

"I don't seem to have much of an appetite any more," said Bryn, as we approached the kebab house. "I think a stiff drink would be more in order."

"Yes, absolutely, a drink."

Next to the kebab house was The Half Moon Tavern, a magnificent specimen of Victoriana with its etched glass windows and long polished mahogany bar that shone like a mirror. It was almost empty of customers, except for a few lone drinkers who sat like statues, which only added to the museum-like atmosphere of the place. The barman was reading an evening newspaper, his head bowed over it, his forearms folded in front of him, resting on the polished wood.

"I shall regret this in the morning but they have this stuff on tap," said Bryn, coming back from the bar and planting a brimming pint on the table along with my schooner of port. "Fullers ESB. Tastes phenomenal but they don't call it brain damage for nothing. Appropriate, wot?"

He was feeling sorry for himself and trying to get over it by laughing at himself. So I had a choice. Say more or say no more, and, as usual, I plucked my decision out of the air. I took a big swallow of port — a sublime tawny — Bryn had chosen the best. That settled it.

Bryn raised his glass to his lips and drained a few inches of his beer.

"All right," I began, speaking faster than usual, "I don't really want to talk about this much more but you do know him, the — the person I was with today. Well, you don't know him, but you have actually seen him."

Bryn did not look at me, but reached for his glass again.

I continued more slowly: "He was the man, sitting at the bar, in the Strand Palace Hotel, that evening when you took me to the Hundred Club."

Bryn carefully put down his glass, stared hard into space for an instant, frowning, scouring his memory: "Him? You slept with *him*?" he said loudly, making the barman look up from his newspaper.

And my feelings of sympathy for Bryn instantly hardened into a fierce obstinacy and a mass of sharp retorts crowded into my mind.

But before I could retaliate, into the pub, with theatrical timing, walked Phil and Angie, and Angie was obviously pregnant. They saw us and came over.

"Just the bloke I wanted to see," exclaimed Phil, smiling. He shook Bryn's hand. "Hullo, Lowri. What you both drinking?"

Bryn asked for another pint, I told Phil I'd hardly touched mine, and Angie said, "I'll have a Babycham, Phil." He went to the bar.

Angie saw me looking at her rounded stomach. She looked down at the bulge and patted it gently: "I know," she said. "I decided to have it. Phil said we should get married and there's plenty of room in his flat now, so I changed my mind about — about the other thing."

"Oh, you are brave," I said warmly. Then, in order to give Bryn a chance to compose himself and finish the drink he already had in front of him, I asked, "When's the baby due?" By the time Phil came back from the bar Bryn's glass was empty.

"You'll never believe this, but it's due on Phil's birthday."

"She's not kiddin'!" laughed Phil. He placed a pint in front of Bryn and a shallow champagne glass full of a pale gold fizzing liquid in front of Angie. "I'll be thirty and the baby'll be nought!"

"Cheers, Phil," said Bryn, and greedily raised the second pint to his mouth.

"Not a minute too soon, eh?" replied Phil, with a knowing glance at Bryn, sensing that something not entirely pleasant was going on but acknowledging it humorously. He was good at that.

"Let's have a toast to the baby," I suggested.

"Great idea," agreed Phil.

We all picked up our drinks and extended our arms to clink glasses in the centre as if we were the points of a compass, north, south, east, west: "The baby!"

And with fatalistic bravado, I downed the remainder of my drink. Phil immediately jumped up to get me another and I did not stop him.

"You said you wanted to see me?" enquired Bryn, when Phil had sat down again.

"Yeah — you play trombone, don't you?"

"That's right."

"Well, I started playing drums again, a bit more seriously, you know, just to make some dough, with the baby on the way, and this new band I play with was askin' me if I know anyone who plays brass."

Phil now had Bryn's complete attention: "What kind of music?"

"Standards mostly. Jazzy stuff but nothing freaky, unless you wanna make a solo out of it and really stretch yourself. These guys are open to experimentation but there's no pressure. It's mostly straight standards with a few bursts of improv so we don't die of boredom."

In the slight pause that followed, I turned to Angie: "Do you have any names lined up for the baby?"

"Well..." began Angie "if it's a girl I want to call her Willow but Phil isn't very keen— "

"And if it's a boy, we'll call him Stumps!" Phil interrupted.

"He's just saying that, he doesn't even like cricket," Angie grinned apologetically.

Ignoring the interruption, Bryn asked Phil, "Where do you guys play?"

"Tufnell Park Hotel, every other Friday, eight till ten."

"Really?" said Bryn, obviously impressed. "You chaps must be pretty good."

"Well, if I do say so meself, we've gone down well the times we've played. And they pay us well."

They continued to talk about music and I turned to Angie who was sipping her drink very delicately, reminding me of the advert with the sweet little animated fawn leaping about in a forest and the ad's caption: *I'd love a Babycham.* I said, "I think Willow is a lovely name."

"Yeah, only Phil thinks it'll sound really daft with his last name — Willow Miller."

"So you really are getting married?"

She nodded. "Next month. Registry office."

"You know — you don't have to take Phil's last name. It's just a tradition, a convention. It's not required."

Angie's pale pretty face became serious. "Don't think Phil would like that very much… "

"What's your last name?"

"Percy."

"Well, that sounds much better, doesn't it? Willow Percy." I sat back, pleased with myself, confident of a minor victory.

"Yeah, that's really nice," Angie replied, with a weak smile. "Only….you'll never guess what Phil wants to call it if it's a boy."

"What?"

She turned and looked me straight in the eye: "Have a guess."

"Oh no," I said, trying to hide my disappointment. "You mean…"

"Yeah!" she exclaimed, delighted at being able to joke about the whole thing. "Percival! It's 'is grandfather's name! If we have a son, he'd be Percy Percy!" We both burst out laughing.

"Nice to see the girls 'avin' a good time," beamed Phil, turning to us and then back to Bryn, who said nothing but managed a very small smile.

After Phil and Angie left, Angie apologising for feeling tired and dragging Phil away — Bryn seemed calm again though not in any hurry to close the gap between us.

He went to the bar for a third pint without asking if I wanted another drink.

When he came back to the table I said, with as much enthusiasm as I could muster: "That sounds great, doesn't it, playing with Phil's group?"

"Please don't patronise me," replied Bryn with maddening emphasis on each word.

"I wasn't— "

"Look — I — I'm sorry, but it may take me a while to absorb what you told me, okay? To take it in."

I became flippant because I was on my second schooner of port — I could feel its effects on my judgement — and bitterly regretting having told him about Nick: "What's to take in? It's no worse than you and *Simone*," I enunciated the name outrageously.

Bryn's face grew thunderous. "Not quite, it isn't. I saw that guy and I just can't believe you would— "

"So I have to get your approval for my choices?" I protested. "I don't remember that being mentioned."

"Bloody hell, no!" Bryn downed a third of his pint. The alcohol was beginning to get the better of us. "But the idea was that we'd be open about this stuff. Why didn't you tell me you knew him, that night when you saw him at the Strand Palace. Instead of — slinking around."

"Slinking around?" I could not help myself, I was laughing at him.

Bryn stared hard at the table and I realised that while I was now ready to look at the whole thing as if it were all a huge joke, he was unable to take that point of view, a completely novel state of affairs between us. At the same time he was making a huge effort not to allow our disagreement to escalate. His silence irritated me, then impressed me, then the reason for it abruptly became clear to me and I understood what was going on. Bryn was angry because Bryn was hurt and embarrassed, hurt because he cared so much, and embarrassed because his open marriage theory was not working. He had failed his own test.

I also understood that the only bond between Nick and me was the sporadic and very temporary indulgence of our own burning lust, and I had to acknowledge to myself that, forced to make a choice between Nick and Bryn, I would choose Bryn every time. Every time. Nick was perfect open marriage fodder.... my bit on the side, and no more.

I suddenly found myself envying Phil and Angie and their messy adherence to conventions. After thinking myself so far above them, even pitying them, I could see that they were acting in a much more mature fashion than I was. They were making a commitment to a combined future, a commitment I was still avoiding.

The pub was filling up and as more bodies squeezed around the tables Bryn and I were forced to sit closer together so as not to look as if we were hogging too much space. There seemed to be an unwritten law about these things.

A middle-aged man and woman sat down at our small table. They looked as if they had been married since birth, they both had exactly the same bored dyspeptic expression on their faces. The man was a stolid individual with a stomach that bulged out over his belt. The woman looked as though she got the same tight perm every month.

When I moved up closer to Bryn my proximity brought about a softening of his mood. "What's his name, anyway, this bloke of yours?" he asked, in a low voice.

"Nick."

"Nick," Bryn repeated, his mouth a tight little slit as if he were uttering the single most objectionable word in the English language.

"See-moan," I countered, sensing a shift in his attitude.

There was a brief pause while he silently decided whether or not he wanted to play this game. Then: "Ew, Neek... " he squeaked.

"Ohh, See-moan," I groaned.

The foulness of our argument had dissipated, we were on the same wavelength again. I suddenly felt exhilarated, as if I was about to jump off a cliff and fly.

Bryn clutched my left hand in both his: "Dahling, dahling Nick," he gushed.

I stroked Bryn's arm with my right hand: "Simone, my dearest dearest," I whispered hoarsely.

The man with the bulging stomach looked at us from the other side of the table. "Them two need their eyes tested," he said to his wife.

"Either that or they need their 'eads read," she said.

All this was for our benefit, and being the focus of their attention had the effect of drawing us still closer together and further lightening Bryn's mood. He grinned at them: "If you must know, we are both saving up for a sex change," he threw out, and we all laughed. Then, standing up, he said to me, "Come on. Let's go before we make complete fools of ourselves."

As we left the pub, the man with the swollen gut called out, "Good luck, mate! You're gonna need it!" and he laughed loudly.

Driving back from the Half Moon, Bryn and I were silent, We lapsed back into our separate trains of thought, giving each other the necessary space to look back over recent developments and assess our reactions and feelings. As we pulled up outside the house in Sylvester Road, Bryn broke the silence: "You know, you are free to do whatever you want. Don't ever forget that."

"Listen to this," said Bryn, making straight for the records when we were inside. He slid one of the LPs out of its sleeve and put it on the turntable.

I heard a plaintive melody on a single stringed instrument, no orchestra. It was one — no — two violins, a viola, then a cello....a string quartet....sounding to my ears as if something was missing — a near-deserted village as opposed to the bustle of a city. I felt I had to explain my lack of enthusiasm: "It sounds a bit — thin."

Bryn was appalled: "Thin! How can you say that? This is the Amadeus, the crème de la crème."

I shrugged my shoulders. "It just sounds so — empty," I insisted, not wanting to be argumentative but determined not to be bullied. "Skeletal. As if something is missing....it doesn't — transport me."

Bryn gave a snort of exasperation, took the record off, chose another and put it on mid-track. The glorying strains of a Brahms symphony filled the room, the fourth — commanding, potent, teeming with instruments.

"Now that's more like it," I exclaimed, smiling, and Bryn was immediately happy again. He stood in the middle of the room, laughing, waving his arms around, conducting. In one of the more strident passages, he shouted, "Never smile at the brass!" and I realised that he was more drunk than sober.

After the chord that concluded the first movement had sounded, he calmed down somewhat. Still standing in the middle of the room but not looking at me, he said, in a distant voice: "Would it be — very tactless to say I'd like to make love to you?"

Because of the way he asked, with such delicacy after what I'd told him earlier, I went over to him and instead of answering, put my arms around him and kissed him.

After a few moments of silence, I said "I'm all yours."

"La crème de la crème," muttered Bryn, running his hands up and down my arms.

We went upstairs, took off everything we had on except our socks and began to make love, with Bryn sitting on the edge of his bed and me in his lap, facing him — things moved along rapidly like that. There was an urgency in his lovemaking that had never been there before. Afterwards we dived gratefully under the covers.

Later, when Bryn was asleep beside me, I thought about something Camus wrote in one of his books, that after living for one day, a man could spend the rest of his life in prison, he would have so much to think about, he would never be bored. Perhaps. Not all days would bear that kind of scrutiny, I thought, but the one I had just lived through....all that emotional turmoil....I resolved that in the morning I would buy a proper journal and write it all down, every bit of it: *See the little mark on that rock over there? That's mine. I made it.* It wasn't enough that I was born, lived and would die, I had to leave something of myself behind, I had to. As if it is possible, not to — leave something behind.

In the morning I awoke, filled with a familiar, expectant energy, something I had not felt for a long time, a reminder of the times I'd awoken in my college dormitory room, the curtains closed against the daylight and last night's make-up smudged around my eyes, with no clear plan or direction in mind but filled with an inexplicable sense of power and possibility. Was it my imagination or had this always happened on a cold winter morning, when the bed was so snug and warm it was like my own little nest and it hadn't been long since I had been born and my legs might not function if I tried to get out, but if they did — if they did, I could do anything.

A bittersweet feeling....because it was accompanied by memories that refused to fade: Stan Coleman's long, suntanned legs and enormous smile — he was my first lover in college, destined to be usurped almost immediately; sliding down a haystack into the outspread arms of Joanna, a college friend who also, though I was reluctant, became my lover and was also swiftly usurped; the idiotic posed photographs taken at the end of term, five of us sitting cross-legged, staring intently at a battered aluminium kettle. And the time I almost lost a finger when Stan and I tried to move a huge oblong block of stone into my room because I thought it would make an interesting ornament. At the last moment, we lost control of it and it dropped to the floor, trapping one of my fingers. Joanna came rushing in when she heard me cry out, she and Stan heaved at the stone and then the three of us stood for a few seconds staring down, transfixed, as the scarlet blood poured across my palm.

Gone, all gone.

I pulled my right hand out from under the covers — yes, it was still there, the scar along the side of my middle finger. And I wanted to cry, because my life was slipping away. I was going to get to the end of my life and have nothing to show for it — not a thing.

Gone, all gone....except for the scars.

The sadness of remembering was so strong that it overpowered the feelings of expectancy and suddenly, with a sensation like that of physical pain, I craved a place of comfort, a place I knew and liked, where I could let down my guard and relax and not be asked to explain myself and not have to make decisions about how I was going to live my life, a place that felt like home....even if it wasn't.

After we had gone out together a few times, Miles took me home to meet his parents. They lived in a village called Botley about ten miles east of Southampton, very rural, very pretty, the front gardens of the cottages and houses were a mass of colourful flowers and Miles's parents' place was no exception though the house itself was much grander with a gravel drive that swept around and ended at the front door.

Miles' mother insisted I call her Jean but I was never able to call Miles' father anything other than Mr. Hodges, partly because of the way I had been brought up, partly because I was in a strange house, but mostly because I was a little in awe of him, he was so big and blustering and majestic, like a character out of a Dylan Thomas story. What fascinated and impressed me most was the way he refused to observe the accepted rules of social engagement. When Miles introduced us, he gave a grunt of acknowledgement, looked me slowly down and up, and down again, without smiling — he seemed to have no compunction about staring — and his first words to me, spoken loudly, were: "Those shoes don't look very comfortable."

"That's why I'm taking them off," I replied, kicking my shoes merrily across the floor of the kitchen.

This impetuous behaviour clearly appealed to Miles' father, because he gave a huge guffaw. Miles and his mother joined in, delighted I had risen to the occasion. Looking round slyly, Mr. Hodges added, "Let's hope everything else she has on is comfortable enough," and his eyes glittered like a weasel's. This had the effect of instantly quenching all the humour in the room and there was a moment of absolute silence which I interpreted simply as embarrassment on account of an unruly relative.

"Right then, who's for a cup of tea?" asked Jean, swiftly, and Miles' father subsided with a growl.

It was an old house, probably hundreds of years old, with five bedrooms, wood panelling everywhere, and all the floorboards in the place creaked, especially when one walked up the stairs and moved about on the first floor. The handles on all the inside doors were forged iron latches, shoulder-high, which made the place feel old-fashioned and rustic, like a farmhouse. A long thin chain with a small, smooth, torpedo-shaped white porcelain pull at the end of it hung down from the cistern high above the toilet in the W.C. That was what Mr. Hodges called it — the W.C.

In the kitchen a vast white gas range took up half of one wall. Casement windows, with a double sink, draining board and counters below them, ran the length of the south wall and overlooked a very productive vegetable garden. In the adjoining sitting-room were two armchairs and a huge sofa, all covered in very worn, very dark brown leather, like the furniture in a gentleman's club. There was a beaten brass coal scuttle next to the fireplace, chintz curtains in the bay window. I liked the place immediately....although I was sure it was full of ghosts.

When I sat in that airy kitchen, chatting to Miles' mother while she made pots of tea and cucumber sandwiches, or measured out ingredients for a cake or, if it was Sunday, prepared vegetables, basted a joint of meat in the oven, and whisked batter for Yorkshire pudding — all the things I had watched my own mother do — I experienced a sense of ease that was unlike anything I had felt before and I began to understand the true meaning of having a home.

When I was very small — long before I started school — everything was cooked on an open coal fire in the blackleaded grate or in the grate's small oven. One of my earliest memories was of my mother carefully positioning a saucepan on the glowing coals so that it was level and its contents would not spill.

We had a fire every day, even in high summer, because that was also the way we got hot water. In the alcove on the left side of the grate was a glass-fronted oak bookcase where my books of fairy stories rubbed shoulders with the New Testament, an atlas, my brother's novels, a small untidy pile of stationery and several thick books with leather bindings that I never opened.

Set into the alcove on the other side of the grate was a big wooden cupboard. It was painted to match the living-room trim and contained a shiny copper cylinder as tall as I was and as thick as a tree trunk. This cylinder was full of water which was heated by the fire. We called it "the tank". When someone wanted a bath, the first thing my mother would say was, "Is the tank hot?" and one of us would open the cupboard door to find out, pushing a hand in under the layers of clean laundry in which the tank was usually swathed, "airing". As big as this water tank was and no matter how hot the water, we were only allowed eight inches for a bath in the long clawfoot tub.

Yes....a fire every day.

After I became a teenager, home was a place where I was always on edge, uneasy, waiting to deflect the veiled insults which passed for conversation or defend myself against the next blunt criticism — (*What's that muck you have on your eyes? Where have you been till this hour? You better watch out for that boy, he's after you.*) Home was the place where I needed my armour the most.

"I'm going home," I'd say, at the end of each college term, when anyone asked what my plans were, and the excitement and optimism that accompanied this statement were genuine because travel was a big part of it. I travelled hopefully: hope disappeared upon my arrival.

"Lowri Mai!" my mother would exclaim, and she would try to kiss me but I would not allow it. When you have been pushed away for so long, you can't expect to be pulled back again at a moment's notice. *I am in my own space now, you can't hurt me any more.* And she would turn away with a tight shattered look on her face and I would have to pretend that nothing had happened — oh, my armour was very strong in those days, because the memories were still so strong — *No need to cry, Mam. There's nothing to cry about.*

I'd go into the living-room, drop my overnight bag on the carpet, sit in one of the armchairs by the fire and wait for the battle of emotions to begin. Because it wasn't true that she couldn't hurt me any more; if anything it was worse than ever....no-one could hurt me more than she could. But I had become expert at not showing it.

A fire every day....and so little warmth.

In Miles' mother's kitchen, there was no fire but there was warmth, and carefully, without fuss, hardly daring to believe it, I tentatively began to dismantle my armour and breathe freely.

I trawled through all these memories as I got out of Bryn's bed and started to move around the room, getting dressed. "I think I'll go to Southampton this weekend," I announced.

"Yeah?" replied Bryn, looking up at me from the bed. "What for — another slinky assignation?" He chuckled, then put his hands to his head and clutched his temples. "Christ, my head."

"Don't be cheeky," I said. "I just want to look up a friend — a woman. No-one you know."

On Friday, I made a telephone call, hired a car, picked it up after work, and on Saturday morning drove down to Botley to look up Jean Hodges, whom I had not seen for years. It no longer mattered that she was not Miles' mother, but his grandmother. That was all in the past. Now Jean was just someone I had once felt comfortable with, someone who I hoped would be glad to see me without wanting too much from me. That's what a friend is, after all. Someone who just lets you be, who accepts you for the flawed being that you are — and trusts that you are prepared to do the same for them.

After Miles and I had — faded — yes, that was the word, faded, for that was how it felt to me, as if a scene once clear had gradually drifted out of focus, becoming more and more vague and colourless. Jean remembered my birthday just once afterwards, enclosing with the card a note telling me that Miles had found a job in Luxembourg, was drinking too much and putting on weight — and was busy chasing women no doubt, though she omitted any mention of that. After I read the note inside the card I felt a twinge of interest, a passing concern, a whiff of nostalgia, then nothing.

All in the past.

I drove into Southampton city centre then took the road for Hedge End and Botley. There was a new flyover bridge spanning the Solent and for a little while I did not recognise anything and thought I had lost my way. Then the road was familiar again and I could drive without having to concentrate so hard. For the last mile or so I enacted in my head the scene out of "Un Homme et Une Femme", one of my favourite films, where the Jean-Luc Trintignant character drives south to see his old girlfriend and anticipates their meeting:

She'll come to the door — we'll smile — no, she'll look surprised, I'll smile — she'll ask me if I want coffee, invite me in — with the un-forgettable soundtrack music in the background, haunting, in-sistent — *Dah…dah…dah…da-da-da-da-da, da-da-da-da-da…*

What a fascinating, pointless game it turned out to be…. because Jean wasn't in. I asked in the village butcher's shop if she still lived in the village and received a guarded affirmative from the man behind the counter. I went back to the house and walked round.

It was the same house and yet not the same: it was clean-er, smarter, it looked more modern, freshly painted. I tried the front and back doors, which were locked, and decided to wait for a bit. I sat in the car and read *The Guardian* until my excitement had worn off, then wandered around the house again, starting to get bored and restless. I told myself I would wait for another half an hour, then leave. I continued to sit there, trying to find something else worth reading in the newspaper.

Minutes later, a white Ford van rolled up and a friendly face with sparkling blue eyes appeared at the window, a man's face.

"Looking for Jean?" he asked, brightly.

"Yes!" I replied, throwing the paper, unfolded, into the passenger seat, my original interest immediately restored.

"I'm Norman." And he got out of the car. He had on white overalls which were covered in splashes and splotches of paint, and grubby from constant contact with tools and working hands.

After I told him who I was and we were shaking hands, his expression changed and became more quizzical, so I knew that Jean must have mentioned me at some time. He told me she was out for a while but would be back soon and invited me in for a cup of tea.

And after over five years, there I was, back in the kitchen where I had felt so much at home, wondering what I was doing there and who this man Norman was.

The place had been considerably updated, there was a new stove where the range had been, a large new refrigerator next to it, everything was freshly painted, and the warmth that I remembered seemed to have evaporated.

"So you're the famous Lowri," observed Norman, as he filled the kettle at the gleaming kitchen sink. "I was wondering if I'd ever get to meet you. This place looks a bit different, doesn't it? Did you know that Jack died?"

"Jack?"

"Jack Hodges — Miles' father. The old bastard finally kicked the bucket, year before last, and not a minute too soon, in my opinion, evil old sod, 'scuse my French. So Jean got the place done up — I did most of it, in fact." He turned and grinned, showing that he was willing to accept a compliment but he wasn't pushing for one. He plugged in the kettle, came and sat on the other side of the kitchen table: "I'm living here now. Jean and I are — well, let's say we're as good as married."

That explained the response at the butcher's shop. Jean and this man were *living in sin*....village life and its medieval standards. But Norman was at least ten years younger than Jean, perhaps more, and not an obvious match for her, with her tailored clothes, her careful make-up and regularly tended hair.

"Before you ask, she's fifteen years older than I am," said Norman, as if he sensed what I was thinking, though it was probably what anyone would think. "Jean didn't want to get married again, she didn't see the point, and if that wasn't bad enough, the people in the village think I'm just after her for her money. Stupid sods. I've got my own painting and restoration business — I've done work for half of them — but they still look down their noses at me. What they can't understand is that I actually love the woman. She's a thoroughly wonderful person and she hasn't been treated well. And she has plenty of life left in her, I can tell you." He managed to make this sound touching instead of prurient.

"Milk and sugar?"

"Just milk, thanks,' I said. "So — where is Jean exactly?"

"Oh, should have told you." He turned, his eyes sparkling again: "She's gone to Gatwick airport — to meet Miles. He decided to come over for a couple of days. They should be here any minute."

Suddenly my thoughts were in complete turmoil. I could not quite believe that I had chosen that day to go there or that my reaction to Norman's words was so strong. My feelings bounced all over the place and one of those feelings was — no, it couldn't be true, it couldn't be love, it was not possible that I still loved Miles. Was it? That was all in the past.…*Dah…dah…dah…da-da-da-da-da*.…but what was it then?

Norman chuckled and said, significantly: "Just fancy — you choosing today to come down."

This only added to my confusion. The man seemed able to read my thoughts. "Another cup of tea?"

"Um, no, thanks," I said, and smiled automatically.

He said something about emptying out his van and left the room, leaving me alone with my thoughts.

Miles never actually said goodbye. After telling me that his father had raped Nessa so that Nessa was not Miles' sister but his mother — correction: his sister *and* his mother — this grim fact brought us closer together for a short while. And after I had shared some of his pain and recovered from the shock, I accepted the situation and found it only added to the heat of my love for him. It meant a great deal that Miles had confided in me something so personal, so life-changing. No, that wasn't what came between us. Nor was it Jean or Mr. Hodges, neither of whom had any qualms about Miles and I sleeping together when he came home from York after getting thrown out of university. I stayed there in the Botley house, Miles and I had our own bedroom and I was treated like a treasured daughter-in-law. What came between us, ultimately, was the fact that Vanessa, having conclusively thrown me out of her house for becoming involved with her *little boy*, was equally conclusive about my not — under any circumstances — returning.

While he looked for work locally, Miles went round to his sister's house regularly but what he and I had together meant more to him than any of the diversions at Tim and Nessa's.

However, he was developing into a man, with all the attendant interests and desires and, gradually, this ratio was inverted: instead of leaving Nessa's early to come to me, he began to bring our evenings together to an earlier and earlier close so that he could go there. Sometimes I would ask him, choosing my words very carefully, if I could go with him, but Miles thought it "inadvisable", which was no doubt his tactful way of expressing Nessa's fiat: "That woman is never to set foot in this house again."

We began to have very unsatisfactory conversations, when I would get upset because it was clear he was trying to talk a distance between us. The situation at Nessa's was protected from any observation by or interference from me and, naturally, other females were now available to this charming, considerate — and sexually experienced — young man; the exquisite irony was that he was trying to release himself from me because he had scruples about his wandering eye.

I found a new flat and moved into it, taking Felicity the tabby cat with me. I bought my first little car. I was trying to build a new life of my own. Miles' visits became more and more sporadic. It no longer made sense to accept Jean's invitations to Sunday lunch as Miles usually wasn't there, he spent most of every weekend at Tim and Nessa's. Sometimes, to torture myself, I would drive past Nessa's house in the evening, and feel a knife turn in my heart when I saw Miles' battered Cortina parked outside.

So Nessa triumphed. And who could blame Miles for wanting to spend so much of time at the house where a loyal group gathered in front of the television on Sunday nights to watch

Rowan and Martin's Laugh-In and *Monty Python's Flying Circus* and laugh themselves silly? Added to that, the house was the unofficial home of *The Loose Cannons*, the local amateur dramatics society. Tim ran the society and they liked to present musicals. When I was still living in the house, I would wriggle with pleasure as they all crowded into the house after a show, shouting one another's praises, singing, chanting lines, jostling and laughing, before going into a brief reprise of their on-stage routines — *Hey, big spender!*

One evening Miles and I had arrived back at Tim and Vanessa's — this was before I received my marching orders — and as we stood in the hall removing our coats and calling "Hullo!" to Vanessa, the entire cast of *Guys and Dolls* burst through the front door, led by Tim, and started singing *Sit down, you're rocking the boat!* They were instantly loving and lovable, full of fun, talented. And some of them were very beautiful, so that being around them, you felt that perhaps some of it would rub off on you. They were irresistible, a family of lively troubadours. I had felt immediately at home in their midst.

No, I couldn't really blame Miles. I lost him to life.

Norman came back into the room, a pile of folded, paint-splashed canvas in his arms. After several more agonising minutes of waiting, there was a steady crunching of the gravel in the drive as a car rolled up.

"That'll be them," said Norman and went out through the back door, while I, shivering with apprehension, slid into the sitting-room to try and prepare myself for the encounter. Faced as I now was with the prospect of seeing Miles again, the events of our time together flew through my head like the days of a man's existence glimpsed before he dies.

From the shadowy side of the sitting-room I looked out through the bay window at the arrivals. A familiar figure, Jean, emerged from the passenger side of the car, Miles from the other door. Of, course, she had let him drive from the airport. That was one of his passions — driving. And I was — had been — another.

Miles had got fatter, his face was rounder, though Norman told me he'd lost weight so god knows what he was like before. I had thought my main concern was going to be whether he still liked me or not. Instead I found that the big question in my mind was whether I still liked him. Yes, was the answer....but in a different way. He was — the past. My heart was awash with memories, with feelings of nostalgia, sentimentality....but not with love. And I almost collapsed with relief.

Norman must have immediately told Jean I was there because she came bursting into the room with a bright searching look on her face, saw me and exclaimed: "Lowri! What a lovely surprise!"

Miles came in more warily, smiled uncertainly and said hello. His light brown eyes, the slight opening of his mouth and almost imperceptible intake of breath before actually speaking, the softness of his voice and his hesitant way of talking — as if it were somehow tactless to speak at all — struck a gentle blow which did no real damage. Inside my head, a voice like that of my old grammar school headmistress issued orders: *Come along, speak up, show that you, too, have moved on, free of the past, go ahead, speak up, now's the moment....*all this in a few seconds...

Before I could utter a word, "Miles is home for the weekend," said Jean, abruptly, superfluously. "He comes over every other weekend — to see Chrissie, his new lady love."

He had a girlfriend — of course he had a girlfriend....another small blow.

Jean had always been pragmatic. When she learned that Miles and I had finally drifted apart for good — she was the first person I told — she had no qualms about revealing her true feelings: "I didn't want Miles to settle down with the first girl he went out with," she said, and her honesty had jolted me along towards acceptance of the split.

Now here she was once again, opening things up, putting the necessary cards on the table, clarifying the situation.

Miles said to his mother, "I'll go and have a bath, Mum, then I'll be off out." He smiled at me and started edging towards the door: "It was very nice to see you," he said, shifting from foot to foot before leaving the room, an indication that the situation was difficult for him, a difficulty which he did not try to hide, which meant I could still like him.

Jean gave a theatrical sigh, "Well, I'm parched, I'm going to make a pot of tea." Then, raising her voice so that Miles could hear as he went up the creaking stairs, she called out, "Will you two be staying here tonight or at Chrissie's?" and Miles called out in reply, "Here."

"I suppose I'd better make the bed up then," said Jean. Turning to face me she said: "Right, come along into the kitchen and you can tell me what you've been up to for the last I-don't-know how long."

Miles and his current girlfriend were going to do what Miles and I had done, spend the night together in a bedroom upstairs, and once again Jean accepted this without question. My usurping was complete: here was the final small blow….and the walls were still standing.

After my visit to Jean, I drove round Southampton for a while, revisiting places that held the sweetest memories. I sat in the car for the longest time, parked outside 57 Howard Road, where Miles and I had lain so happily in the double bed of the garden flat, stroked the cat, made love and dislodged the cat, then — laughing — patted the bed so the cat would jump up again. I tried, unsuccessfully, to recall the flat's telephone number….I thought it had been branded into my brain forever.

I decided to stay in a B and B overnight. That way I would start the next day with a good meal inside me, a full English breakfast. I had a childish liking for the strong tea that was also a feature of such a meal, and for the way it was served, piping hot, in a tea-pot of stainless steel or brown earthenware, complete with cosy. After one of those breakfasts one had no need to eat anything until evening.

Jean had tactfully not invited me to stay overnight even though only three of the five bedrooms in the house would be oc-cupied. She no doubt sensed — correctly — that for me to sleep alone with only the thickness of one bedroom wall between the bed in which I slept and the bed in which Miles and his girlfriend were entwined would perhaps be intolerable, too strong a re-minder of the time when I had been the woman in Miles' arms.

The next morning I phoned Bryn to let him know I was all right and because I wanted to hear his voice. In spite of the un-conventional aspects of our relationship, he nevertheless repre-sented normality to me, he was a kind of anchor. I did not ask him what he had done the previous evening because I did not feel strong enough to hear him inform me that he had been with another woman.

"You had a phone call," he said, "Mohammed from Kashmir."

"I don't know any Mohammed," I replied.

"Well, he certainly sounded like he knows you, said he'd try again tomorrow. Probably wants to sell you something."

"Well, he can take a flying leap, whoever he is."

"That's the spirit. Fancy a curry this evening?"

"Yes *please*," I said, glad to have something to look forward to. "I'll be there in a couple of hours."

I drove back to London, crawling at twenty-five m.p.h. when stuck from time to time behind a Sunday driver, and doing a steady fifteen miles an hour above the speed limit when the road was clear.

My thoughts wound back over the events of the previous day and all the emotional jolts to which I'd been subjected and I wondered how, in similar situations, other people dealt with their feelings and how — if — they managed to control them.... and whether or not there was any point in doing so. There was, after all, a certain purity in following the dictates of one's heart, it produced a clean straightforward feeling, as if all traces of hypocrisy, control, detachment, neutrality and, above all, pretence, were washed away and one was left with a fundamental motive which was fuelled by — by what, that was the question. I did not have an answer. All I knew was this: I believed in those impulses that came straight from the heart, relied on them, trusted them, awaited their call to action and followed their imperatives. Something either had meaning or it did not....

but then this was exactly the attitude that had always landed me in trouble. After all, what are good manners but the restraint of our baser instincts?

These abstract thoughts washing around in my head meant I was absorbing the fact that there was no more Miles. I had accepted it in the abstract, in theory, but my emotions had not yet relinquished their grip. Now I had to accept it in reality.

There was absolutely no doubt in my mind that I still liked Jean. She had remained straightforward, open, and not afraid to call a spade a spade. Not like my mother, who was either incredibly blunt or maddeningly obtuse in her communications. When asking or answering the simplest of questions, she used either a rapier or a confusion of cloaks and veils just as it suited her, so communicating with her was like playing a game whose rules you could never master because they were continually being changed. The carpet was either pulled abruptly from under your feet or you were expected to quietly raise a corner and sweep everything underneath as she dictated. It was impossible to prepare for both eventualities and the struggle to try and do so was exhausting. Eventually, the challenge was so difficult it seemed to me inhuman, and withdrawal became the only option. *Leave me alone...*

Just before Kingston-upon-Thames I decided not to take the by-pass and instead drove into the middle of town where I stopped at a café for a cup of coffee. I was only a dozen miles from Bryn's house but it was a symbolic moment, taken in order to fully observe my loss before returning to my normal life. No more Miles, I was sure I'd accepted it now. No. More. Miles.

I stuck the newspaper into my handbag when I left the car to go into the café. Feeling a little more calm, I pulled it out and idly read the parts I'd missed. I read my horoscope, which predicted: *If you are ever going to get a windfall, this will be the year.* Part of me ached for this to be true, another part of me scoffed at this random prediction, while still another part remained unmoved, knowing the danger of craving swift, easy solutions to life's exigencies and ennui.

As I turned the corner into Sylvester Road, I felt my mood shift and my spirits lift when I thought about having a curry that evening. Then my brain made a crucial connection: I realised who Mohammed was — not Mohammed from Kashmir, but Mohammed from *The* Kashmir, the owner of the Indian restaurant Ian and I had frequented in Gloucester. Mohammed, who had always beamed at me when I entered the restaurant, who seemed to take a real pleasure in gently pulling out my chair for me to sit at a table, who always complimented me on how I looked and told Ian more than once what a lucky man he was, which always delighted Ian. Tall, slim, probably well educated, always impeccably dressed, smelling very faintly of expensive cologne, single, with the most charming manners, Mohammed was a very attractive package but one that had never interested me because he was simply the very hospitable owner of a restaurant where Ian and I liked to eat. And yet he had phoned me. He must have found out from Ian that I had left and got Bryn's phone number from him. And why was he phoning? Any fool could have answered that question.

Well, well, I thought, as I pulled up the handbrake and reached for my overnight bag, *the Lord giveth and the Lord taketh away….and giveth again…*

"There's a letter here for you, from Alfred Marks," said Bryn as soon as I walked into the house. "I didn't tell you on the phone, in case it wasn't good news."

It could only be about the job with RHM, working for Mr. Tree.

After the events of the last two days my conviction that I had the job was less certain. If the letter contained a refusal I felt incapable just then of surviving another jolt to my mangled emotions. "Okay, thanks," I said.

"Don't you want to open it?"

"No."

"But— " Bryn began to protest.

"*You* open it."

Bryn walked into the kitchen where there was a small bureau on to which he tossed his bills after opening them. I heard the tearing of an envelope flap, the crackle of unfolding paper, a few seconds of silence.

"It's yours!" Bryn called out. "You got the job!"

"Does it say when they want me to start?"

"Beginning of next month."

After my visit to Botley I fell into an emotional limbo. As I had three weeks to wait until I started my permanent job I stopped temping and tried to write some poetry, poems about events from my childhood, schooldays, the angst of adolescence.

Time stretched itself out yet activities became compressed and compartmentalised. Every event — a piece of music or a meal or a TV programme — had a distinct beginning, middle and end and was then immediately history. I had never experienced life in such a clearcut way before. Everything was in present tense.

My involvement with Mohammed certainly had a very distinct beginning, middle and end.

He phoned me the day after I came back from Southampton and was keen to come up to London and take me out. We had three encounters in quick succession and things degraded very rapidly. Perhaps he had set himself a time limit. Within the space of two weeks I was treated like a queen, then a run-of-the-mill date, finally I was one of the hoi polloi. At the beginning he wined and dined me in one of the most expensive Indian restaurants in town and afterwards we danced the night away and drank champagne in the fabulous exclusive night-club at the top of the Hilton on Park Lane; in the middle we had a meal in one of the many popular Indian restaurants in Bayswater where everybody went because the food was good but cheap, followed by a whisky in a nearby pub; at the end we sat in Mohammed's sports car and ate hamburgers from a street vendor's stall and drank canned beer. My descent was so precipitous it almost made me dizzy.

My naivety often hampered my understanding of a situation: in this case, I had not bargained for his having a specific agenda which was probably the search for a suitable wife or at least for sex. I enjoyed his company but found, close up, that I was not the least attracted to him — his breath smelled strongly of garlic, he was very critical of the British and he was forever looking at himself in mirrors and admiring his reflection in shop windows. And he made not the slightest effort to disguise his extreme annoyance that I would not go to bed with him.

So — three strikes and I was out. Part of me was glad that it had been so simple and swift.

A certain coldness set in between Bryn and me after my brief fling with Mohammed: the liaison was so insignificant to me that, although Bryn knew I was with Mohammed on those three occasions, I hadn't bothered to tell him a single detail about any of them. It had meant absolutely nothing to me — I was glad it was over so swiftly — but perhaps Bryn would have liked reassurance of this, would have liked to hear the words, "It didn't mean a thing."

Bryn continued to rehearse with the Goldsmith big band every Thursday, and invariably came home very late from these rehearsals, so late that it told me all I needed to know....but he no longer offered any explanation of these protracted evenings.

We had an unwritten rule that neither of us would bring any other "party" to the house, something we adhered to, but I think I might have preferred to know with what — I should say with whom — I was not even trying to compete. And perhaps Bryn felt the same way. Our openness had evaporated. We were both aware the other person was being entertained by others but these events were no longer discussed. Bryn did not enquire about my encounters and I did not enquire about his. We went about our daily life like two individuals who happen to inhabit the same space but whose lives are not really intertwined....and things cooled between us.

It was the phone-calls that bothered me most: Julia, Genevieve, Isabella, Cassandra, one woman after another with a name that held a whiff of sophistication. Never a Sue or a Pat or a Linda. "Is Bryn there?" "Who is this?" "This is Antonia..."

In spite of all this, Bryn and I moved together into Bryn's new house, in Gubyon Avenue and I, having temporarily lost interest in everything connected with the opposite sex, spent many evenings alone, reading an Edith Wharton novel. In the peaceful sitting-room on the top floor of the house, the room whose windows had glowed with dim light that night Bryn took me to look at the place for the first time, I played at being a little old lady and the only thing missing was the poodle.

"And what will *I* throw myself into?" asks one of the eponymous Buccaneers in the Wharton novel, when a young man she has her eye on announces that he is taking off to South America for a couple of years.

"I thought," he replies stiffly with typical upper crust aplomb, "women usually threw themselves into marriage."

One evening, after Bryn had demolished a whole bottle of wine with dinner — I was drinking lager, dinner was French bread, cheese and olives — he became effusive and started to reminisce about his past conquests, about the circumstances in which they had occurred and why those affairs had invariably been short-lived. We had spent the day pushing furniture around and emptying boxes, trying to decide what to put where. Now Bryn was feeling nostalgic: the Sylvester Road phase of his life had ended and this had prompted him into conducting an overview of his life up to that point.

"I've come to the conclusion my standards are too bloody high," Bryn said, in a despairing tone, as if this were a truly crushing weight he had to bear. "I was at a party once and picked up this really sexy woman, she had long — *really* long — hair. I really fancied her, I loved the long hair and she had a great body. Well, when we woke up next morning she said she'd cook breakfast, and do you know what she said?" — the corners of his mouth turned down — "She said, 'How about some strangled eggs?' Strangled eggs!" He gave a violent shiver as though an icy blast had swept through him. "She thought she was being funny but I was absolutely appalled and I couldn't get rid of her fast enough. So that was the end of that." He gave a sigh and echoed his opening statement, shaking his head ruefully, "My standards are just too bloody high."

And yet he put up with so much from me. It was limitless, his tolerance....the sarcasm, the total lack of interest in house-work, the drunkenness, the lack of co-operation, the uncontrolled spending (of my money and his), the insults and aggression, towards him and sometimes towards his friends....he put up with it all, with only a rare outburst of protest — well, once in six months, that's rare, isn't it? Yes, with me, he was endlessly patient.

I began working for Oliver Tree, which boosted my confidence and gave new purpose to my life, even if getting up in the morning was a perpetual challenge.

An unexpected bonus of the job was that I found myself sharing an office with another executive's personal secretary who was exactly the same age I was and we immediately became friends. Jazmin was a white West Indian, born in Barbados, a Caribbean island I had visited in my twenties and fallen in love with, and this seemed to connect us in a meaningful way. I think it soothed her homesickness to be able to talk about her distant island home with someone who also had fond memories of the place — the endless stretches of pale hot sand, the potent rum punch, the high white surf at Crane Bay, the jungly island interior, and the delicious flying-fish that lay on one's plate like a diminutive pair of baggy trousers, flattened, breaded and deep-fried golden. We talked about the way the sunlight reflected like strips of silver off the palm trees, about the sea breezes and about the cockroaches which were the size of baby mice and were a beautiful burnt-orange colour.

One weekday lunch-time Jaz and I were walking along Victoria Street to the tube station in order to make the one-stop journey to Pimlico on the Victoria line. From there it was a three-minute walk back to the office. We had just spent our lunch-hour shopping for clothes — we wouldn't have dreamed of wasting this interlude on eating — and were each carrying a small harvest of carrier bags from the boutiques around Victoria.

Jaz's company suited me perfectly, as I think mine did her: we were the same height and she was as slender as I was, perhaps even moreso, my hair was now long and unashamedly dyed red, her hair was short, an elfin cap, and bleached blond. The way we dressed undercut any impression that we were either cheap or sheep; neither of us was enslaved by what was fashionable, we each had our own highly customised version of current trends. Neither of us showed much bare skin, certainly no cleavage — we had none — and we both wore just enough make-up to show that we knew it was necessary for a woman to put on a "face" in the big city but also that it was essential to allow one's own natural features to play the biggest part in the presentation. We each lived with a man who was solvent, supportive and encouraging but also independent and occasionally troublesome, and we each seemed to have the same amount of self-confidence which meant there was no competition between us. Not since I was a teenager had I had a female friend with whom I was quite so comfortable and at ease. We even had similar taste in popular music — David Bowie, Frank Zappa, Dollar Brand, Ian Dury and The Blockheads.

…And it was not long before I discovered that she and her boyfriend took every type of drug imaginable.

That was the only significant difference between us: Jaz and Rupert routinely took every drug available *except* alcohol and nicotine — "so unhealthy," she said — while Bryn and I routinely partook of all kinds of alcohol and smoked cigarettes (though Bryn's consumption far outstripped mine) but no other drugs. But Jaz was keen to share all her drug experiences. She told me the first time she smoked opium she promptly "threw up" but then immediately tried it again and "did better second time." Her commitment to illegal substances was a source of fascination to me and she in turn was impressed by the fact that I drank alcohol every day and liked classical music.

So there we were, sauntering back to work after a non-existent lunch, looking aimlessly ahead or around at the shop windows, still hoping to see one last something we might want to buy. Suddenly Jaz gave a little yelp, stopped dead, dropped her carrier bags, bent down and picked up what looked like a piece of coloured paper off the pavement in front of us. This item turned out to be four five-pound notes, crisp new ones neatly folded in half, money that someone had obviously dropped through who-knows-what unfortunate circumstance. Our pity for the person who suffered the loss was sincere but short-lived. I said, "Lucky you!" and we both squealed with delight.

"Oh my gahd," drawled Jaz, staring down at the slim wad of cash, separating the notes. She had an accent that made you think she was American, except that she used peculiar idioms which didn't sound American at all. "I haven't found money for longti'." This meant "for a long time", one of her favourite native Barbadian expressions.

"Lucky you!" I said again, and there was only a trace of envy in my voice. It could have been me who had found the money but it wasn't — too bad. And I thought nothing more of it.

Next morning, the moment she arrived at the office Jaz came over to my desk, slid a small white envelope into my IN tray and covered it with a sheet of company letterhead. She bent her head towards my mine: "That's a couple lines of Charlie," she whispered, pushing out her lips to pronounce Charlie. "We got some last night with that money I found."

"Oh, thanks," I said, as casually as I could.

That evening I told Bryn about the cocaine and asked if he would like to try it with me. For both of us it was the first time and we were very excited. Added to that I was glad to be reminded of one of the things I liked best about Bryn — that he was completely open to new experiences. And no matter how high-flown the experience — and Bryn was capable of flying really high — his feet somehow remained planted firmly on the ground, so I felt safe experimenting with him. It helped draw us closer than we had been for the last few weeks.

Jazmin had told me, "The Charlie is good stuff, hardly cut adawl," and although I was not familiar with drug jargon I immediately understood that this meant it was pure and probably potent.

Bryn cleared a space on the kitchen table, went to the bathroom for a razor blade and a mirror and, while I chopped up the slightly lumpy, crystalline white powder and shaped it into two straggling lines, Bryn rolled a pound note into a tight hollow tube. We took a line each, snorting the two halves of it briskly into one nostril then the other, using our dampened fingers to lap up the remaining crumbs and rub them into our gums —

where had I learned that? Afterwards we stood and grinned at each other, suddenly feeling very pleased with ourselves. There was nothing quite like trying something completely new with Bryn, especially something illicit.

"I don't feel anything, do you?" I said, frowning.

Bryn said nothing, but from his expression, his eyes slightly narrowed and his mouth a straight line, I could tell he was listening inwards and also waiting for a change.

Another thing I liked about Bryn was that at times like this he didn't talk too much. Some people might have found this unnerving — "But what's happening? they'd have wanted to know, "What's happening? Aren't you going to say something? We need to talk about what is or is not happening — don't we?" To cover their nervousness.

"Give it a minute," he said.

A few silent seconds passed.

"I don't feel any different," I protested again, then I could feel my eyes widening, and I added, slowly, "...oh yes I do."

"So do I," said Bryn, smiling. "Nice, innit?"

"Yeah, innit?" I echoed and we both laughed nervously.

We went down the pub — and then the talking started. We had only one drink each but we got completely drunk on conversation. The words tumbled out of our mouths as if they had been piling up behind some invisible barrier that had finally burst open. We kept drifting off the subject or, rather, veering sharply away from the subject and coming back to it before veering away again, and Bryn seemed to have a joke on every single topic that popped up in the conversation. He would start laughing before he told the joke then we'd both laugh as he continued, even before he got to the punch-line and when he finally came to the punch-line, we would both stare at each other, goggle-eyed for a second, pretending we didn't get the joke, then collapse into more laughter. Life was a wonderful game that we were playing to perfection and we relished this uncanny ability we both had to be intelligent and lighthearted....while, of course, feeling enormous unspoken pity for those not so blessed....oh, the entertainment and enlightenment — and self-delusion — provided by the brain's substance-powered excursions into new territory.

In fact, that cocaine evening brought Bryn and me together again. In the beginning, when I was living in Phil's flat, Bryn and I had seen each other most evenings. After I had moved out from Phil's flat into Bryn's Sylvester Road house we had started going out drinking every evening, only missing an evening when he was rehearsing with the big band. Going down the pub was as automatic as sitting down to breakfast when you were a child — it was just what you did, it was established and you did not even think to question it. Bryn and I would come home from work, shift gears, regroup, shrug off the working day mentally and physically and then it was time to go out. That part of the evening was set, unchanging; the only thing that changed was the particular pub we chose and what we talked about when we got there.

Then things had begun to change. Perhaps Bryn had decided to claim for himself what he had given me, which was space: the space to visit Ian in Gloucester, go to Southampton, have three dates with Mohammed. Or — the more likely possibility — relations between us had cooled because I was not giving him any real information about any of those events. I had started treating him in the way that was most familiar to me, the way I had learned to treat my parents in order to avoid any possible criticism, telling them as little as possible when they showed any interest in my personal life...."Did you have a nice time?" "Yeah, it was okay." End of conversation. And Bryn had adopted a similar approach. Say nothing.

Now, at one stroke, we had both returned to that earlier more agreeable plateau, the one on which we had both wept to the strains of "Nimrod" in front of the TV. And I was happier than I had been in a long time.

About a month later I came home from work much later than usual because there had been an incident on the line at Victoria and two trains had been cancelled. The resulting combination of frustration and boredom had left me exhausted and irritable.

As soon as I opened the front door, Bryn's voice rang out, from upstairs, "Don't move, I'm coming down!" and there was the noise of leather soles hurriedly descending the uncarpeted stairs. *Now what?* I thought. *After the bloody awful time I've had getting home?*....all I could think about was the first beer I was going to drink.

"What's going on?" I asked, remaining obediently rooted to a spot three feet inside the front door.

Bryn appeared.

"Your mother rang— " he began, then, as he saw my expression start to contract into one of horror, "No, no, it's not bad news, well — it is a bit....come in here," and he opened the door to the downstairs sitting-room.

"It's Gareth, isn't it?" I said, picturing my brother's racing car whirling off the track at Silverstone, bursting into flames, two men running towards it with foaming fire extinguishers, the crowd of spectators with greedy faces, craning their necks to see….a charred body being pulled from the wreckage…

"No, no, it's not Gareth, Gareth is fine, as far as I know. It's your uncle Gwilym."

I blinked.

"He had a heart attack this morning, it was bad, he….well…. he didn't survive."

"Uncle Gwilym?" The youngest of the four brothers. I felt a rush of regret — the last of my father's family gone. All four brothers, now dead. "Was Mam upset? When did she ring?"

"About an hour ago."

"Does she want me to ring back?"

"No, she just wanted to let you know about it. And the funeral is on Wednesday."

"Oh," I said. It was something I would never become used to — someone dies and before you know it, before you've had time to absorb it, there's a funeral. For a split second I saw myself sliding my arms into the sleeves of a black coat.

"It's all right," said Bryn, comfortingly. "She said she doesn't expect you to go. But listen, this is the good part. Your uncle left a will and guess what?" Bryn was beaming at me now: "His house is to be sold and all the nephews and nieces are to share the proceeds. That's what he wanted. And that includes you!"

A single drop of bright yellow fell into a colourless pool, suffusing it like sunlight.

"His house in Bwlch?" I asked, bemused.

"Is that where he lives?" asked Bryn.

"Lived," I corrected him, feeling myself becoming warmer by the minute and wanting to cry with gratitude. "He stayed in the family house because he never married, the big house where they were all born. We used to go there when I was little and— "

"Well, it'll be sold now," said Bryn, "and you'll get some dosh out of it. How many cousins do you have anyway?"

I ran through the names in my head: David, Gwyneth, John, Glyn and Brenda. And Bethan and Gareth and me. Eight of us. And suddenly my lucky number, which had always been five, was eight. *A windfall...*

Time passed — slowly, the way it does when you might prefer that it pass quickly. I was not really conscious of waiting for the money or, more precisely, of waiting for the changes that a sudden substantial injection of money into one's life can bring. I was not impatient. What I did think about was what I might be able to do with it. Doing certain things takes money; you suddenly have money, now you can do them. What are you going to do? What do you want to do? Finding answers to these questions swiftly turned into a kind of illicit pleasure, a drug I could partake of at any moment, for as long as I liked and as intensely as I liked.

I had been reading Jack Kerouac's novel, *On The Road*, and fantasized about making a coast-to-coast freewheeling trip across the USA like the one Jack and Neal Cassady had made. I also yearned to write a book, perhaps one like Kerouac's....but in both cases I doubted I would be able to realise my ambitions. Travel....write....these were romantic dreams, dreams I had always told myself I would have to modify, tailor to my resources, perhaps abandon altogether. Now they might be possible.

One evening Bryn and I stood in the King and Queen in the Edgware Road, talking about what I could do with my inheritance money when I received it. Bryn listened closely as I told him what was on my mind, that I wanted to stop working and travel, really travel, go somewhere I had never been before, write about it.

"I know some people in Washington DC," I said, "I could go and stay with them, see New York, explore the East coast a bit..."

Bryn took the final swallow of his pint and put the empty glass down on the bar.

"Why stop at that?" he said. "Why not stay over there, see a few things, go to the West coast as well, bum around for a while." He gripped his hands around my upper arms, smiling, and gave me a gentle shake. "You can *afford* it."

"You think so?"

"Do it!"

Bryn was a genius at knowing when to give a little encouragement and as soon as he said it, I knew it was what I should do, what I had wanted to do all along. I mentally revised my decision. I would stay with Molly and Ray in DC for a week, go to New York, see the East coast and then head west, with no timetable, just an atlas and some money. I smiled a tight little smile and tapped a finger against my chin, because my interest and enthusiasm were beginning to gather strength.

Bryn looked thoughtful for a moment, then said, "You know, there's this bloke in California that Dexter knows, they've been friends for ages — you could probably stay at his place."

"Really?"

"Wouldn't hurt to ask. I'll give Dexter a ring as soon as we get back home. Want another?"

"Okay."

"Let's have something special." Bryn waved his hand at the man behind the bar, who was polishing wine glasses, and addressed him in a regal voice: "I say, Ted my man, bring us something special."

"What d'you fancy, mate? Roast swan?" replied Ted, with a butler's smirk.

"Something special to drink," I said, hoping for a better answer. "What do you suggest?"

Ted put down the glass he was polishing, slung the cloth over his shoulder and approached us: "You both like gin?"

We looked at each other and nodded.

"How about a martini?"

"Perfect," said Bryn. "Two martinis, very dry."

"Couple of Winston Churchills coming up," grinned Ted.

"What's he talking about?" I asked Bryn, when Ted had turned away to make our drinks.

"There's a lot of argument about how to make a martini. Some people like it very dry — meaning lots of gin, very little vermouth. Ted and I got on to the subject when I was in here once and he told me Churchill was a big martini drinker. The story is Churchill liked his martini so dry he used to pour the gin into his glass and then just glance across the room at the vermouth bottle."

We both laughed.

"Celebrating, are we?" enquired Ted, bringing the cocktail shaker and two glasses over to where we were propping up the bar. We watched as he put ice into the stainless steel shaker, measured gin into it, plus two drops of vermouth, shook it for a few seconds then strained the contents into our glasses.

We drank to my good fortune, clinking together the edges of our martini glasses.

Bryn studied his drink: "I wouldn't mind having a couple of these," he said.

"Me too!"

"No, I mean — well, yeah, it's good isn't it? But I was talking about the glass, the design, isn't it beautiful? I'd like to own a couple." He held the glass out at arm's length to admire it, the distinctive shallow cone shape, and there was genuine longing in his voice.

That night I had a dream. Bryn was in it, he had lost weight, was slim, had a new very short haircut and had on a fashionable long black leather coat, completely out of character for him, with some equally trendy gear underneath. He also had a wife — the jolt of seeing such fashionable clothing on Bryn was nothing compared with the shock I got from discovering he had a wife.

In the dream we met in a supermarket just as I was putting a packet of frozen peas back in the wrong freezer compartment — I'd always disapproved of people who did that. I was talking to Bryn but he seemed uninterested and was not responding to any of my questions so, to hide my embarrassment, I started acting foolishly, flinging the hat I was wearing into the freezer and laughing too loudly. One of my school girlfriends appeared, Val or Norma or Janice — it was very vague the way things are in dreams — and she intimated that Bryn's wife was pregnant, so I asked Bryn — it was suddenly vital that I knew — if it was his wife's idea to start a family. He immediately said, "Oh no, I really wanted a child," and for some reason I felt sick to the pit of my stomach. I continued to clown, in desperation now, to cover up my horror at this sudden burst of passion and commitment.

Bryn eventually left to join the lady who was his wife, she had been striding round the supermarket filling a metal shopping trolley the whole time Bryn and I had been talking. My girlfriend — it was Val — and I went outside into the car park and it was unexpectedly night, and raining. We took a couple of minutes locating the car and as I stood, fumbling with my keys, another car came by with its headlights full on and windscreen wipers slapping. It slowed down as it went past us and I shaded my eyes and saw Bryn in the driver's seat. For an interminable second our eyes met and his face on the other side of the rainswept car window had a mournful expression that spoke to me of all the things we'd had between us over the years, the closeness and trust and the shared history....and then he parted his lips and in the instant before the car roared off, lights blazing, he mouthed the word "Goodbye" and I woke up, trembling uncontrollably.

A few days later Nick phoned to tell me he was coming down to London the following weekend and could we meet. We agreed on a time and place — The Coal Hole on the Strand, "for old time's sake", he joked, adding that he would be staying in a hotel in Sussex Gardens, near Paddington station, and we could go back there afterwards.

Sussex Gardens was the long, tree-lined street that originated just north of the Lancaster Gate entrance to Hyde Park and then leaned to the north-east to join Edgware Road at right angles. The elegant Georgian houses, once home to wealthy families and carriage folk, were now small hotels, guest houses, B and Bs, commercial establishments, maintained in varying degrees of cleanliness. In the light-deprived basements where servants once toiled — freezing in winter and roasting in summer — and complained about "them upstairs", guests now consumed their breakfasts in rather spartan surroundings that reflected the moderate tariff charged for an overnight stay in a convenient central London location.

After I put the phone down, I pictured myself strolling along Sussex Gardens, holding Nick's hand, both of us enjoying the balmy evening after a good dinner and smiling as, savouring its delay, we silently anticipated the moment when we would tear off our clothes and fall on to the bed, ready to devour each other. The phone rang again and I gave a violent start, jerked from my reverie. It was my mother, telling me that I would shortly be receiving a letter from a solicitor with instructions regarding what I had to do in order to receive my share of Uncle Gwilym's money.

"Now you do exactly what they say in that letter, mind," she ordered. "As soon as you get it now. No messing about."

"I will," I said, in my most long-suffering voice.

Two days later I received the notification about Uncle Gwilym's legacy. I was to send details of my bank account to the firm of solicitors in charge of distributing the funds and the money would then be deposited, "in the sum of five thousand pounds". My heart stopped momentarily. At my current job I was earning just over three hundred pounds a month. I kept staring at the words, *the sum of...* Suddenly this, to me, colossal four-figure sum represented freedom, freedom to stop working, freedom to do what I wanted, travel, write. And then, like smoke dispersing, everything else faded into insignificance....Nick, Sussex Gardens, my new job, Jazmin, Pimlico, even London itself...

Bryn saw me off at Heathrow and as I walked backwards, smiling, waving, my one small suitcase bumping against my legs, I somehow knew that everything would be different the next time we met....but I could never have imagined how much.

The roar of the plane's engines changed and suddenly we were lifted up over Washington DC, lifted up into the sky with the ponderous lurching climb of the packed 747 jumbo and I knew my trip was over. I was finally leaving the landmass of North America after spending the last two months wandering over its surface. I looked down through the small oval window at Washington DC receding below; it became less and less like a real city that has sounds and smells and smoke and traffic and people moving about, and more and more like a map, flat and geometric. I thought about the long tedious journey ahead, my bulging suitcase in the hold, and the amazing two months of travel that had just ended. I wanted to feel something but all I felt was numb.

I had bought two martini glasses from Macy's in New York. They were crystal, exquisitely cut, I dared not pack them with my cargo luggage. As I walked through the airport concourse to my departure gate, a small boy pointed at the glossy brown Macy's bag and said, at the top of his voice, "If you haven't seen Macy's, you haven't seen New York!" ...The power of advertising.

Bryn was at Heathrow airport to meet me. I immediately noticed that he had lost weight, had a new short haircut, was wearing uncharacteristic black corduroy dungarees, and looked fit and well. He had brought along a bottle of champagne and as soon as we had put my luggage in the boot of the car — Bryn glanced at the Macy's bag but made no comment — and dropped into the front seats, he pointed the bottle through the open window, released the cork towards the sky and poured foam into the two champagne flutes poised ready on the dash.

"I'm back!" I shouted, holding up my glass, grinning.

"She's back!" exclaimed Bryn, equally loudly, and clinked his glass against mine. We knocked it back in one and he poured again. He laughed: "I have to go to work this afternoon!"

"I don't," I said, and giggled like a child.

"So, how was America?"

"Oh my god, where to start!" I protested.

I had written regularly and at length while I had been away — this question was a way of getting me to talk. I launched into where, what, when, how and why, spilling out a flood of superficial information with scarcely a pause and all the while Bryn nodded and snorted and said "Yeah?" After half an hour of this, I began to feel like a listener myself and, bored with the sound of my own voice, I lapsed into silence, explaining to Bryn that I was exhausted after the journey and promising to carry on with the story later. We were now driving through the middle of the morning rush-hour so Bryn made no protest and concentrated on the traffic while I succumbed to jet lag. I was back.

The streets of London were threaded with cars and taxis and buses and delivery trucks. Motorbikes, needing less of the road, negotiated the spaces between vehicles or streaked vehemently ahead in the stretches between traffic lights. Indicators flashed on and off as vehicles chopped and changed lanes, and drivers looked for small advantages. Unsmiling faces only feet away from one another stared straight ahead at red traffic lights and there was much jerking of gears and handbrakes when the lights turned to green. Taxis darted in and out, intimidating other drivers, while buses, in their own specially designated lanes, surged forward when the rest of the traffic stood still. Hard to believe there were any tourists on the road at this hour — everyone seemed to know exactly where they were going and drove with the immaculate economy that comes from familiarity with the streets, lights, turnings and the price of petrol. I loved the mobile jigsaw of London's rush-hour, the way a mass of traffic clamouring around an enormous roundabout would filter off towards the exits, cars slicing between other cars at unbelievably acute angles with bumpers and wing-mirrors whisking by only inches from other bumpers and wing-mirrors. Chopping, slicing, whisking, all very precise, with unsmiling faces; it was like Japanese cooking, with the addition of diesel fumes. On the rare occasion a vehicle broke down, the flow of traffic still did not stop; hazard lights went on, the bonnet went up, and the sea of vehicles swarmed around the obstacle without so much as a pause, the other drivers thinking, *Some poor sod's broken down* and grateful that it wasn't them.

Bryn put on Radio Three and I heard the mellow cultured voice of Patricia Hughes announcing a symphony by Haydn. As we stopped and started in the traffic the sound of the orchestral strings filled the car, soaking into me like water into a dry sponge. I had missed music.

"It's good to hear some decent music again," I said.

"There's a performance of the Elgar cello concerto on at Greenwich tonight," said Bryn. "Wanna go?"

"Oh yes, yes, yes."

We smiled at each other, pleased at having something to look forward to so soon.

"I missed you," said Bryn, sensing a good moment.

"I missed you too," I said, wishing I meant it as much.

I remembered how we had stood in the King and Queen in the Edgware Road, talking about my trip to America, drinking our Winston Churchills....(*Why not stay over there, see a few things, go to the West coast, bum around for a while. A couple more of these, Ted, when you've got a minute...*)

Eventually the slow movement of the Haydn began filtering out of the radio, creating a lull which Bryn felt obliged to fill.

"So how was the Grand Canyon? You did see it, didn't you?"

"Yes. I sent you a postcard, didn't you get it?"

"Yeah, but, you know....you can't tell much from a postcard."

"It was absolutely incredible. It's so huge! Makes you feel like a — like a little worm. I got up at dawn to look at it and I took a photograph — in that pale orangey-pink light that you get at dawn, you know? That was the only photo I took, I hope it comes out. The place was so still, that was the thing that moved me most, standing on the rim of this vast canyon and everything was so still."

"I must see it some day," said Bryn, half to me, half to himself.

"Yes, you must. You'd be knocked out by it." I realised that by expressing myself this way, I had missed the opportunity to bring us together again, to regard us as a couple, if only in words. I should have said something about the future that involved both of us. The space between us created by my prolonged absence continued to exist.

When we got to the house, Bryn stopped just long enough to help me take my things into the house, change his clothes, drink a swift cup of coffee, then he went off to work and I collapsed gratefully into the familiar bed.

I had seen a lot of the United States of America: the White House, Arlington cemetery, the Smithsonian, the Lincoln Memorial while in Washington; from there I went to New York, excitedly rode the Staten Island ferry, trembled at the top of the Empire State and wandered around Times square, which was a great disappointment, the way I imagine the bustling, seedy, somehow smaller-than-expected epicentre of all capital cities always is; travelling west I had seen the wheatfields of Kansas, the Gateway to the West in St. Louis, Mount Rushmore, the Wall Drug dinosaur, the Rocky Mountains, the Continental Divide, the Great Salt Lake, the Golden Gate — but all that is another story.

Under the gaze of the famous faces carved in rock at Mount Rushmore I had met another lone traveller, a young man from Florida who was making his way around the country, looking for a place in which to settle down. We had spent a day and a night together and on the strength of some very tenuous arrangements, he had actually managed to catch up with me two weeks later in a small town in northern California, having covered a totally different route in the interim.

Convinced fate had thrown us back together and not questioning it, we went on the road together and for the next five weeks explored as much of the country as we could, hitch-hiking, riding Greyhounds and Trailways, staying in cheap hotels, hostels, camping, before his money ran out.

I had mentioned Eric in my letters to Bryn but I had not given him any details. Or, to be more accurate, I had not expressed to Bryn my true feelings because I was not even sure of them myself. Had it been just another holiday romance?

That evening Bryn and I went to the concert in Greenwich Town Hall and heard an impressive performance of the Elgar cello concerto. A storm blew up outside the hall during the last movement and the streaks of lightning, rolls of thunder and the rain lashing against the windows added a theatrical dimension to the performance, making it extraordinarily dramatic, as if that was the way Elgar had intended it. The lightning flashed, the thunder roared, the soloist bent into his instrument as if competing with the elements, and Bryn and I turned and looked at each other with widened eyes.

Afterwards we had a few drinks with the members of the orchestra that Bryn knew, then it was time for the curry. The current favourite was the Surma in Lordship Lane. It had fallen out of favour for a long spell a couple of years earlier, apparently, after a diner found a dead fly in the chopped onion, but it was the only curry restaurant in the area that had a tandoor oven and eventually — inevitably — the aroma of tandoori cooking lured people back.

Dexter was in the Surma, with two other men I did not recognise, seated at the table just inside the door; I walked through the entrance almost on to Dexter's plate. He leapt up from the table, shouted my name, and gave me a hug that almost crushed me then stood there, beaming his welcome while Bryn and I hovered just inside the doorway of the restaurant, until a waiter scuttled up with two menus.

Dexter insisted we sit at his table. Extra chairs were brought and, after introducing everyone, Dexter organized the seating and immediately began to bombard me with questions. I tried to give some impression of my travels, but I was inhibited by the presence of the two unknown men.

When the waiter came up to take our order, I was glad of the interruption and allowed myself to be derailed. Dexter kept the conversation going, talking about his trip to California the previous summer and the history of his friendship with Chris and Jeff.

These were the brothers with whom I had stayed, one in Carmel, the other in Willits, when I reached California.

Bryn continued to drink throughout the meal. By the time we were saying our goodbyes to Dexter and his friends outside the Surma, he was decidedly drunk. I put my hand on his forearm: "Bryn, let me drive."

"No, I am quite capable," he replied, in a voice that did nothing to help convince me....still, it was a short drive and the roads were wide and well lit all the way, so I stopped protesting and we got home safely. In fact Bryn was the only person I ever felt completely safe with in a car, whether he was drunk or sober — I think this had more to do with his protective attitude towards me than his driving skills.

We climbed the four flights of stairs to the living-room at the top of the house where Bryn immediately spotted the bottle of Jim Beam I had brought back for him. "Ah, just what I need, a shot of boybun," he said, striding towards the bottle.

Although it was well after midnight, the two of us settled down to drink bourbon and, oddly enough, Bryn began to sober up. He was waiting for me to tell him. We played an album he had bought called *Art Pepper and Friends* and laughed and joked and he told me what had been happening while I had been away. He was now playing with Phil Miller's group and with the Goldsmith big band, he had finished paying for his car, a friend of a friend had cut his hair, he had been running every day, which explained his weight loss, he had been moved to a bigger office — but all the time he was really waiting for me to tell him.

"I have to tell you something," I said, finally, in one of the pauses between tracks.

"I know," said Bryn, quietly. The close-knit saxophone harmonies of *Four Brothers* filled the room. It was thrilling the way human beings could play that way, as if all were being guided by the same hand. "The guy from Florida." A statement, not a question.

I nodded.

"Well, I guessed as much, from the way you kept mentioning him in your letters." He sat very still, as if suddenly frozen. I went and sat beside him. He closed an arm around my waist and pressed his face against the side of mine and we stayed like that for a while, with the music tumbling and bursting from the speakers then Bryn relaxed his arm and stared into space: "I introduced you to jazz," he said, and I realised that he was crying.

We slept in separate beds that night and Bryn went off to work next morning without disturbing me. Perhaps he thought I was asleep, still recovering from the plane journey.

When he returned from work, I showed him some of the photographs I'd taken on my trip, a censored viewing, with many of the shots of Eric removed. Then Bryn said he had to practise for a gig with the big band the following evening. He went down to the room with the piano while I spent an hour on the phone, calling friends to tell them I was back. Afterwards, I dutifully called my mother and arranged to visit the following day.

Although we were in separate rooms — on different floors of the house in fact — doing completely dissimilar activities, I still felt very close to Bryn. Coming back to him was like coming home to a safe existence: he had been my base, my security, a raft on the choppy unpredictable sea of my life. Now a storm had blown up in the form of my American adventure, producing a wave that threatened to dislodge me, and even though I wasn't sure if I would sink or swim, I was certainly considering the possibility of letting go of that raft. And I would perhaps be swept away to my doom, all the while looking back longingly at my former protector.

It did not occur to me to try and identify what might have held me back from leaving or to admit to myself that, whatever it was, it was important....and had always been lacking.

Bryn had always been a firm believer in the concept that one should not have to work at a relationship and I had never made much of an effort because it had not been necessary; whatever it was that worked between us — worked, and was presumed to be indestructible.

Now, without warning and with stunning abruptness, the positive parts of our daily existence, the aspects that we had enjoyed and taken for granted, were simply not there any more and the relationship was mortally threatened.

I went to bed before Bryn returned so I left him a note saying I was off to Wales next day and suggesting we meet for a drink at Paddington Station before I left.

Next morning, after Bryn got up — I was still in bed — I heard the post drop on to the hall floor inside the front door and I could tell from the way Bryn picked it up and flung it back down again before leaving the house to go to work, that there was a letter for me from America.

It was a thick airmail letter, four pages long, full of longing and frustration, with a photo enclosed, showing Eric staring straight at the camera, arms folded across his chest, unsmiling. Towards the end of the letter, he wrote: *I want to be with you, either here or in London, I don't much care, but I want us to be together again.*

At lunchtime I met Bryn for a drink in the bar at Paddington station before I caught the 125 to Wales to see my mother. Bryn drank gin and tonic and chatted about inconsequential things. I was sure he was still upset about the letter I had received that morning but my not broaching the subject seemed like kindness rather than collusion on my part. Our life together was being disturbed by the existence of someone on another continent whose place in my life had not yet been defined

I knew he had been devastated to hear what had happened — *she's found someone else* — but I still had no idea how he would react to the rest of the story, since I also had to tell him that I was considering going back to America to live with Eric so that we could explore in a more normal setting a relationship that had developed against the background of constant travel and all the excitement and turbulence that went along with it.

I had finally admitted to myself that I was not prepared to write off the affair with Eric as just another holiday romance.

To tell someone you are no longer theirs is one thing; telling them that this entails removing yourself thousands of miles away is another.

So I watched, stiff with sadness and guilt, as Bryn clinked the meagre amount of ice in his drink and talked about the inability of the drummer in the big band to provide a steady beat.

As we were leaving the station bar, Bryn stopped to say hello to a woman who worked in the building where he worked. Looking at her middle-of-the-road clothes and not-quite-matching shoes and handbag, I was reminded of my chronic morning dilemma over what to wear to work and hoped I would never have to work in an office again, though I dared not swear to it. After all, what else was I equipped to do?

Everything that could have gone wrong at home did. After the initial sweetness — my mother's smiling face as she opened the front door to my brisk double knock and the warm kiss which I forced myself to allow — relations between us, as always, rapidly soured and crumbled.

By the middle of the second day I had retreated to my childhood bedroom, wounded by her inability to accept my actions and intentions, and disgusted with my own inability to remain calm in the face of her criticism. I threw myself on the small hard bed, weeping with fury and frustration. I had travelled solo all the way across America and back but was incapable of holding a civil conversation with my own mother.

After a while I forced myself to go back downstairs and make myself a cup of coffee. My mother studiously ignored me and carried on watching television. Neither of us spoke. Mug in hand I plucked my shoulderbag off the settee beside her and went back upstairs.

Next morning, after exchanging barely a handful of sentences with my mother, I went back to London.

"Peter Sellers has died," said Bryn, when I joined him at the breakfast table next morning.

I was finally comfortably back on British time again He was drinking black coffee and reading *The Guardian*, his usual way of starting the day, except on Sunday when it was *The Sunday Times*.

"Oh no!" I cried, using the shock of the news to release some of the confusion and sadness I now felt when Bryn and I were in the same room together.

"Heart attack," he added. "He was only fifty-four. There's some important-looking post for you."

It was a large buff envelope, containing the Decree Absolute of my divorce. So at last it was official, I was no longer married. No more marriage, no more Ian. No more Peter Sellers....and soon there would be no more Bryn. I looked at him as he continued to peruse the newspaper and, overtaken by feelings of sympathy, I said in a half-whisper, "I'm so sorry."

"Yeah, it's a shame," sighed Bryn, still looking down at the newspaper. "Hell of a funny guy. Did you know he could play the ukulele really well?"

"No!" I exclaimed and suddenly, because my heart was bursting with mixed emotions, I started laughing, because that ukulele represented the absurdity of existence, it epitomised everything about being alive that was marvellous and maddening and ridiculous.

Bryn looked up, put down the paper and started laughing too. We were on exactly the same wavelength, we were one mind, the way we'd always been — just like that time he'd shown me the picture of the punk and the piglet. We couldn't stop laughing. Bryn stood up and we roamed around the kitchen briefly, every few seconds throwing our heads back to laugh anew and bending over to lean on the kitchen table, shaking, because we were now laughing uncontrollably. And I thought, *He's right, there will never be anyone I can share these things with the way I can with him.* And I knew he was feeling exactly the same way. The thought of what I might be giving up went through me like a knife.

And then, just as suddenly, Bryn stopped laughing. He gave a little sigh, came over to me, hugged me briefly, turned away with his head down, took three short steps, then turned back to face me: "I might as well tell you now," he said. "I've been putting it off..."

I was no longer laughing. His serious tone was terrifying.

"What's that?" I asked, my voice shaking a little.

"I'm getting married."

I blinked and my mouth fell open but I was suddenly mute.

"I've been trying to find a way to say it but... "

"Who?" I heard myself say.

"Rebecca....the woman I was going out with in college."

"Re-becc-a," I said softly, drawing out the name.

"While you were away, I had this thought — just out of the blue — that I'd like to find out what she was doing now, you know — blast from the past and all that — so I got in touch with her — while you were in the US."

I said nothing so he went on, making his voice sound casual so as to reduce the significance of what he was saying: "She was really pleased to hear from me. She's got a ten-year-old son — she got kicked out of college because she was pregnant — I don't know if you knew that — and she — well, she was really pleased to see me."

How to describe the way people talk at times like this?... They so much want to share certain information — information that is important to them — while at the same time they know that what they are saying is the last thing the other person wants to hear. And yet this awareness does not stop them from say-ing it....because the feelings of that other person are no longer important, that consideration has slipped into second place....or perhaps it has disappeared altogether.

Part of me was relieved, relieved that Bryn had someone to turn to, somewhere to go to have the huge gap I was about to leave behind me filled, and part of me was more sad than I had ever been in my life before.

"But — isn't she already married?" I asked. "If she has a child?"

"She's a single parent — the guy who got her pregnant dumped her but she had the kid anyway."

"So it's not your child."

"No. I stopped going out with her because you arrived back on the scene and she immediately started seeing this other chap — and he must have been a bit more of a man than I was." Bryn gave a tiny self-deprecating snort.

"You must still like her then."

"Yeah," said Bryn, keeping his expression neutral.

"And she must still like you."

"Yeah," said Bryn.

"When?" I asked.

"When what?"

"When are you getting married."

"Not sure. Soon."

I managed a very small smile, not a smile at all really, it was just the attempt one makes in situations like that to turn up the corners of the mouth....because you can feel the great surge of life pulling you forward, at that moment you can really feel it. And you need a convenient mask to put on, while you try and work out what your emotional reactions are to such life-changing developments.

Bryn remained standing, leaning back against the kitchen counter while I sank down onto one of the dining chairs, thinking, *Coffee — I need coffee. I'll feel better if I have a cup of coffee in my hands.*

Then I thought of something else, the obvious question, and I knew I should not ask it but I did: "And will it be an open marriage?"

Bryn shrugged and pulled his closed mouth to one side, perhaps to indicate that this was a question he would soon be asking himself....or perhaps he was not about to admit this was something that would not change. Or — of course — it was no longer any of my business. He replied, with finality but without animosity: "What do you care?"

A tense fragrant silence filled the room. And I thought, *There is no such thing as an open relationship — there is only a relationship that has holes in it.*

"Look," said Bryn, flinging his arm out, as if to throw off any bad feelings that threatened to develop, "we should be celebrating — we are acting as if someone has died! I want to celebrate what's happening to me — *and* what's happening to you. This is the next phase, we are both going on to the next phase in our lives. And christ knows how it's going to turn out, but it's actually happening and we'd better accept it— " he looked at his watch, "I have to get going or I'll be late for work. Look, let's — this evening — let's go to Davy's."

He came over and gripped my upper arms — exactly the way he had that evening in the King and Queen in the Edgware Road when I was trying to decide on my American travel plans — then looked into my eyes to remind me of the first time he had taken me there — how long ago was it — almost a year? — and once again shook me gently and said, "It's time I took you to Davy's."

"Well, I should think it is," I replied, softly, and, though we smiled at each other, this time the mood was subdued, because now I knew what Davy's was and where it was....and we both understood that this time we would be going for a completely different reason; this time we would be parting — for good.

My heart was a jumble of confused emotions: I knew what I was most inclined to do — move to America to be with Eric — but I had no idea how this was going to be achieved. The prospect of concluding my life in London and embarking on a life in the USA was like looking at a mountain and not knowing how to move it. But I had to leave, that was clear.

Late one evening — Bryn was out drinking with one of his fellow musicians from the big band — I watched the first part of a television dramatisation of some of the events of the Holocaust. In one scene an older woman, soon to go to her death, befriended a young girl who had been severely shocked — to the extent of being almost insane — after seeing her parents brutally killed by the Nazis. The old woman, doomed yet selfless, sympathetic and loving, put a blanket around the girl's shoulders, gently placed the girl's head against her own shoulder and embraced her, humming softly. As I watched this scene I asked myself why had that never happened to me, why had I not known, as a child, the *physical* expression of love, that powerful phenomenon that, without words, would have reassured me that not only was I loved, supported, wanted, but that I was worthy of these things.

Was it true that I hadn't experienced this....or was it that I had simply forgotten it? Surely my mother had sometimes taken me in her arms and enfolded me with her love and warmth? Hadn't she?...Had she?...

I sat there, frozen, searching deeply in my memory for the slightest recollection, the smallest echo, of having been comforted in that way, but nothing came and the conviction that such an event must never have taken place grew until I was utterly dejected. Nothing can make up for the emptiness of a feeling like that, no change of scenery, no new relationship, not even money. And what happens to a person who is convinced of this sad fact, even though it may not be true? She spends her life searching for that experience — no, that's not it — she spends her life running away from the lack of it, from the intolerable feeling of being unloved by the one person who is supposed to love you. Now I had the opportunity to run as far away as I possibly could and I was going to take it.

We both dressed casually. I wore navy-blue corduroy jeans that flared out at the ankle and a pale-blue knitted silk top with a laced-up scoop neckline and long sleeves that ballooned out at the wrist. Bryn wore his black cords with a black lambswool sweater.

We ordered smoked mackerel, French bread and a bottle of the nouveau Beaujolais that had just been released. Bryn started talking the instant the waiter turned away from our table after taking our order:

"The nouveau beaujolais is supposed to be really good this year. I can't wait to try it."

I said nothing, not knowing how to react or what to say, incapable of being suitably nonchalant....because there it was again, the great surge of life pulling me forward. There was a rule I had never understood and thought I would never accept, that one must allow oneself to be dragged along by the passage of time without looking too closely at the effects of the events that pushed time forward. *Keep moving* seemed to be the over-riding imperative....but how does one keep moving — how does one begin to move — when one's emotions are tethered?....how does one do that?

Bryn took a deep breath, sensing my unease. "I'm sorry. Didn't mean to be a clod. All right, look, I won't beat about the bush. You deserve some kind of explanation. This is going to sound like a criticism and it isn't, okay?, but....well....the thing about Becca is that — I'm just going to say this, okay, I don't mean to hurt you — but it's probably one of the main things — well, it's *the* main thing — that contributed to what must seem like the amazingly short time it took me to — to — to decide I want to be with her. I'm honestly trying to soften the blow of all that and anyway I want to explain. I want to be — I'd like to be....I feel I owe it to you... "

I had never before heard Bryn sound so hesitant and ambivalent so I guessed that he was about to say something he knew I wouldn't like, that would upset me, even hurt me.

...After all my concern about having to explain to him about Eric, I thought bitterly, here was Bryn, about to tell me something I did not want to hear, something that was going to change things even more than they had already been changed. Part of my mind, the part that just watches and observes, coolly, as if the living of my life was some kind of abstract exercise, looked on with disinterest. I was to be judged and given a score — a failing score — by a particular person, the one person out of all the other people in the world to whom I felt closest....what superb irony!

Although I was consumed by curiosity, it suddenly occurred to me to ask, "Why did you cry when I told you about Eric?"

Bryn's face lit up: "I was relieved! When you came back from the US I felt terrible because I was going to have to tell you what had happened to me. I mean — it was bad enough I had to tell you that I had picked up with Becca again but then, then I had to tell you that I wanted to get married! So when you told me about Eric, I knew you'd be leaving, so it was a load off!" He looked sheepish and lowered his voice: "Sorry....I should have said all this that night — instead of letting you believe that you were breaking my heart — well, you were breaking my heart but not for the reasons you were thinking. I knew I was going to have to tell you. I just didn't have the guts right then."

The wine arrived at our table, giving me a few minutes to consider what I was going to say next. The waiter filled our glasses and we both watched closely as if we were going to be tested later on the details of this small event.

"So what's this main thing then?" I demanded — roughly, because I was scared of the answer — reaching out to pick up my wine glass. I needed something to do with my hands.

"She loves me."

I suddenly felt as though I had been dealt a blow just above my heart. I replaced the glass on the table very carefully, before I started trembling — because I knew that was coming next — and chewed at my lips. Then, after taking a deep breath so that my voice would be level, as normal-sounding as I could make it, because the trembling had just started, I said: "And I don't." A statement, since there was obviously no doubt about this.

Bryn also took a deep breath but I could tell he was completely calm: "Well — no you don't. You never have."

Every human being has so many different voices: there is the one that cajoles; the one that tries to understand; the one that rages; there's the carping, complaining voice and the voice that registers delight — or indignation or sorrow or stubbornness or sympathy or the thousand other reactions that human beings are capable of....and then there is the one that is absolutely honest, because honesty is called for....though the temptation to avoid it may be very great. There is no mistaking that voice, because it is used so infrequently.

"I've always known it but it didn't seem to matter because I loved you so — so tremendously. You were the only person I'd ever loved. It was never really like that with Olivia" — this was the woman he had been engaged to very briefly and disastrously two years earlier — "even though that thing nearly broke me in two." He gave a bitter little snort. "All the other women were mainly for sex. I wasn't looking for any kind of replacement for you, you must know that, and anyway you know how amazingly fussy I am. So I didn't give *being* loved a second thought."

The food arrived and we both ignored it, ignored it so completely that someone looking over at us might have thought we hadn't even noticed it arrive.

I stayed silent so that he would keep talking.

"The thing is — Becca loves me. I felt it immediately and it was like the lightbulb thing, you know — Aha! — and I just couldn't fight it. I didn't want to fight it. I found out what I'd been missing and there was no going back."

…You find out what you're missing. And once you find out, a line is crossed and there is no going back…

I was so shocked by his statement that I remained silent. Even if I had opened my mouth and tried to speak no sound would have emerged. Because it was true and I had never truly acknowledged it. Here was the irrefutable, heartbreaking truth: Bryn was friend, parent, lover, protector, confidante, soul mate even, but not my own true love. Bryn was everything to me except the man I loved. Love....without it, what do you have?

Well, what did it matter now, as Bryn had clearly found the one thing he had *not* had — someone who loved him. Bryn's voice intruded into my thoughts:

"I have no regrets....I still think it was a good idea for us to try — again."

The waiter, having noticed that neither of us had touched the food, came over and asked, delicately, "Is everything to your satisfaction, sir?"

"Uh, oh yes, yes," said Bryn, "we're — uh — yes, fine, thank you."

The waiter retreated and Bryn went on: "My view — it's one I've held for ages — it was actually the cause of the bust-up with Olivia because she thought the complete opposite — my view is that there shouldn't be any need to *work* at relationships. It either works or it doesn't and each person should be able to do their thing, whatever that might be. That's why I have never been interested in making people do things, moulding them to suit me. I'm really passive in that way. The reason things have worked as well as they have between us is because I've basically let you do whatever you wanted to do — and I probably would have gone on doing that....if you hadn't gone off on your trip."

"But you were the one who encouraged me to go!" I protested.

"I encouraged you to go because I could see that you really wanted to. Look, we should eat something or the waiter is going to have a nervous breakdown."

We lifted our cutlery and started to move food from our plates into our mouths.

After a minute Bryn added: "I wanted you to do whatever made you happy. It never occurred to me to try and dissuade you from going for my sake — that would have been self-defeating. You wouldn't have been *you* anymore."

And that phrase echoed in my head, *You wouldn't have been you anymore*, while in another part of my head, a little voice asked, with the utmost innocence: "And who is that exactly?"

It was to be our last meaningful conversation. At that moment something ended and if I were to try for the rest of my life I should never be able to express adequately what that something was. I can only say I experienced a profound sense of loss, perhaps the same indescribable sense of loss that courses through a child's body when it discovers it can no longer rely on the solace of its mother's breast. The child is still loved....but from a great distance and what it actually feels is the removal of the most comforting sustenance in the world. And like the process of weaning, this separation from Bryn was necessary, a connection that had to be broken....because bloody Nature had designed things that way.

Nostalgia, regret, sentimentality — call it what you like, it does not stop it being real. Bryn's caring and concern for me had lifted me above the most familiar feeling in my life, that of having no home. Now I understood it at last. The feeling he had given me was one of — of having a safety net....of having someone to turn to, someone who cared absolutely. *If I fail at this, I can always...* Now I was going to have to walk the tightrope of my changing life without it.

Bryn went off on a two-week holiday in Greece with Rebecca and — luxury of luxuries — I had the house to myself. It was a relief not to have to disguise my mixed feelings. I wandered round the house, taking stock of what I might take with me to Florida. There now seemed to be no other choice what to do next.

Letters and cards flew back and forth across the Atlantic — phone calls were prohibitively expensive. The words "I love you" were written and read over and over again and I was fairly sure I meant them. Eric's letters became more and more insistent that we should be together again. Sometimes they contained words that I found distasteful, words that hinted very strongly at his need for sex and I forced myself to respond in a similar vein, grateful that I only had to write my responses and not say them or put them into action. And the frustrating time difference between continents added a sense of disjointedness to our communications. Sometimes I ached with the need for some kind of certainty.

I went to see a film called *Heartbeat* about Jack Kerouac and Neal Cassady. Nick Nolte's portrayal of the charming, irresponsible, driven, doomed, alcoholic, womanising Cassady was brilliant but the film made me uneasy because I found myself identifying very painfully with the way Kerouac lived his life, through other, stronger people. When the actor playing Kerouac said the line, "When have I ever known what I've been doing?" a deep dissonant chord was struck inside me.

It was still too early to think of myself as a writer and not as a defunct secretary but the money I now had was opening up the possibility of a new life. Money buys all kinds of things: possessions, possibilities, options, change....freedom. And of all these things, freedom is the most frightening, because you have to work out what to do with it...

Bryn and I had one last memorable evening together. I had received my inheritance, I had bought my ticket to fly to Florida, I had my visa to stay in the USA for six months, I had sent ahead a trunk containing my painfully pared-down belongings. All that was left was a few days of waiting.

Bryn suggested one last evening down the pub, nowhere special, just one of the locals. We went to The Clockhouse. We drank beer. He chatted to a few of the regulars. I didn't talk much.

When we got back to the house in Gubyon Avenue, we climbed the three flights of stairs to the top room, Bryn wanted to listen to an album he'd bought that day. He went straight over to the record-player and put on his new acquisition, an LP of JJ Johnson, the American jazz trombonist, a recent discovery of his. Bryn was now playing regularly with Goldsmith's big band during the week and with Phil's group on weekends and

his own trombone lay on the sofa where he had left it after prac-
tising earlier in the evening. When JJ Johnson broke into a solo, I
picked up Bryn's trombone and started to mime Johnson's solo.
I knew enough about trombone-playing to be aware of how to
make my performance somewhat convincing: when Johnson hit
a high note I pulled the slide close in to my mouth and when he
played a very low note, I extended the slide a long way out. My
realistic gestures so impressed Bryn that he gave a great guffaw,
which encouraged me to continue, then he started laughing and
couldn't stop until the track came to an end and I replaced the
trombone on the sofa. He was laughing so hard there were tears
rolling down his face.

"That was tremendous!" he exclaimed and beamed at me.

...I can still see the slanting walls and the wallpaper Bryn
and I had chosen and hung together, with its striking Art Deco
motif, a repeating pattern of large yellow and white bulbous
shapes, vaguely flower-like, against a dark green background.

...Thinking about it now, I realise that what Bryn gave me
was a sense of security that came from no other source — certainly not from my parents — and therefore the absolute freedom to be myself, without the filters that had always been so
necessary. And I knew in my heart that, even though any number of consoling things might appear to take the place of that
feeling, I would never experience it again.

Now I had agreed to go and live with Eric in Florida, I had no
way of knowing what I was letting myself in for, and no way of
finding out....without actually doing it. I was about to relinquish

completely my life in England. And my emotional reaction to this prospect was an unhelpful combination of the desire to flee without looking back and complete paralysis from fear of the unknown. I had put into motion something that could not now be reversed: my immediate future lay on the other side of the Atlantic, but exactly how I would fare in this transformed future was a complete unknown.

If it worked out well, fine. If not, then the one person I knew I could turn to was — no — was no longer — Bryn. No more safety net, no more lifesaving raft, no more haven. That certainty had been obliterated. I was used to throwing myself off the edge of cliffs....*Ladies and gentlemen, this next trick is impossible!*....but this time the person who had always held the invisible lifeline was no longer there.